THE
ALTERED

THE ALTERED

MARIA DEVIVO

4 Horsemen
Publications, Inc.

DEDICATION

For Babaysh— You always know what I want to hear, what I don't want to hear, and what I need to hear. Thank you for your eagle eye.

For Rooney – From day one of this book, you've had my back. Thank you for encouraging me to push forward.

For Morgi – it's always for you, and always will be for you.

CONTENTS

Chapter 1 1
Chapter 2 15
Chapter 3 29
Chapter 4 42
Chapter 5 55
Chapter 6 68
Chapter 7 81
Chapter 8 92
Chapter 9 103
Chapter 10 112
Chapter 11 124
Chapter 12 134
Chapter 13 148
Chapter 14 165
Chapter 15 174
Chapter 16 186
Chapter 17 197
Chapter 18 208
Chapter 19 220
Chapter 20 230
Chapter 21 241
Chapter 22 251

Chapter 23 262
Chapter 24 274

Book Club Questions. 283
Author Bio. 285

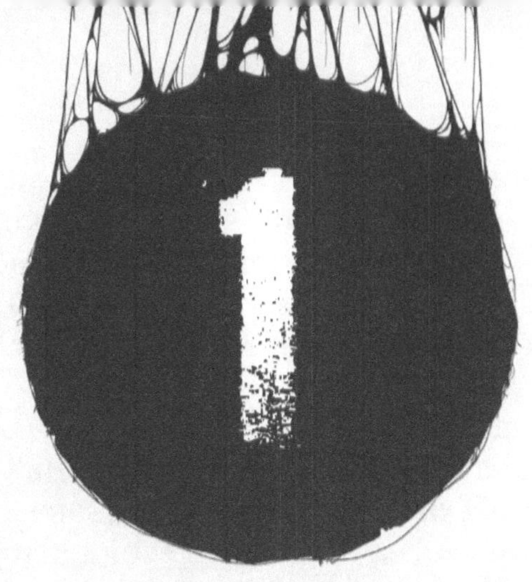

ALWAYS LIKED THE SOUNDS THE HOUSE makes when it wakes up. There's that kind of weird silence followed by the gradual tones and shifts through the walls. Usually, the roof creaks when the first light hits it, and the floorboards crackle. Even though the house is only ten years old, it still makes those morning settling noises like it's stretching its arms to start the day, readying itself for the onslaught of feet and hands that will soon make their way over every inch of it.

The first person to wake up is my mom. Always. She has some weird internal clock thing going on and swears to God that ever since my sister Sydney was born she can't sleep past 6:00 am. Ever. She's loudly fussing with brown paper bags for our lunches for today. I've told her a thousand times that I end up throwing it out. I mean, really, what high school senior do you know who still brings his own lunch to school? But she does it anyway. I guess she means well. Dad is up next. He has an alarm clock that I hear through the wall. It's a muffled sound, like something underwater. I hear him smack it off, mumble some morning obscenity, and hop into the shower. When the water turns on, that's Sydney's cue to wake up. Her bedroom is on the other side of theirs. The head of her bed lines up directly with the back wall of my parents' shower. Sydney is nine. And loud. She does whatever nine-year-old girls do when they wake up and runs down the hall to meet Mom in the kitchen. That's my cue to get up.

But I don't. Not right now.

I don't want to go to school today. I don't want to sit in some boring classes and hear about some boring stuff I'm not going to need or use at any point in my life. Even seeing Lana Anderson in 5th period isn't enough for me to pull the covers off my body and do my morning routine. I don't have the strength. I don't have the will. What the hell does it matter anyway?

"Griffin!" Sydney yells from down the hallway.

"Yeah?" I yell back after a long pause.

"C'mon, Griffin! We're gonna be late! Mommy says you have to walk with me to the bus stop!" She's such a whiney little thing, but I guess all girls that age are.

"No, I don't! I'm driving!" I retaliate.

She stamps closer to my room. Her footfalls heavy on the porcelain tile in the hallway; the soles of her "grown-up girl" shoes clicking and clacking like tap shoes on a dancer. My bedroom door flings open, and she dramatically exhales. I duck under the covers, hoping she'll just go away, just go away, just go away...

"Don't you reeee-mem-buh?" she says slowly in her annoying sister-voice as she stands in the doorway. "Daddy has to take the car to the shop and needs your car for work. You have to take the bus today!"

I forgot. Now I'm pissed. What high school senior do you know takes the bus to school? She's still standing there—her shoes still tapping against the metal threshold. She exhales again.

"Jesus Christ, Syd!" I say angrily as I throw off the covers and sit up.

Sydney stands in my doorway. Her neck is twisted to one side. Blood drips from the side of her head, making a gentle tapping sound against the metal threshold. Fear grips me for a brief second, and I jolt.

I wake up.

I'm not in my house.

My parents are not in their morning routine mode. Sydney is not nagging me to get out of bed.

Those people don't exist anymore, and it has been quite some time since I've seen them—even in my dreams.

The room I wake up in is white. Sterile. It smells like medicine, like anti-bacterial soap in a hospital or something. I'm wearing a white gown and there's some sticky circle thing attached to my chest. I'm on a metal gurney. This has to be a hospital. The sticky circle on my chest has a wire attached to it, but it hangs on the floor. There are no machines or monitors in the room, very un-hospital-like, but I'm clean. That much I know for sure. There's no stench of death or bile or rotten meat. No smell of infection. I reach my hand up to touch my face. My hands are clean, fingernails cut and probably highly sanitized. When my finger reaches my cheek, rough stubble on the sides of my face, chin, and upper lip scratch at my fingertips. I never let my face get this stubbly—God knows how long it's been since I've shaved. I look down at my right arm and there's a bruise and small hole in the crook on the opposite side of my elbow. Medicine, probably. Antibiotics, fluids, whatever else they give you in a hospital.

I sit up and look around the room. There's nothing here but me, a door, and a mirror, and I've seen one too many movies to know that that's not just any mirror. Someone's there watching me. And wouldn't you know it, the second I swivel my legs off the gurney to stand up, the door flies open and a man wearing a white suit enters the room.

White suit. That day in the city. Flesh in my mouth. Purple gas cloud.

"You're awake. That's good," he says nervously from behind his face gear. His voice sounds almost mechanical, and he's breathing heavily.

I stare at him. I'm not sure if I can talk. I don't really want to, but could I if I tried? Do my vocal cords still work? Am I normal again?

"Dr. Holston will be taking you down to the observation room now that you're up," he continues as he moves closer to me with a jerky awkward motion. Maybe it's the suit, but I swear he's afraid. No. I can tell. He's afraid.

I inhale deeply and smell the sweat coating the palms of his hands. Even though he's wearing those big bulky gloves, I smell it. I smell him. His flesh. His fear. That lightly roasted aroma. It's faint, but I know it's there. I have an awareness of this man's body, but there's an absence of the hunger. I don't have the urge to eat his face, and I don't have the need to devour his entrails. I'm not hungry. Not driven. I have the memory of the hunger, the need, the taste. I have the memory of it all, but I'm not hungry.

"Are you hungry?" he asks.

I roll my eyes.

He gives a slight chuckle. A nervous chuckle. "Can you stand up?"

My shoulders rise in an "I-don't-know" gesture. I'm afraid to open my mouth to speak. Afraid to try. Afraid of what my voice will sound like.

"Can you talk?"

I roll my eyes again.

He moves closer to me, removes his gloves, and places them next to me on the gurney. He seems a little more relaxed as he reaches into his pocket and takes out a small flashlight. Like something from a doctor's office.

"Open your eyes wide," he instructs as he aims the ray of light into my pupils. "Hmmm. Okay. Open your mouth and say 'ah'."

I open my mouth, but no sound comes out. I don't allow it to.

"Okay. Very good," he continues as he removes his face gear and places it on the floor.

My mind flashes back. The last man to do that in front of me got my teeth embedded in his face. I instinctively hiss. Teeth bared. I don't know why I do it. I'm not hungry. It just happened. The man drops his flashlight and backs away stumbling over his helmet. Whatever confidence and sense of security he had mustered up is now gone. His face is as white as his suit.

"Okay... oh... okay..." he stammers as he makes his way to the door. "The doctor will be in shortly."

He leaves. His scent leaves with him.

My head hurts. It throbs. I force myself to stand up and my legs feel wobbly, like they haven't been used in months. I grip the side of the gurney and wait for a minute or two until I'm completely sure my legs will hold up my weight. I look down at my body and realize there isn't much weight to be held. I must have lost about twenty pounds or so. Who knows? Maybe more. At six feet tall and 175 pounds, I was a pretty stocky and physically fit guy. Not an athlete, but I kept myself in shape. That Lana Anderson from 5th period always used to hang around the gym to watch the guys work out, so I kept going there to lift weights and watch her watching us guys. It eventually became my thing. *Lana Anderson*. I wonder what happened to her. I know what happened to me, and I don't think she could have possibly lived through half of that.

I creep over to the mirror, and I know there has to be someone there watching me. There always is. Detectives, doctors, lawyers, witnesses. The two-way mirror is always a reflection and an evaluation. I try to keep my cool, unlike most people in the movies who go screaming up to the glass, fists clenched, demanding answers. But honestly, I kinda feel like doing that myself. Like, I need some sort of answer. Before I even look at myself in the reflection of the glass, I size up the mirror. I size up the glass, letting whoever on the other side know that *I* know that they're there. The way the white suit guy reacted to me before, I'm feeling a little like a badass, and right now that's about the only thing I have going for me.

I believe that even more so after I finally do get around to examining myself in the mirror. The only word that comes to mind is 'horrible.' It doesn't even look like me. I look ghostly, sickly, deathly, and whatever other '-ly' words you can think of. I think they're called adverbs, but I wasn't much for paying attention in English class. The hair on my head is wild. At this length you can really see the red highlights against the light brown color. There's a gauze bandage around my forehead and it makes my hair seem to poof out even more. My beard is getting thick. I've never seen it like this before. I never let it get passed a day or two without shaving. Sydney had once dared me to grow in a goatee. I took the dare but ended up taking her for ice cream and a movie when I lost. I've also lost a lot of weight. I have no muscle mass left, and my skin looks kinda grayish, too, but that could be from anything. I think of Lana Anderson, and I suspect she wouldn't give me a second glance if she ever saw me like this. But if Lana had become what I had been, I don't think she'd care too much about my looks than she would about the way my flesh tasted…

The door opens again, and a doctor enters.

Dr. Holston, I presume. I say in my head with my best British accent.

"Hello," he says in a gentle voice, "I'm Dr. Holston."

I hold back from rolling my eyes, so I nod at him instead.

He's a heavyset man with gray hair wearing a white lab coat. *Seems to be the clothing of choice around here.* He looks at me with an odd expression, one of partial wonder, partial joy, and partial fear. I'm hoping he'll be able to explain to me what exactly has been going on, but as he glances at his clipboard and back at me with rapid movements, I don't get the sense that he's here for a "heart-to-heart."

"I need to take you down to the observation room to run a final test. I promise this will be the last one of its kind. It's to make sure the serum worked and you're not going to have a relapse of the virus. Now you're up and mobile, it's important for us to see what's going on in your brain and in your blood, and if there was any permanent damage done from the virus."

Permanent damage? Did he say permanent damage?

I nod. Unwillingly. Unknowingly. Do I really have another option in this situation?

"It would really be better for us if you could speak..."

I cut him off by shaking my head wildly back and forth. Why am I afraid of my own voice? Can I speak? Was that part of the permanent damage he was talking about?

"Ok. Well, I need you to hop up onto the gurney so I can take you down to the testing site. I'm going to give you a sedative and an anesthetic, so you'll be calm and won't feel anything. Is that okay with you?" He makes this sound all normal, and routine-like, but I know there's nothing normal about what happened to me or what I did to people.

I nod again and inch back to the gurney. I prop myself up and lay back. Dr. Holston takes the end of the wire that's attached to the sticky thing on my chest. I see now it's not a wire, but a small tube. He dips it in a plastic vile filled with clear liquid. He squeezes it a few times, and the liquid is pumped up into the tube. It moves slowly up and snakes around until it reaches the circular sticker. My eyes flutter a few times, and I fall asleep.

When I wake up, I'm in another room. It's an office. It reminds me of Mrs. Roberts's office at my school. She's my guidance counselor, and she was helping me out with college applications and scholarship opportunities. She really had her work cut out for her. I was a smart kid, but with my work ethic, you'd never know. I scored off-the-charts on standardized tests, but my class grades outright sucked. Oh, and to boot, I had no athletics behind me. Getting into a good school was going to be hard, but I knew Roberts was calling in some favors for me. She always told me I reminded her of her son. She knew I was good with numbers and was giving me pointers on what field I should get into. Hotel management? Business? Whatever. I'm 17. I have my whole life to figure that out. Or should I say, *had* my whole life to figure it out. Because Mrs. Roberts *was* my guidance counselor before I got sick and started eating people.

I'm not hungry, but my stomach rumbles something awful telling me otherwise. Really, I'm not. My mind isn't able to process what food is yet. Before getting sick, I would crave a big juicy burger with bacon and pickles and cheese. Well-done. Almost burnt! Wash it down with an ice-cold Coke, maybe some fries on the side. Or Josh and I would go to a baseball game with our dads and get footlong hotdogs smothered in ketchup. Josh would try to impress my dad by putting on his best New York accent and yelling, "Hahht Dawwwgs! Getcha hahhht dawwwgs!" which would of course crack us all up.

Josh...

Before getting sick, I would crave normal food, but once I changed, once I *became*, the cravings were quite different. Raw and warm. Nothing dead, and nothing from an animal. I learned that one real fast. In the beginning, when I was new, I ate just about anything to see what would kill that awful hunger pain. By process of elimination, I came to find the only thing that satiated my hunger was flesh. Raw and warm. Live. Human. But really, there was no true satisfaction. The hunger was always there, always constant. Any scent of human flesh drove me crazy. Like Lana Anderson's perfume. She would sit by the window and Mr. Miller would crack it open so the breeze would come in, and her perfume would fill up that room. It sucked when she was absent cause the room would just smell like dirty gym socks and stale Frito chips. But when she was there, man, you *knew* she was there cause you could *smell* her presence! And of course, you had to look at her. You wanted to look at her, wanted to be near her—to smell that smell, and maybe even *taste* that smell. Live humans did that for me after I got sick. Lana's perfume wouldn't have mattered much. It actually would have been a deterrent. I craved pure, clean, fresh flesh with hot blood pounding against the body's shell. I close my eyes and take a deep breath, and the smell is right there in the room with me, like it never left me, and a part of me twinges with the craving. But I'm not hungry. I don't think my mind can discern between the pre- and the post-sickness meal patterns because there's a part of me that would love a *hahht dawwwg* right about now, but there's another part of me that wouldn't mind a nice hunk of Lana Anderson's thigh.

I must have dozed off because I'm startled when I hear another voice in the room.

"I said, are you with me?" the voice repeats.

I sit up straight. I'm still in the office with the blue walls and beige rug. The couch is black leather and comfortable, and I figure that yes, I did nod off for a few minutes. I was alone when I first woke up after my test with Dr. Holston, and now there's this man sitting across from me in a leather chair. He's wearing a suit. Not a white one, thank God. It's a business suit with a jacket and tie. His hair is jet black, and he's wearing way too much hair gel that should be allowed for men. He has a clipboard in his lap, and he's waving his arms in front of me and snapping his fingers at me.

He whistles. Between the snapping and the whistling, he must think I'm a dog or some other type of animal that can be snapped and whistled at.

"Hey, hey," he says with two quick snaps in my face.

My eyes focus, and I tilt my head at him. He settles back and relaxes, glances at his papers, and looks back at me. His eyes peer above the rims of his thin reading glasses. He can't be more than forty, maybe forty-five years old.

"My name is Dr. Graves," he finally says. "I'm the psychiatrist assigned to evaluate you. This facility has been designated as the Re-Assimilation Center for any and all of the Altered population. After my assessment, which can last an indeterminate amount of time, we will review whether or not you are suitable to rejoin those who have not been infected. You have completed your first battery of physical exams, and according to Dr. Holston, your primary care physician, you have passed with near-perfect results. I have been assigned to you to test your psychological faculties and anything else of a mental nature," he says nonchalantly, again like this is all so normal. Then, he smiles at me. It's a half-smile, really. More of a grin, but it's fake, and very telling.

I immediately know I don't like this Doctor Graves. There's something behind those black eyes and that phony grin that says I shouldn't trust him. Besides, any forty-something year old man who wears that much hair gel certainly can't be trusted!

"Let's get started, shall we?" he asks, but it's not really a question. Graves leans over to the end table next to his chair and presses a button on a small tape recorder.

"This is Doctor Warren J. Graves at the Mount Sinai Re-Assimilation Center. I am here with Patient Number 024. This is session one."

He looks at me and gives me a nod. That fake grin turns up his mouth for a split second, and he is staring at me as if he wants me to say something. There's a second or two of uncomfortable silence, and Graves finally says, "You should start with your name."

I stare back. *My name? Really? That's where you want to start?*

It's clear I'm not responding to this little tete-a-tete. *And I think I amazed myself that I actually remembered something from Miss Dougherty's English class!* Graves looks grave. He's uncomfortable. He's glaring at me. He swipes his big lunchbox hand over to the recorder and forcefully presses the stop button.

"Why are we doing this?" he says with a hard exhale. "Dr. Holston says you check out fine. Physically, you're okay. Can we get on with this?"

Physically okay? I don't feel physically okay. But I'm staring hard at him. I don't like him, I don't like him, I don't like him. He fake smiles again. Bigger than his last two grins. Faker than his last two grins. And it hits me. He doesn't like me either.

And something else hits me: he called this a Re-Assimilation Center. What happened to me must have happened to others, and I kinda need to know what went down. I need to put the puzzle pieces together before the hunger comes back. I'm not hungry, now, but will I be tomorrow? Did I die? Was I brought back to life? Am I really cured? And what happened to Lana Anderson? Right now, this psychiatrist, this snaky, middle-aged, fake grinner is the only one who seems like he would have any answers. Holston and the other white suits don't seem like they're gonna do much talking. So, I dig deep, trying so hard to find my lost voice. Scared to death that the only sounds I'll hear are the familiar moans and groans. Scared that I'll *really* wake up and realize this Re-Assimilation Center is all a dream and I'm back in the city street eating the face of a white suit CDC lab tech.

Graves is clearly pissed. He repositions his left leg behind his right ankle. He's waiting for me to say something.

"Griffin," I finally mutter. My voice is strange and hoarse. Unfamiliar. The sound almost scrapes out of my throat, and I fear the last 'n' sound has a guttural moan to it that scares me half to death. It's all I got. I think it'll be a while before I say much else.

His eyes flash wide for a second and he fumbles his hand for the recorder.

"Again," he says without any emotion. "Say it again, louder, so the recorder can hear you."

He presses the record button, and I get tense. His stares are a little intimidating. I have to dig deeper to find my voice a second time, and I pray the moaning is no longer there.

"Griffin. Griffin King." My voice is deep. Deeper than I remember.

"Okay, Griffin King, Patient Number 024, can you tell me what happened to you? Can you tell me what you remember?" he says with a hint of disgust in his voice.

I nod my head. Images and sounds start to flood back into my mind in shattered pieces, and as I try frantically to work some sort of timeline out in my brain, my voice comes to me, strong and confident because I start to have an understanding of my version of the incident: "I remember everything."

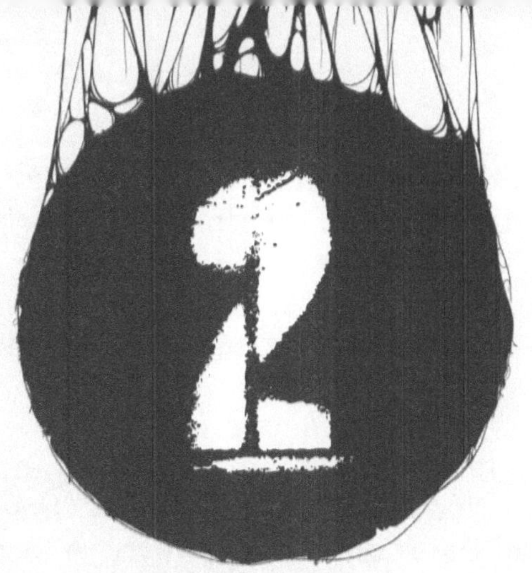

RAVES STRETCHES HIS ARMS OVER HIS head and obnoxiously exhales. "Good, then, I guess we should start at the beginning."

There is disgust in his voice again. Disgust and contempt. He licks his thick lips and narrows his eyes. He's waiting again. There's an impatient vibe in the way he subtly shifts in his seat and drums his fingers against the arm of the leather chair. I see the indentations in the leather and realize this Graves guy is a pretty massive dude. I hadn't noticed it before, but I do now, and I get a weird sensation that at any moment he's going to leap across the coffee table that separates us, pin me to the couch, and choke the life out of me. I've done worse, so I guess I would deserve that, wouldn't I?

"What was the beginning like for you?" he asks with fake interest. I'm not sure what he means by "the beginning." The beginning of what? The beginning of my life? My change? The world? The beginning is a pretty broad topic, and my life seems to have many different beginnings.

"What do you mean?" I answer in a low voice, and as soon as the words leave my mouth, they sound so stupid to my ears. Graves tilts his head down, and he's staring at me again from above the rim of his glasses.

"How far back should I..." I start, but he silences me with a slight hand gesture.

"The *beginning*," he repeats with a cruel emphasis on the 'b' word.

The beginning. The beginning.

I pause, racking my brain for the optimum point in the timeline that could possibly satisfy Graves. My eyes dart around the room for help. I try to locate a visual that would spark some sort of proper beginning, make some sort of connection between the then and the now. The flowers on the desk behind Graves are yellow, and I immediately think of Lana's blonde hair. I shrug my shoulders. I guess that's a good enough place to start. Lana Anderson...

I'd known Lana since I moved to Florida in the second grade. She was always the cute girl in class, the one who all the boys wanted to kiss behind the bookcase. She had blonde curly hair and these blue-green eyes that always reminded me of the beach. I wouldn't say we were friends, though. We were more like acquaintances, and we always had an occasional class together throughout the years. I'm not gonna lie; I thought about her. A lot. Most guys did.

It was a Monday morning in early November. I really didn't want to go to school that day, but the only thing that made the thought of going even remotely interesting was seeing Lana in 5th period. That pretty much would be the highlight of my day, as it was most of my days for my entire school career. I kinda lay in bed thinking about her and wondering if she ever thought about me. There were about six more months before senior prom, and the only way I would go is if she was my date. Otherwise, I had no interest in that pathetic high school ritual.

My whole family was awake. Mom, Dad, my little sister Sydney. I still had to take a shower and do all that stuff, but I wasn't motivated. I was quite content with being in bed with my thoughts of Lana. Sydney banged on my door a few times, which of course I yelled at her for. I had totally forgotten my dad's car went into the shop over the weekend, and I had to take the bus to school. I was so embarrassed. I had finally been freed from the shackles of the yellow prison in August when I turned 17 only to be thrust back into its noisy, gum-stuck clutches. I would have stayed home if it hadn't been for Sydney. My sister was nine and was all about school. She hardly ever missed a day since kindergarten. Even insisted she go when she had the flu a few years ago. I usually drove Syd to her bus stop in the morning and would continue on my way to the high school, but now I had to walk her there. Dad needed my car for work, and Mom was hosting her yoga class at the house that morning. Dad worked in the city as a banker which paid the bills and then some. That allowed Mom to be a stay-at-home-parent, a luxury not afforded by most families.

My cell phone rang, and I saw on the caller-id tag it was my best friend, Josh. His picture flashed on the touchscreen—the one of him winking his eye and pointing at the camera like a big shot. He was a loud and obnoxious clown, but we'd been best friends the second I stepped foot into school here in Florida, so I guess I was used to his crazy antics. He winked at everyone. Guys, girls, teachers, old ladies, you name it. It was his trademark. I don't think he ever admitted it, but I suspected it was because he had one brown eye and one blue eye, and he didn't want people to notice it. His parents got divorced when he was twelve, and I think that added to his need to be the center of attention. I cursed him out under my breath for interrupting my thoughts of Lana.

"Hey," I answered.

"Sup man?" he responded.

"Debating whether or not I'm going to school."

"Dude, when's your car gonna be done?"

"Not sure."

"So, I guess you're not picking me up?"

"You're so dumb, Josh! It's Monday. We literally just dropped the car off yesterday. *Sunday.* Noone even looked at it yet!" I practically yelled at him like he was a child. Sometimes you had to yell at Josh, though. Sometimes he didn't get the obvious, and besides, he knew damn well I wasn't going to go out of my way to pick him up.

"Just sayin'," he whined. "So, you goin' to school or not?"

I exhaled. "I guess I am now!" I said annoyed.

Sydney banged on my door for a third time. "Griff-iiinnn!! Let's go!"

Josh started chuckling on the other end. "Have fun on the *bus,* dude!"

"Shut the hell up!" I snapped.

"Later," Josh said, still laughing.

"Later," I said as I pressed the disconnect button on the touchscreen and threw the phone on the edge of the bed. Suddenly, Sydney opened my door and stood in the entrance, hands on hips, tapping her feet on the metal threshold.

"What are you doing!?" I screamed at her. "I could have been naked, ya know!"

"So?" she responded in her little girl smartass voice. I swear I wanted to smack her every time she had that prissy attitude! "Let's go. Mom's pissed at you." And with that, she turned on her heels and slammed the door behind her.

With Josh's annoying phone call and Sydney breathing down my neck, I figured I had no other choice than to get up and start the day.

I got ready and went into the kitchen. My mom was spouting off some laundry list of instructions for me and throwing a brown paper lunch bag into my hand. The living room was set up with yoga mats, and there was a pitcher of orange juice set out on the breakfast bar that connected the kitchen to the living room.

"I don't eat this," I said handing it back to her.

"Just take it!" she sighed, pressing it back into my hands. "You eat like a horse. You might get hungry."

I rolled my eyes. "When I get hungry, I'll buy lunch at school, ma!"

"I hate that you eat crap school food! Oh, whatever. Sydney," she began as she bent down slightly and kissed my sister's forehead, "you have a fabulous day at school, Peanut. Give em' hell, today!" Mom said, to which Sydney smiled her nine-year-old's diabolical smile.

My family was kinda strange. Both of my parents were pretty much in the genius status, which would explain why my sister and I turned out so smart. But their way of raising us was far different from the way my friends were raised. My parents let us think and speak however we felt, and they treated us like people. If we wanted to eat Oreo cookies for breakfast, they let us because sometimes *they* wanted to eat Oreo cookies for breakfast, too. Sydney and I had very little restrictions put on us. One time Sydney's first grade teacher called my mother to let her know Sydney had called another girl a "bitch" in class. My mother's response was, "So, what the hell do you want me to do about it?"

My mother stood up on her tiptoes and kissed my cheek. She was about 5'2" and always had to reach a little to kiss me or my father goodbye. I half-heartedly put my arm around her shoulder in a "good-bye" embrace and quickly walked out the door trying to create as much distance as possible between me and Syd. Mom was yelling something at my back about watching the news tonight, but I wasn't paying much attention. She was always such a scary Mary, paranoid to the core. I heard her say the word "terrorist," lifted up my hand in acknowledgment, and kept walking. Sydney was right on my tail. Her shoes clacked on the pavement behind me. "Wait up!" she yelled at me. I ignored her. It sucked not having a car.

The bus ride was awful! I felt like the biggest loser sitting in the back of the bus, crammed next to some Freshman kid. I had been driving my car for a few months now, had just gotten out of yellow-bus-hell, only to be thrown back into that bitch's arms! Every time the driver hit a bump, my stomach lurched up into my throat, and looking out the window nearly gave me a heart attack. The world looked fuzzy and jagged from the school bus window, so I closed my eyes and tried to ignore the kid babbling incessantly next to me.

School was the same boring nightmare as it always was. I was lucky enough to get out of 3rd period History because Mrs. Roberts, my guidance counselor, needed to see me about some scholarship application I filled out half-assed. That was double good because 3rd period was one of the two classes I had with Josh, and I was still kinda sour with him for his annoying wake-up call that morning. The shining star of the day would be 5th period, and I told myself if I could hold out until then, it would all be worth it. But when 5th rolled around, I could have taken a shotgun to the face! Lana was absent. I knew it right away, too. The smell of Fritos and sweaty gym socks was putrid. Her perfume smell was not there to mask the horrid odor of high school seniors.

Damn her! I thought, and I was now mad at her too for doing what I couldn't do—stay at home!

So, I hated Lana, hated Josh, hated that stupid bumpy bus ride, hated my annoying sister, hated my mom and her yoga class, hated the damn transmission on my Monte Carlo, hated Mrs. Roberts for giving me a hard time about some stupid Coca-Cola scholarship I would never get. Anything and everything. You name it, I hated it.

Josh asked me if I wanted to go to the gym with him after school. I shook my head and got on the bus. All I wanted to do was go home and back to sleep and erase this uneventful day from my memory.

"Call me," he said to me holding up his fingers to his ears like an old-fashioned telephone. I glared at him from the dirty window of the school bus and thought anyone watching this little pantomime would have thought we were a couple. I knew he did it on purpose because behind him were some hot Junior cheerleaders who were watching us. But that was Josh for ya—always causing a scene and being stupid. I rolled my eyes.

I got home to my mom cooking dinner and Sydney finishing her homework at the kitchen table. My dad wasn't home yet, and the first thing I asked was, "Is the car done?" My mom gave me her "Are you serious?" look, and Sydney started to laugh at me. I shot the brat a look from hell, and she shut up real fast.

"What's for dinner?" I asked, even though I really didn't care.

"Shrimp scampi, angel hair pasta..." my mom started, but I walked away saying, "Okay, I'll be in my room," without letting her finish. I got to my room and plopped on my bed and closed my eyes thinking about how badly life sucked at the moment.

I guess I fell asleep for a little bit. I'm an easy-sleeper, I suppose, cause it seems like all I need to do is close my eyes, and I'm somewhere in dreamland. I woke up with a jolt. There was some kind of "pop" sound in the distance, and everything went quiet and dark. Not normal night-time dark, I mean *dark* dark. The hum of the appliances and cable boxes in the house went silent. The street light outside my window was out. The little green flickering of the battery-operated fire alarm light on my ceiling was the only light around. Living in Florida, power outages were common place. Maybe not so much for November, but they still happened. I heard my mother say to Sydney, "It's okay. It's okay."

I got up and walked into the living room. My mother was cuddling with Sydney on the couch, and my dad was in the kitchen pantry rummaging for the flashlight. "Get TECO on the phone," my father commanded my mother, and she got up to get her cell.

"What time is it?" I asked, still in somewhat of a dream state.

"About 7:30," my mom replied as she balanced her cellphone in the crook of her neck with her shoulder.

"What about dinner?" I asked. I could care less about the power. I was hungry and a little pissed they hadn't gotten me to eat with them.

"Left you a plate in the fridge," she answered as I could hear the extension ringing, "but it won't be any good without the microwave!"

Leave it to my mom to state the obvious. Cold shrimp never hurt anyone.

"Power's out all over the neighborhood," I called over to my dad.

"How do you know?" he yelled back from the pantry. I could hear him cursing under his breath and fumbling with a flashlight. "Ya know, babe," he yelled, directed at my mother, "if you weren't so goddamn unorganized, I might be able to actually find something in a crisis situation!"

Sydney tensed up. She hated it when my parents yelled at each other. I learned to live with it. It wasn't that often, and I was old enough to understand both of them had fiery Italian blood running through their veins. I looked to my mom, who rolled her eyes at Sydney as if to say, "you know your father's crazy!" and Syd's shoulders relaxed. I realized right then I had gotten my natural eye-rolling habit from my mother. Mom was an expert eye-roller, much to my father's chagrin.

"The street's out," I finally answered my father as he stepped out of the pantry flicking the switch on the newly charged flashlight.

"I want to go outside!" Sydney declared.

Mom finished punching in some numbers on her cellphone and disconnected the call. "The automated recording said they were aware of the problem and power would be back as soon as possible."

"What the hell is that supposed to mean?" my dad snapped.

Mom shrugged. "I don't know. That's all it said. It was the electric company recording." My dad went into a diatribe of obscenities, and I grabbed Sydney's hand. "C'mon, let's go outside," I said and led her to the front door.

It was a little chilly that night. It can get that way in November. Not freezing, though, like some of the northern states. It's comfortable that time of year. My mom always wears a jacket or sweater 'cause she's naturally cold all the time. I'm fine in shorts all year round. When we got outside, it seemed like the whole block was out there. This is the usual scene whenever there's a blackout. Ain't nothing like bringing neighbors together like a tragedy, and as far as tragedies go, this barely registered on the scale. The neighborhood kids were running around in the street with their flashlights, some parents were on their front porches surrounded by candles, and voices echoed in the night air. There was always an underlying hint of nervousness as neighbors spoke and chuckled with each other, but overall, the mood was light, fun. My parents followed behind us, Dad with flashlight in hand, Mom with her cellphone.

"Hey Debbie!" my mom called to the lady who lived across the street.

"Hey!" she answered back and came down from her porch.

My mother and father met her half way down the road. "Did you call TECO?"

"How long do you think this will be?"

"It's kinda scary, but kinda cool," was how the conversation went.

Sydney went into the garage to get her bike and circled the rotunda in our cul-de-sac with the other kids. I went inside to eat the cold shrimp my mom had set aside for me.

When I opened the front door, I heard my cellphone ringing so I ran to my room. Josh's idiotic face flashed on the screen once again.

"Dude!" he exclaimed. "Your power out?"

"Yeah, you?"

"Yeah! Must be something big goin' on, cause Lana's power is out too."

I froze. Josh, Lana, and I all lived in different towns but were zoned for the same school district. When there were blackouts, it usually affected one town or the other. Just how far did this thing reach? But that certainly wasn't my first thought. How did Josh know about Lana? Why would she even call him, or why would he call her? Were they dating or something? I didn't know what to say, so I mumbled, "Wow, that's crazy."

"Yeah, well, let me go. I don't want my battery to die. Call me if you need anything, man." And he hung up.

As if this day couldn't get any worse, now I had the thought of Josh and Lana as a couple stuck in my head. Josh was my best friend! Why on earth was he keeping secrets from me!? And what did Lana Anderson see in *Josh*! Weird-o, mis-matched eyes, loud and crazy, no future-goals, probably going to drop out and die in a gutter somewhere Josh! I knew that was going to drive me insane! I lay back down on my bed, staring at the green fire alarm light, trying to disappear in the darkness.

Normally, when there was a blackout, the power was back on fairly quickly. I hadn't fallen back asleep; rather, I was brooding in my own depression fueled fantasies. Okay, maybe I did doze off for a little bit. I picked up my cellphone to look at the time. It was 12 am and everything in the house was as dark and as quiet as it was when the power went out four and a half hours ago. I figured everyone had gone to sleep, but then I heard voices coming from outside and realized everyone was still awake. I got up to see what was going on.

Sydney and her friends were sitting on the curb of the rotunda going to town on cartons of ice cream in their laps. My parents were sitting in the candle-lit driveway on the lawn chairs. Debbie and her husband Stuart from across the street were with them. My mom and dad were sharing their own carton of ice cream, and Debbie and Stu were eating ice cream sandwiches.

"Hey, stud!" my mom said when she saw me staggering out of the house.

"What the...?" I moaned.

"Ice cream party!" Debbie exclaimed. "Had to salvage something. Lord knows when this power will come back on!" She laughed and smiled. Stu took a huge bite out of his ice cream sandwich.

"Ma!" Sydney yelled over to my mother. "Can I stay home tomorrow!?"

My mother's face narrowed slightly. She slouched her body forward and whispered, "What time is it?" to me.

"Twelve," I answered with no emotion.

"Hmmm…" my mother said, making her voice louder so Sydney and the whole block could hear, "we'll have to see how everything goes, okay?"

"Okay," Sydney answered and continued to dip into her vanilla bean carton.

"Griffin," my mother coaxed, "come sit down. Have some ice cream with us."

The smile on her face was so pretty. She looked young and happy like she was having the time of her life. My mother was such a good and caring soul, and when she asked someone for something, it was hard to ever turn her down. I nodded my head and sat on the concrete between my mother and father's lawn chairs. My father handed me the carton of Chocolate Mudpie Madness and scuffed up my hair. I took the spoon and dug in. I was really hungry by then, and the ice cream really hit the spot. Mudpie Madness. My favorite.

We sat out there for about a half hour more, talking and laughing, my parents telling their "remember when" stories, eating up all the ice cream in the neighborhood. It was pleasant in the darkness, light-hearted and fun. There was a collective gasp when the power popped back on, and the street lights sprang to life. The houses started to hum again with all their appliances, computers, and cable boxes.

"Guess that's over with!" Debbie said clutching her chest. For all her laughs and smiles, I had suspected she was scared.

"Guess so," my mother said standing and folding up the chair. "C'mon, Syd, get your ass in bed! School tomorrow!"

"Aww, Maaaaa!" Sydney whined.

I looked at my father, and we both shook our heads and laughed.

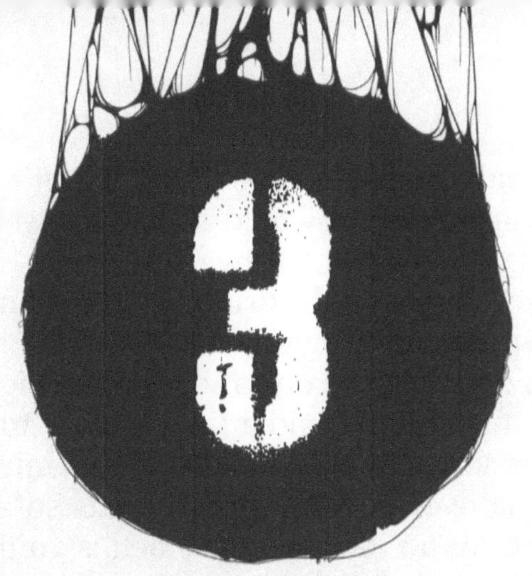

3

RAVES IS NOT IMPRESSED. I SEE IT WRITTEN all over his face. But he said he wanted me to start from the beginning, so I guess I kinda did. Anyone else who went through what I went through would classify the first blackout as the beginning. I don't think he does, though.

"Is that good enough?" I ask. "Is that what you wanted?"

He looks down at his clipboard and scribbles something feverishly. "Uh, yeah," he says without looking at me. He flips the pages over a few times. "Did you say the blackout lasted from 7:30 pm to 12:00 am?" he asks.

"Yes," I answer with authority.

"Are you sure?" he questions.

"Yes," I repeat, my voice raising in volume a notch.

"How can you be sure?" he presses.

"Because that was the same time the 2nd blackout took place," I answer matter-of-factly.

Graves stops and nearly drops his pen. "Wait," he begins, "you experienced a second blackout?"

Okay, so I know something he doesn't know. I want to stick my tongue out at him and say "nah-nah-nah- nah-poo-poo," but I don't think that would be appropriate or would go over too well right now.

"Two nights in a row," I say.

"Hmmm," he says as he drums his thick finger against the leather armchair again, "that's pretty interesting. Most of us only had the one and then the big one."

I'm confused now. And a little pissed, to be honest. He's sitting here, not even looking at me, mind you, and he's mulling over how many blackouts so-and-so had and I still have no idea what the hell is going on, what happened to me, what happened to other people. And then there's a little rise of hunger in my stomach, a growl so loud it forces Graves to look at me from atop his stupid glasses.

"Hungry?" he asks, and I'm so confused and upset that I instinctively clench my teeth together and make a horrible hissing sound. Not at him though, more like a wince to myself, but it's enough to make his eyes flash. He grips the side of the leather chair, not in fear though, in readiness, like if I make one little movement, he will pounce on me.

"Listen," I say, trying to break the sudden tension, "I'm trying to tell you what you want to know, but I'm really confused about everything and..."

"Just continue," he interrupts with another wave of his hand. His eyes are dead locked on mine. He's examining me, watching me, waiting to see if I'll try to attack him. But I'm not hungry. Not for his obviously booth-tanned skin and his slick black hair.

"You want me to..."

"Yes, pick up where you left off."

"But wait," I say. My voice sounds a little desperate, and I wish it didn't.

He glares at me hard.

"Did I die?" I ask, and the words come out of my mouth before I have a chance to control them. The thought of being dead has been in my head from the moment I was attacked. If I was dead, then maybe all the horrible and terrible things that I did—people I killed, people I ate— would kinda seem justifiable or like it didn't even happen.

"No," he replies nonchalantly. "No, you didn't die. Please continue."

My chest rises a bit as I inhale the reality of his words. I'm not stupid, though. I knew that would be his answer. I guess I was hoping for a miracle. I guess when you've done what I've done, you're kinda outta miracles.

"Okay," I say on my exhale. And I proceed with the second piece of the timeline...

The next morning was not a normal one for us. We didn't go about with our normal wake-up routines and scripts. It was all a little chaotic and rushed. Dad had gone to work early, taking my car yet again. *Another bus day for me*, I thought. When I made my way into the kitchen, the TV was on, and Mom and Syd were eating breakfast. There was a plate of French toast waiting for me at the breakfast bar, and Mom nodded to me to sit down and eat. Even though she must have had four hours of sleep last night, Sydney was all bright-eyed and bushy-tailed, as usual, and was talking rapidly about the blackout.

"The news people keep talking about the Blackout of 2003. Why's that?" Sydney asked my mom.

"Because it was pretty bad," she answered as she stirred her coffee.

"Well, what happened?" Sydney pressed.

"August 14th," Mom began, "we were living in New York at the time and the power grid failed. So, we were without power for about two days."

"Two days!" she exclaimed. "Wow! That must have been scary!"

"Ya know, I'm surprised they're comparing this little blackout to the 2003 one," Mom said after settling down a little. "This was only for a few hours."

"You know how the media has to sensationalize everything, Ma!" I interjected.

"I guess you're right," she said as she pushed back her hair from her face. "You two better get going!"

The bus ride was as agonizing as the day before. The whole way, all I kept thinking about was how I was going to confront Josh about the Lana situation without looking too conspicuous. Would he even understand what I was talking about? Would he even pick up on why I was angry? Was I angry? I didn't know. I knew I was irritated beyond belief, and I felt kinda betrayed by him for having conversations with Lana Anderson and not telling me about them.

The second I stepped off the bus, the buzz was all about the blackout. I could have cared less. I went to my locker, got my stuff for the day, and went to class. I saw Josh bopping his way into 3rd period and my stomach almost fell to the floor. A part of me wanted to smack that obnoxious smile off his obnoxious face. He came waltzing through the door in his usual style: sunglasses on the bridge of his nose, winking and pointing at all the girls and making an obnoxious clicking sound with his tongue. I saw a few of the girls mouth the word "gross" to each other and a glimmer of hope stirred within me. Maybe Lana mouthed the same word when she saw Josh, too! I could only be so lucky.

Josh sat down next to me in the back of the room. "What up, dawg?" he said as he moved his closed fist to my hand for a bump. I closed mine and pounded him with a little more force than usual. His fist jolted back in a wince of pain, and he gave me a strange look. "Easy, easy, killa!" he said as he opened his fingers and shook out his hand.

"Sup, bro?" I answered without acknowledging the intentional force of my fist bump.

"Nada," he responded. "When did your power kick back on last night?"

"Midnight," I answered. "You?"

"Same. My dad and I ate all the ice cream in the house."

I snorted and grinned. "Us too."

There was an awkward pause, and I was trying to find the moment to ask about Lana. I started to say, "How'd you know about..." but the bell rang, and the teacher stood up from his desk to start the class.

Things didn't get much better the rest of the day. It was another uneventful snooze-fest. Lana was out again. I had this strange feeling she was avoiding me, but quickly got rid of that idea. How could she be avoiding me when she barely knew I existed?

When I got home, Mom was putting dinner out on the table. Hot dogs, corn-on-the-cob, pickles. One of my favorites. I threw my book down and took my seat. Dad was home early that night. No mention of when my car was going to be fixed, either. Sydney was blabbering away about some stupid writing contest she entered, and after hearing about the "no word" on my car, I think the only words I spoke were, "Pass the ketchup."

A little while after dinner, I went into the family room so I could go online. We only had one computer we all shared—an ancient desktop—but we all had different settings and passwords to get into our files. After I logged in, I went straight to one of the social networking sites that I belong to. It was one of those sites where you connect with your friends, their friends, and the rest of the god-forsaken world. I wanted to see if Lana had logged in and posted something about her not being in school. She had accepted my friend request last year, but we didn't post anything to each other's message boards. We weren't "friends" like that. Well, anyway, the site was down. I got this weird error message that said I was unable to connect to the server. I tried some other websites that I frequent, and they were down, too.

"Internet's down!" I screamed into the family room.

"What?" my dad yelled back.

"Internet's down!" I repeated.

"What about the phone?" he replied.

I picked up the cordless that sat next to the monitor on the computer desk and pressed the "talk" button. The dial tone immediately blared in my ear. "Phone's okay!" I yelled back to my dad.

"Hon! Get Brighthouse on the phone! The Internet is not working!" I heard my father yell at my mother. He hated talking to people on the phone, especially customer service-technical support type people. When that type of situation arose, it was always my mother's duty to take charge. I heard the other extension in the house "beep" to life and my mother punched in the numbers of the cable service provider. She must have had them memorized because here in Florida, something was always going wrong: Internet out, cable not working, electricity getting funky. Always something. Always giving my father something else to complain about, too. I heard him cursing to my mother in the living room, "And get someone on the phone! No more recordings!"

My mother responded, "Whatever," and the sound of her New York accent rang heavily in the air.

I smiled to myself and shook my head. Figuring it would take forever and a day to get the Internet up and running, I clicked the start button to temporarily power down the computer. The last thing I noticed was the time, 7:30, before the "pop" sound came again with the eerie silence right behind it. I heard Syd squeal in her room. I heard my father yell out, "Jesus Christ!" to no one in particular, and I heard my mother rush into Sydney's room saying, "It's okay. It's okay!" as if to a hurt and scared animal. It had happened again. Another blackout. I looked out the front window and the neighbors were starting to filter into the dark cul-de-sac, but their facial expressions were a lot different than they were the night before. Debbie and Stu (with their daughter Ashlyn in tow) walked across the street to our house.

"Dad!" I called my father who was back in the pantry fussing with the flashlight. "Dad, the Marshalls are coming up to the house."

"Jesus!" he groaned. "Don't answer the..."

But the bell rang, and my sister went racing down our porcelain tile foyer to open the door. There was desperation in Debbie's voice as she asked my sister, "You guys okay over here?"

"Yeah, yeah, we're okay," Sydney said, "Ma! Miss Debbie's here."

My mother came bustling down the hallway and stood at the front door. She never invited the Marshalls in, and I think it was partly to do with the fact that my father hated having people in our house. I got up from the desk and followed suit. Sydney clutched my mother's waist in a death grip. I stood behind them looking at the worried faces of our neighbors.

"A little weird, don't cha think?" Stu said with his eyes flashing wide. Debbie's pale face forced a smile on her chubby cheeks.

Mom made a nervous shift, as Sydney's grip tightened on her. "Not too weird," she said half-heartedly to help lighten the now ominous mood. "Ya know, it is Florida..."

"It's November, Maggie," Debbie huffed. "In your eight years of living here, when has this ever happened in November?"

Sydney and Ashlyn stared at each other with fierce fearful glances, so I put my hand on Syd's shoulder and tried to usher her away from the door, but she was locked on tight to my mother. There was no budging her.

"It's terrorists!" Stu declared.

"Now, Stu..." Mom interrupted as the word "terrorists" made my sisters fingernails dig into her rib cage.

"I'm telling you, Maggie," he continued.

"Really, Stu, let's not get all bent outta shape..." my mother insisted, her deep New York accent coming out strong.

"He's right, Maggie!" Debbie interjected. "The Internet has been wonky all day, my phone service has been going in and out, TV doing weird stuff. Our cells are out, too!"

Upon hearing that, I turned on my heels and raced for my bedroom. I grabbed my cell and looked at the touchscreen to look for any texts or voice messages or missed calls. Maybe an SOS text from Lana? Wishful thinking as there was nothing. Nothing. I hit the keypad and dialed Josh's number. He picked up with a "Hey."

"Hey. Power out again?"

"Yep."

"Here too. Call ya later."

I hung up and raced back to the foyer. "My cell's working fine," I said, winded.

My mother rolled her eyes at Debbie and Stu. "See! You guys are getting all freaked out for nothing. Listen, let me go help Jack with the flashlights. Go home and try your cells again. Call TECO. If you need anything, come over to get us." And with that, she gently shut the door in their faces.

"Mommy!" Sydney squealed with terror.

"What the hell did they want?" my father called from the living room although we all knew very well he was hiding in the wings, listening to every word.

"Nothing, nothing," my mom said, brushing him off.

"Mommy, I don't wanna go to school tomorrow. I wanna stay home with you," Syd continued to whine.

"No, ain't nobody staying home from..." my dad started to yell, but in an instant, there was a deep hum in the house, and everything sprang back to life once more.

●

I pause to swallow. All this talking is making my throat dry, and I wish I had some water or maybe even a Coke.

"Your neighbors?" Graves says glancing at his notes. "The Marshalls?"

"Stuart you said the father's name was?"

I nod.

"Why did he say it was terrorists?"

I shrug my shoulders. "How am I supposed to know that?"

"Well, is there any indication he would know if it were terrorists or not? What did he do for a living? What was his nationality? Did he act suspiciously? Do you know if he had any criminal activity going on?"

Graves gives me rapid fire questions that make my head spin.

"How am I supposed to know all that? He was my neighbor. My weird-o neighbor."

Graves flips to a blank page on his clipboard, and I see him write in big letters STUART MARSHALL at the top. "Weird, how?" he asks as he licks his thick lips in frustration.

I'm agitated. I shift in my seat, and my thirst is becoming almost unbearable. "I don't know. He was weird. Everyone on the block was weird. People are weird. What do you want me to say? I think they were German or something. They had blonde hair, so I guess they were. He was a postman. The wife, Debbie, sold Avon stuff from home. I guess they were average people. I don't know. Why?"

As I speak, Graves jots down some notes underneath Stu's name. "It's just that it's curious he would mention terrorists."

"Curious? Why? *Was* it terrorists?"

Graves looks around the room, and he begins to tap the edge of his pen against the clipboard. My question has obviously made him uncomfortable, threw him off guard a bit.

I pursue the issue, "Well, was it terrorists?"

"It's not really a concern of yours, and I..." he begins to deny me an answer, but my body feels hot, and I start to grip the sides of the couch.

"Then why are you writing my dead neighbor's name on your stupid paper and asking me about terrorists?" I yell, my voice getting louder and louder, my body feeling hotter and hotter.

He keeps looking over to the sidewall. There's a mirror there that I notice for the first time. One of *those* mirrors. Someone's watching us, and he keeps glancing over there as if he's looking for some sort of sign or validation. But he doesn't answer me, and I can't control the rising heat in my body. My eyes flutter in the back of my head, and I blink rapidly to try to maintain focus. I'm losing control; the familiar feeling of rising heat and a wave washing over me, letting go, and releasing, giving into an unseen urgency that detached my conscious self from my fog-gloom self. My knee rapidly bounces up and down up and down, and I have one last thought of tearing out Graves's heart with my bare hands before I flash my teeth and growl like some primal animal.

The phone on Graves's desk chirps, and I'm broken from my instinctual trance. How Graves reacted to me, I'll never know, but my body relaxes, and I become cognizant of my surroundings.

Graves looks up at me. There's a line of sweat rimming his hairline. I get a sense he was ready for me, ready to take me down if I had attacked him. His fingers have left impressions in the arms of his leather chair, but not like they had before. These are deep, like he was half- standing while I was having my freak-out, half-standing and putting all his muscular weight down onto those leather arms. Half-standing and ready for me.

"As a matter of fact, it was." And he says it just like that. Matter-of-factly. No emotion. No affect. As if he was reading something in a newspaper, or book.

Terrorists.

Graves says the word "terrorists" like it's no big thing, and I want to scream at him for being an idiot. I want to leap across this coffee table and bite *his* face off.

"What did they do? How did they do it?" is all I'm able to muster up.

"The Big One. The Big Blackout. They shut us down from the inside and crippled us. That gave them the chance to release the virus. Popular belief is that the intent was to kill all of us, but it didn't work that way. Something failed when the chemical was distributed. Some people died from exposure, some people were unaffected by it, and some people were..." and he pauses to give me a hard stare, "...changed."

Changed?

"I was changed? Changed like how? Changed like what?" I say waving my hands around the air much like my mother does... did... when she was over-excited.

"Changed," Graves repeats.

"What? What? Like an animal? Like a freak of nature? Like, like, like a zombie?"

Graves pauses and thinks over what I said. "For lack of a better word, yes, like a zombie," he responds in his uncaring, unaffected voice. I hate that voice.

Zombie.

That was really the only word I could use to describe what had happened to me, but it was the last word I was willing to admit to. I remember watching all those B-movies as a kid, and then the more big-budget ones when I got older: *Night of the Living Dead, Dawn of the Dead,* even the comical *Shaun of the Dead.* Films where "...persons who have recently died have been returning to life and committing acts of murder." Changed. I was changed. Things that I did, I did when I was changed. Graves said I didn't die. I didn't think I died. I could have only been so lucky. Still, the word "zombie" doesn't sink in with me. I remember all those movies I saw over the years, and I take the word in association with what happened to me, and I can't make the connection.

"So," Graves says, interrupting my thoughts, "can you go on or would you rather stop and pick this up later?"

"No," I answer. "I'll go on. Can I just get something to drink?"

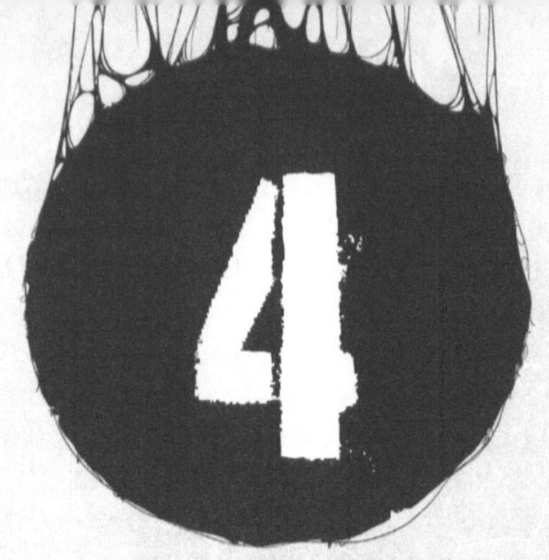

GRAVES HANDS ME A PEPSI CAN, AND I TAKE a swig. The carbonation of the beverage is like a mouthful of sand grating down my throat, and I realize it must have been ages since I drank a soda—or anything besides blood, for that matter. Although it tastes awful (I'm actually partial to Coke), it does its job of eliminating the dryness, and I'm ready to go back to my story. Because, really, it is a story. And I speak these words as if I was telling a friend about a movie I just watched. They're just words about events that may or may not have happened, and I'm still not quite sure what I'm doing here or even why I'm talking to this imperious man in front of me.

Graves presses the stop button on the recorder and flips over the tape. I had almost forgotten my words were being captured.

"Dr. Holston is going to want you to eat something and get settled in your dorm in a little bit, so I think we'll go a little while longer," Graves says before he presses the record button again.

"Where is this place?" I ask. "*What* is this place?"

"I told you. It's the Mount Sinai Re-Assimilation Center."

I shake my head. "No, I mean, where are we? Location."

Graves breathes deeply. His barrel chest rises majestically under his white, crisp shirt.

He must work out, I think. *Or maybe killed a lot of people.* It's obvious every time I ask him a question, he gets annoyed. He doesn't want to answer me; he wants to figure out whatever he's trying to figure out. I hate looking at him because when he looks back at me it feels like daggers in my brain. His stares make something deep inside me shudder. Like, he's mentally murdering me with each glance. I take another sip of my soda.

"When everything went to hell, Mount Sinai in New York was about the only medical facility functioning at full capacity," he answers. "They stepped in and took over. They were the only ones capable of doing it. Hence, the name. We're in the old Brandon Regional Hospital in Florida. It's strictly a Re-Assimilation Center."

"What does that mean, because you say it like I'm supposed to know what that means, but I have no clue what you're talking about," I interject.

Graves's face narrows in contempt, and he doesn't answer me.

"Let's continue please," he says as he loosens up his tie. It's one of those fancy jobs. Looks like the material of one of Mom's purses. Some designer something or other. It's blue and brown and flowery. Not something I would ever wear, but on Graves it works. He's one of those guys who seems to be very particular about his appearance even if the Apocalypse just happened. "What happened next?"

Even though the second blackout didn't last nearly as long as the one the night before it, it was enough to have everyone rattled and on edge. The Marshalls had insinuated the idea of terrorists and that certainly was not an unpopular speculation. Sydney had begged my mother to stay home from school, and even though my dad was against the idea at first, he allowed it. With my car still in the shop, I was forced to take the bus for the third day in a row. I swore if my car wasn't done by the afternoon, I was going to stay home, too.

The buzz around school was even louder than yesterday. It was hard for the teachers to keep everyone on task because the conversations all centered around the blackout. Some neighborhoods had lost power for a few minutes; others were out for a few hours. It seemed there was also widespread mechanical disturbance. Some people lost cell service, some Internet, some even lost use of their microwaves or ice makers. In 1st period physics, Andy Gregors led the conversation about a possible EMP, but the teacher dispelled that theory. An electromagnetic pulse would have taken out everyone and everything; power would not have been restored. Andy was one of those conspiracy theorists who always fought with the teachers. I couldn't stand him, but I will admit it, all the stuff going on was definitely strange. Strange enough to make me forget about confronting Josh about Lana. However, there was a glimmer of hope in 2nd period when my mom texted me to say the car was ready! "We'll get it when Dad gets home from work," it read. Finally! Things were getting back to normal.

I could only be so lucky.

Third period rolled around, and Josh bopped in like always. We sat in the back like we usually did. He was all talking about the blackout like everyone else was. Josh was a sheep like that. If the school conversation was about lollipops and puppy dogs, he'd be front and center on the topic. Josh loved to feel involved, like he was a part of the bigger picture, like his opinion actually mattered and made a difference in people's lives. I was not that naïve. I had a pretty good sense of my ineffectual existence for someone my age.

"Lana's out again," he announced as my eyes widened. How did he know? When did he talk to her? What the hell was going on with them?

"Oh, yeah?" I responded, trying to play it cool.

"Yeah, she..." But before he could continue, there was a weird, all-too-familiar "pop" sound, and the room went dark. Some preppy girls in front of us screamed. The teacher immediately stood up and flipped open his cell phone. I reached into my back pocket for mine, and Josh did the same.

"Out," he said.

"Me too," I answered.

The class started to get a little panicked. One of the preppy girls started to cry. The teacher went over to the classroom phone and dialed the main office. He held up his hand as if to silence the class, "Guys, guys, guys," he said over the teenaged mumblings, "let me see if I can get the front office people on the phone. Don't freak out; we'll get this all straightened out."

"What the hell?" Josh said, and I could see he was starting to get into panic mode, too.

I shrugged my shoulders.

"My car's fixed," I said. I guess I was trying to take his mind off the situation. I guess I was trying to take *my* mind off the situation.

"Sweet," he replied half-heartedly. "No more yellow bus for you." But there was a sound of fear rising within the timbre of his voice.

"Try your phone, Alicia!" one of the cheerleader girls said to the now hysterical preppy girl.

"It's not working!" that Alicia chic screamed, and the teacher yelled from the front of the room, "Will somebody shut her up!" and then went back to his conversation with the front office people on the internal school phone. He said "okay" and hung up.

"Here's the situation," he declared as the room quieted down. "Power's out all over. The principal said if it doesn't come back up in about two hours, the bus company will dispatch the buses and send you guys home for the day. Not a bad deal, if you ask me," he tried to force a chuckle to lighten the mood. "Until then, we have to stay put. No changing classes, no bathroom, no water."

There was a collective grumble and someone from the opposite side of the room yelled out, "And no work!"

That sent everyone into hoots and hollers and applause. The teacher nodded his head and put his forefinger to his lips as if it was supposed to be a secret, but we knew no one in the building was doing anything right at that moment. No changing classes. No bathroom. No water. No work.

The two-hour time limit expired, and we were instructed that the buses would be arriving shortly. The kids who walked to school or drove were dismissed to go home. There were only a few of us hanging around waiting for the buses to show up.

"Hey man, do you think I can ride the bus with you and hang out at your place for a while?" Josh asked. "My dad's supposed to be working late and all, and without power and no cells, I'm gonna be pretty bored."

No, you're scared, I thought.

"Sure," I answered. "We'll go get my car when my dad gets home. My mom and sister are at the house. Eat over."

"Thanks," Josh said with a sigh of relief. He was my best friend. Did he really think I was going to say no? Unless he knew that I was annoyed with him for dropping hints about Lana...

We all filed onto the bus. Me, Josh, a couple of Junior girls, and a few Freshman boys. Josh and I were the only Seniors. I didn't know any of the other kids. I'd seen the Junior girls around school, but I didn't know them. Josh, of course did his trademark finger point and wink when they came on after us. They smiled and giggled. Most younger girls did. Maybe it was because they were flattered from getting attention from a Senior, or maybe it was a nervous, uncomfortable giggle. Who knew? Josh sat across from me in the back. I propped my head against the smelly vinyl seat and stared out the window. Josh took out his phone and popped in his earbuds to listen to his downloaded music. "Wake me when we get there," he said loudly. I gave him the thumbs up sign flicking my wrist with an obnoxious motion.

I started to think about Lana and thought I would leave her a message on her webpage to see if she was okay, but then I rolled my eyes when I realized the power was out!

Lana. What the hell do you see in Josh? *I* was supposed to be the one to take you to the prom. *I* was gonna rent a nice limo and do the whole corsage thingie. *I* was gonna dance like a fool on the dance floor with you. *I* was gonna pull out your chair for you when we sat down to eat. *I* was gonna be the one to open your bottle of beer at the after-party. *I* was gonna be the one to...

My head thumped against the glass of the window, interrupting my thoughts. The driver had made a sudden sharp turn, and I perked my head up to see what had happened. The other kids on the bus didn't seem to notice. Josh's sleeping body had naturally moved with the rocking of the bus, but for me, who was lost in thought, I was jarred into reality from the abrupt movement. The driver's CB radio crackled to life. I could see his hand in the rearview mirror reach to pick it up. His hand looked unsteady, and for a split second I thought he was shaking. But that could have been from my vision and the shakiness of the bus. I don't normally pay attention to the radio blather, but for some reason, at that moment, I did. Of course, it sounded like a lot of static and incoherent words. Like on the trains in New York. I remember going into the city with my parents when I was a kid and the conductor got on the loudspeaker. I looked at my mom and said, "What did he say?" She answered, "Change at Jamaica." But what it sounded like was completely different. I guess my mother was able to understand it because we had to get off our line at Jamaica station and board another train. When I was a kid, I thought I had to be a grown up to understand the train conductor, so that's why I always ignored the bus CB transmissions.

I wasn't ignoring them then.

The driver was shaking because after some static filled words from the other end of the radio, he made another sharp turn, this one more forceful than the last. I looked out the window and saw we were not on the normal bus route. The bus increased in speed. Josh woke up, took out his earbuds, and looked at me with his hands outstretched in a "what the hell?" gesture. One of the Freshman kids yelled out, "Hey driver! Cut it out! You're making me sick back here. I'm gonna blow chunks!" The boy sitting across from him started laughing. Then I heard the driver say, "What about I-75?" into the walkie, and the response from the other end was a clear-as-day "No!"

Another sharp turn.

The other kids were starting to get anxious. I could tell their conversations were becoming more rapid and sing-songy.

"Is this the way you normally go?" Josh asked as he looked out the window.

"No," I answered, and I could hear fear in my own voice. The bus ride was normally a half hour from the school to my stop, but we had gone some other way and were a good 45 minutes in the opposite direction. "I think we're somewhere near Mulberry."

"Mulberry!" Josh exclaimed. "No way, man! That's impossible!"

"I'm serious. I must have drifted off to sleep…"

Then, without warning, the voice on the CB came on in a high-pitched wail that startled and silenced the whole bus: "Oh God! Oh God! Get out of there! Get out of there!" The driver violently swerved to the side of a dirt road, flung open the door with the handlebar and raced out of the bus into the nearby field. Immediately, we filled up the left side of the bus and watched as the driver disappeared into a thick of trees.

"He left us!?" the Freshman kid screamed. "What the hell?" Josh repeated.

I shrugged my shoulders. We were literally in the middle of nowhere. I had never been up that way before. Never seen any of the surroundings, and to be honest, it wasn't much but dirt road and woods.

"Anybody know where we are?" I yelled out to the entire bus.

"Yeah. I think so," one of the Junior girls responded as she tilted her body into the aisle. "There should be train tracks near here if I'm right. We're in Mulberry. Close to the industrial section. My dad used to work out this way."

"You guys know what's going on?" the other girl said.

"No," I answered.

"Where do you think he went?" the one in the aisle asked.

"Maybe he had to take a leak!" Josh joked and the girls giggled.

It was possible, but after hearing that scream from the other end of the radio, I didn't think it was probable.

"Let me try the radio," I said as I made my way to the front of the bus.

"Dude," the mouthy Freshman yelled to me, "why don't you drive us home!" and his buddies laughed with him.

"If I knew how to drive a bus," I replied, "but we're out of luck there."

"Anything on the radio?" Josh said as he came up behind me. I nearly jumped out of my own skin. He laughed, recognizing he had scared me. "Relax, buddy! Only me."

I ignored him and shook my head. "Just static."

Josh grabbed the door handle and pulled it shut. "I always wanted to do that!" he chuckled. I glared at him. Each second that passed made me more uncomfortable. My mind was starting to race, and the weirdness of the blackouts, the bus ride, and Stu's talk of terrorists all flooded my mind at once.

"We can't stay here," I whispered to him. There was a small battery-operated digital clock on the dashboard. It was 3PM. "If we get to the train tracks and follow them a bit, we might be able to get to State Road 60 before dark. Then we can hitch a ride or something from there."

"Leave?" he yelled, and I grabbed his hair and bent his head down to "shush" him.

"Yes. Leave. We can't stay here in the middle of nowhere. Who knows what the hell is going on out there? Who knows where the driver ran to or why he left us. I don't want to stay here to find out. It's gonna get real dark in a couple of hours."

Josh mulled it over for a second. "What about the others?"

I shrugged. "I guess if they want to come, they can, but really? Do you want those Freshmen tagging along with us?"

Josh looked back over his shoulder, and I glanced up into the rearview mirror. The Freshman boys were picking their noses and wiping their fingers on the backs of the seats, laughing all the way. To think that I had laid my head back on my seat while they were probably painting the vinyl on the opposite side with their nose gunk made me wince in disgust.

"I see your point," Josh said flatly. "What about the girls?"

"Think Sydney times two," I paused for dramatic effect, "in the dark."

"Another point taken," he answered nodding his head.

"Hey, guys?" one of the girls asked. "Anything going on?"

"Yeah, listen," I said as I stood up, "Josh and I are gonna go see what's up. Try to get help or something."

"No way!" the other protested. "You're not leaving us here alone! Let's all go together!"

Josh and I glanced at each other.

"We're gonna try to get to State Road 60 to see if we can flag someone down or something," he added.

"Yeah," I continued, "it's probably gonna be a real long walk from here. Probably not worth your effort if we're gonna get someone to come back and pick you guys up."

"Dude," the ring-leader Freshman boy said, "get us help. I'm staying right here!"

"Yeah, man," one of the other boys echoed.

"Why don't you sit tight, babysit the litt'uns, and don't worry about a thing," Josh said in a calming, quasi-flirtatious way to one of the girls. She had an "I-don't-know" expression on her face, but after he pointed his finger at her and gave her a wink, her face lit up and she nodded her head.

"Okay," she said, her brown curls bouncing up and down around her face, "just hurry back!"

"And get us some grub, man! We're starving!" the head Freshman said as the others continued their laughter.

"Shut your face and shut the door behind us!" I commanded him as I pulled the handlebar on the door. I looked at Josh. "I always wanted to do that!" I exclaimed and he smiled wide.

"See! I told ya!" he responded as we both hopped off the bus.

The Freshman boy was right behind us to close the door. I heard him yell something about being the King of the Yellow Chariot as we walked onto the dirt road. I rolled my eyes.

We walked solemnly along the unfamiliar dirt road. There was an eerie silence in the air. No cars drove by. No familiar town sounds of kids playing in their backyards or riding their bikes on dusty trails. I kicked the dirt in front of me with every step I took, trying to count the particles that rose up in puffs at my feet. Every now and then, I looked over my shoulder behind me to see if anything was going on. The bus was starting to become a big yellow blur. Josh had turned around and was walking backward so our faces met, and he could keep an eye on the bus.

Suddenly he stopped and pulled on my shirt. "Look, man! Someone's running to the bus!"

I turned and looked. We must have been about three blocks or so away, but it was all open field and land surrounded by some trees, so we still had an unobstructed view of the bus.

"You think that's the driver going back?" I asked.

"Yeah. Probably is," Josh replied as we watched the figure who looked like our bus driver race around to the door side of the bus.

"Hey! Hey!" Josh cupped his hands and screamed. "The kids are still in there! Come swing by and pick us up!"

The driver stopped, and it looked like he turned his head toward us. I breathed a sigh of relief and bent forward to put my hands on my knees.

"See, man, it's all good! I told you he had to take a leak!" Josh reassured me as he patted my back.

I spat into the dirt. "Yeah, some leak that was! Maybe it was more than that!"

We laughed as I straightened out my back. "When ya gotta go, ya gotta go!" Josh playfully declared, and we watched the bus door open, and the driver get on.

"Stupid Frosh kid with the big mouth," Josh complained referring to the obnoxious Freshman boy on the bus. "Glad he had the sense to open the door for the driver. C'mon, baby, rev that engine and come get us!"

But the engine didn't rev.

Instead, the sound of horrifying screams shot out into the air. We both froze as we watched the bus sway slightly from side to side. There were growls and moans and screams and screams and screams and screams. I shook Josh's shoulder as if to snap him out of his frozen trance, but it was his hand that was locked tight onto mine. I looked at him and saw his face was as white as a ghost. The only thing I was able to say was "Run."

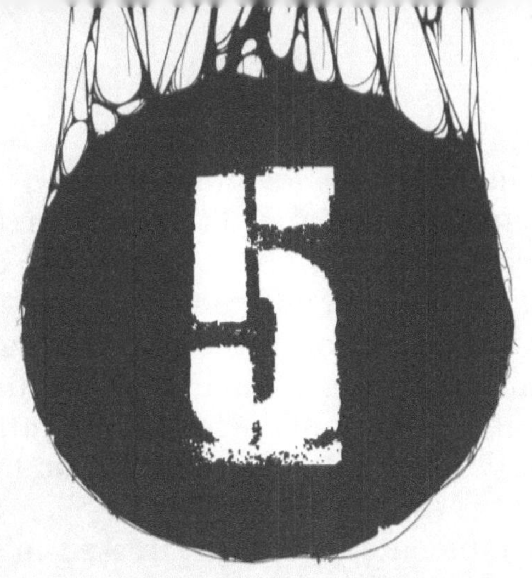

I STOP THERE BECAUSE I DON'T HAVE ANY-thing left in me. I can't go any further 'cause my heart is pounding with each breath I take, and I'm afraid if I let myself talk about Josh and what happened, I'll die of a stroke or something. The room is getting warmer. I'm still thirsty. Graves is looking at me with his big black eyes like he wants me to continue. Are his eyes really black? Or are his pupils so insanely large that they consume the entire circumference of his eyes?

"Oh," he says as if some imaginary light bulb has gone on inside his brain, "you done for now?" I feel like he should be patting my head like a little dog or something. His tone is so condescending; it makes me want to throw up.

I nod my head. I'm done with him, with this, with the interview. Graves stops the recorder, gets up and walks behind his desk. He dials a number on the phone and says, "Patient 024 is ready for pick up," and hangs up.

Patient 024. Whatever that means. I'm a number to him, even though I told him my name and probably repeated it a few times when I was telling him parts of my story. But no, to him I'm still Patient 024. That gets me thinking—does my number mean something? Are there 23 others like me? Is there anyone after me? I'm still sick; I know it. I feel it. I can sense that there's something in me that's different, changed. And maybe that's why I'm unable to ask the questions I need to ask, or to formulate clearer thoughts and sentences. Like, there are still remnants of the fog swirling around in my mind. I need to rest. Maybe I need to eat, too. But I'm not hungry...

Within moments, two men dressed in police uniforms and a doctor I haven't seen before at the door. The doctor motions for me to get up and follow him. I obey his non-verbal command and leave the office without saying another word to Graves. The doctor leads me down the corridor, through some heavy metal doors that need swipe cards to open, and into what looks like an old maternity ward. He opens a door and leads me into a pale blue room with white curtains. The room is made up nicely, and looks pleasant enough, unlike the white walled prison I woke up in this morning.

"This is your dorm," the doctor says as I step into the room. He stays by the door, and I see he's holding a key ring. "You have everything you need. There are clean clothes in the dresser, the bathroom is to the right—you'll find soap and clean towels in there. The TV works, but there are only a few stations up and running, and they mostly play old sitcom repeats. There is some reading material on your nightstand, and the orderly left you a tray for dinner. Dr. Holston suggests eating slowly; it's best to pace yourself in your condition. If you need anything, there's a nurse's station down the hall. Press the intercom button on the wall, and they will answer you to determine your needs or answer any questions.

Dr. Holston will be in tomorrow morning around 9 am for morning examination and will then take you to your session with Dr. Graves. Have a good night." And with that, he closed the door and locked it behind him.

Locked in.

I survey the room a bit more. It's a fairly basic hospital room with a TV hanging from the ceiling and a hospital bed with buttons for adjustments. My dorm. I don't think this is what I had in mind in the way of a dorm. The dorm I had planned on going to would have smelled like Ramen noodles and had pictures of half-naked women on the walls. Instead, I get framed pictures of happy families with puppy dogs, a copy of *Catch-22* on the nightstand, and a blue tray of food at the foot of the bed with a pitcher of water next to it. I sit down on the bed and open the lid of the tray. Some sort of chicken looking meat, mashed potatoes, and string beans. It smells good. My old senses kick in, the senses I had before I was changed, and I pick up the fork and curiously prod the food on the plate. I used to like chicken and mashed potatoes. I wonder if I still do. I raise a forkful of meat mixed with the potatoes and open my lips, anticipating the flavors that will explode in my mouth. I pace myself, like the doctor suggested, but all I keep smelling is the strong iron scent of blood, and my mind is telling me that no, this isn't a piece of chicken; this is a hunk of that little girl's calf, and no, this isn't a glob of starchy mashed potatoes; it's a glob of white muscle from that young man's bicep. I start to chew, and these thoughts keep coming to me, like my brain is tricking my mouth or something, and I start to gag, start to feel a slight surge of vomit rise up in my throat. My stomach growls again, and I'm determined to keep the food down.

I will not throw up, I will not throw up, I will not...
I throw up.

In my mouth.

The acidy bile is mixed with the chicken and mashed potatoes, and I spit it out into the napkin next to the tray. It's no use. I put the cover on the tray and place it on the nightstand. I pour myself a glass of water, chug it down, then lie on the bed with my arms folded behind my head.

The pictures in the room are a little disturbing to me. No, a lot disturbing. They're of happy people smiling and playing: a mother and father holding hands looking lovingly at their blonde haired blue eyed perfect children. A Hispanic looking woman kneeling down in front of a German Shepherd, laughing as the animal licks her face. Lovingly. A black father pushing his son on a swing. Laughing. Lovingly. It's weird. These people could very well have been people that I killed.

Wait. Did I kill them? Do they know these are the people and animals I mutilated? Did they put these pictures in here as some cruel joke to remind me I've messed up big time, I destroyed lives, I ruined families, I...

One of the boys in the pictures looks like Josh, and I'm completely convinced they are playing a game with me, that this is all going to end in my execution or something. The novel, *Catch-22*, why would they leave that here in my room? Are they sending me a message with that as well?

Josh...

I know I'll have to get into it tomorrow with Graves, but at least I have a night to figure out what I want to tell him and what I do not want to tell him. I close my eyes to try to hide from the faces of my maybe victims on the walls. I hope either I or they disappear when my eyes are shut. Maybe both. But the second I shut my eyes, Josh's face pops into view. I can't escape him, or that night, or what happened, and I know Graves isn't going to let me escape it tomorrow either.

Josh...

He annoyed the hell out of me, but he was my best friend, and for some reason I have an overwhelming sense of guilt and pain and hate every time his face flashes in my mind. Even more so than the guilt I feel about my mother and sister and what happened to them.

Josh...

I tighten my lids, hoping to increase the darkness behind my eyes, but it's no use; there's his face and his opened bowels, and his gnashed chest. Then his voice starts to echo, and I remember the things he said, no *screamed*, and I know there's no stopping the floodgates from releasing the memories.

Josh....

"Run," I said to him in a calm voice, although the fear and anxiety was at an all-time high surging throughout my body.

He was terrified. White. Ghostly. Sickly. But I knew he understood because he nodded his head and started counting. On "three" we ran. I'm not sure how long or how fast, but it was a while. My instincts took over. It was either run or faint, and once I knew Josh was comprehending the severity of what we witnessed, I knew running was the option my inner self was choosing. My inner self—the primal, human condition that forces us to survive or gives us over to the hands of death. It's quite fascinating what the body will do to survive 'cause isn't that what it's all about in the end anyway?

So, we ran. Ran. Ran. The thumping of my feet against the dirt road flooded my ears with rhythmic bass sounds. It drowned out everything around me. I was about fifteen feet away from him when I realized Josh had stopped running and was bent over, hands on knees, vomiting. I skidded to a halt, turned on my heels, and jogged over to him, my feet still at a racehorse's speed trying to slow down.

"What the hell?" he screamed as he spit up the last remnants of his stomach. I could tell he was crying, too. Tears streamed down his face and mixed into the puke puddle in front of him.

"Dude," I said with a hushed but anxious voice, "we gotta keep going, man! Who knows if he's following us or not!"

"Griff! What the hell did he do!? What the hell was that!?" he shouted.

"Josh, lower your voice!" I commanded. "C'mon, we gotta keep going!"

"Did he kill them? Did he see us? Why did he do that? What the hell is happening?" His voice was fragile and desperate, like a child, like a scared and lonely child. Not the confident jokester Josh who could talk to and wink at everyone. Not the self-assured Josh who even had the moxie to somehow know what Lana Anderson was doing.

"Maybe, I don't know," I said, getting more nervous and anxious each second, "we did yell at him, and I think he looked at us right before he got on the bus."

"He's gonna come after us! Do you hear a bus coming? Do you hear a bus?"

I wanted to slap him in the face, slap him out of his hysterics and bring him back down to reality with me, but then I realized I did hear something, an engine sound, barreling down the dirt road.

"Get over! Get over!" I ordered him to step out of the road. Josh fell to the ground and clutched his knees in the fetal position. The cuff of his jeans now dipped in the puddle of his vomit.

"It's the bus! It's the bus! Oh, God, it's the bus!" he moaned as he rocked back and forth.

I looked down the road behind us and saw headlights approaching out of the blue twilight horizon. Not a bus. But a car. *Help?*

"Not the bus, Josh! Get up! I think it's a car! It might be help," I yelled, frantically dragging him up. I stood out in the middle of the road and waved my arms back and forth and up and down, and for a second I thought about all those scenes from different horror movies when the damsel in distress flags down a beat-up pickup truck on a deserted highway only to find the driver is the stalker who's been after her, and just then I felt like I was in one of those movies as a surge of fear gripped me again.

I shook it off when the car got closer and pulled over. The driver rolled down the window, and I approached with hesitation.

"Hey," I said as I looked into the cab at the driver. The driver was a man, and there was someone slouched over in the back seat directly behind him. "My friend and I need a ride up to State Road 60. Can you give us a lift?"

"You guys hurt?" the man said.

"No, but there's some weird shit going on, and we really need to get the hell out of here, like now!" I answered with urgency.

The driver's eyes quickly darted back and forth between the person in the backseat and me. "Get in," he said as I heard the door lock pop up. I immediately opened the door and slid into the front seat. Josh gave me a look like he wanted to ride shotgun, then resigned to the back. The driver peeled off before Josh had the door completely closed.

"I'm Doug," the driver began, "and that's my buddy, Rob," and he thumbed to the backseat. He had on a workman's jumper, and his face was stained with grease. His hair was brown and greasy, and he had a full beard.

"Griffin," I answered, "and Josh," and I mimicked Doug's gesture to identify my friend in the back.

"We were working at the gas station," Doug started in a heightened, frantic voice. "The power went out. We were all kinda hanging around for a while, waiting for it to come back on, ya know? Then this guy comes tear-assing through the place, all wild and crazy. He starts knocking over the displays and acting all out of control. I told Rob he must have been on some PCP or something to be acting the way he was."

"Was he a bus driver?" Josh said gripping the back of my seat and moving closer between Doug and I so he could better hear the conversation.

"A bus driver?" Doug answered as if he didn't under-stand the question, "Nah, he wasn't no bus driver. Some guy in regular clothes. I think he had a gun or something and was looking to hold us up. Drug money probably. So anyway, Rob back there thinks he's gonna play hero and take the sonuvabitch down. I told him not to do it, but he went for it anyway. That guy was really strong and came charging at Rob and bit him on the neck."

Josh turned his head to the man in the backseat next to him, and I too peeked over my shoulder. Rob moaned quietly. He was still bent over, but I could see he was holding the side of his neck. In the darkness of the car, black inky pools of liquid decorated the carpet of the floor.

"You need to get him to a hospital, man!" Josh exclaimed.

"That's where we're going, my friend," Doug responded. "Right, buddy? Gonna get you to the hospital; then I'm gonna come back and find that guy and kick his ass!"

Rob moaned his response.

"We'll go with you," I said, figuring that would probably be the safest place to be.

"Fine by me," Doug replied and pressed his foot a little harder on the gas pedal. Josh gripped the seat a little tighter when the car accelerated forward.

"So, what were you saying about a bus driver?" Doug asked.

I rested my head against the seat as Josh proceeded to tell Doug the entire story. I didn't feel like talking much. I was still catching my breath and processing. The screams I heard coming from the bus still echoed in my head. They were chilling screams, and I can only imagine what happened to those kids we left behind. I shook my head as if to shake the sounds away.

"You okay, man?" Doug quietly asked me with a little panic in his voice. Then I realized: Doug was a bit jumpy. A little too jumpy. Anxious. A little too anxious. Like, when he first pulled up to us on the road, he asked if we were hurt. Not, what's the matter? I guess I had thought he had been through something pretty bad, too, like us, but the more I thought about it, the more I grew suspicious of toothless Doug. I was starting to feel like those chics in the horror movies again. Did I just get in a car with my killer?

"Fine, I'm fine," I answered, clearing my throat. "So, he starts running back to the bus..." Josh retold the story with wild hand gestures when suddenly, Rob in the back screamed out Doug's name. It was a jarring scream, and in my head I saw a vision of the kids on the bus. Doug violently swerved the car to the side of the road and put it in park.

"What's the matter, man!?" he yelled into the rear-view mirror.

"I... I... it... hurts!" Rob yelled back and I covered my ears for it was so loud.

"We're almost there, buddy!" Doug replied, trying to maintain composure, but Rob started making gurgling sounds in his throat and coughed up blood onto the back of the front seat.

Josh winced. I did, too.

"Okay, okay, let's have a look at ya!" Doug said maintaining his calm stance as he opened the door and got out.

"Wha... wha... what are you doing?" I said raising my voice.

"Yeah, man, he needs help, bad! We don't have time for this!" Josh interjected.

"It's okay, it's okay," Doug answered as he opened Rob's door and eased his body onto the ground, "I'm just gonna have a look at him."

Josh and I looked at each other perplexed. He mouthed, "What the hell?" and I shrugged my shoulders. Doug talked to Rob in a hushed voice, and I could see from the opened door he was petting his hair.

"Hey, man!" Doug called to Josh. "Dude in the back seat. Come help me stand him up."

Josh went white again and his eyes went wide. A wave of terror crashed over his face. "Nah, man, just get him back in the car and let's go. I'm no doctor, man, but I don't think it's such a good idea to..."

"Please!" Doug pleaded. "He says he wants to try to walk around."

"Um, I really gotta agree with Josh, Doug," I offered. "Your friend doesn't look like he's in any shape to..."

"One of you get your ass out here and help me! I helped you two sorry sons of bitches; now I need you to return the favor! Don't make me come and drag one of you out! Let's go!" There was an eerie malice in Doug's voice that made us both tense up. Josh stared hard at me.

"Listen," I whispered, "I'll slide into the driver's seat. You go out and help them. Stay close to the car door. If anything weird happens, jump back in and I'll pull away."

"What kind of stupid plan is that?" he pleaded through gritted teeth.

"I don't know," I said, "it's the best thing I got right now. I wanna get to the hospital and get away from these freaks."

Josh sighed heavily. "Alright!" he snapped as he got out of the car, and I moved my body into the driver's position.

Josh walked in front of and around the car to where Doug was sitting on the ground holding Rob's body up in his knees. Rob's hand held his neck tightly as the blood streaked down the fronts of his fingers and down his wrist and forearm. There was a lot of blood, and it was browning, drying. Rob obviously had been bleeding for some time. I glanced down at his workman's jumpsuit and took notice of the classic retro name tag stitched into the fabric. It read "Wayne," and like in a slow-motion horror movie, my stomach dropped. I quietly moved my hands to the keys in the ignition and tried desperately to get Josh's attention. I hoped the expression on my face would signal to him that we needed to bail out of there without letting Doug know something was wrong. I waited impatiently for my opening.

"Thanks, man," Doug said to Josh as he approached them.

"Yeah, yeah, no problem," Josh answered nervously.

"Just get on the other side of him and help me prop him up to his feet," Doug instructed as he bent over and hoisted Rob's underarm underneath one of his shoulders.

Josh walked around Doug, leaving my sight for a half second, and tried to mimic Doug's actions. "Dude, he's like dead weight," Josh griped as he struggled to position Rob's body against his.

"Just get him…" Doug started to say, but all of sudden, Rob let out a bloodcurdling scream and shot straight to his feet.

"Buddy! Buddy! You okay?" Doug yelled in hope and desperation.

Rob tilted his head to one side and let his hand drop down from his neck. The gaping hole between his ear and collarbone oozed with blood and fluids. Josh was frozen. He took one step backward, but that was about as far as he could get. Doug made a move toward Rob, but Rob reeled back and shoved Doug so hard he went flying back and landed on the ground. I didn't move a muscle. I was frozen, too, but my hand stayed steady on the key in the ignition.

Turn the key, let's go, turn the key, let's go.

Josh made an attempt to run around the back of the car and get into the passenger side seat, but Rob was on him in an instant. I heard him moaning, no, howling, as he pounced on Josh taking him to the ground. I poked my head out the window to see what was happening. Rob was straddled over Josh's legs. His head moved up and down up and down up and down with feverish motions. He snarled and gurgled as Josh writhed and screamed beneath him. I heard squishing sounds, tearing sounds, opening sounds, wet sounds, emptying sounds.

"No, please! Stop! Please! Griffin!! Help meeee! Oh, God! Mom! Mom! Mom-meee!" his terrified and agonized voice rang out as Rob continued his visceral assault on Josh's lower cavity.

Sprays of blood misted the air.

And I did nothing.

I heard the pleas, watched the mutilation of my best friend, and did... absolutely... nothing.

I started the engine of the car. My hands shook horribly, and I thought for a moment I would never be able to get the car started. For the first time I thought about my own mother and what must be happening at my parents' house, and I knew I had to get home as quickly as possible. From the headlight's glow, I could see Doug sitting in the dirt on the side of the road, his face agape in horror. He was watching, too. He did nothing, too. I turned hard on the wheel and swerved out of his way, careful not to hit him. Careful not to hit my mangled best friend. I drove away hurriedly into the night until the only screams I could hear were the ones from inside my head.

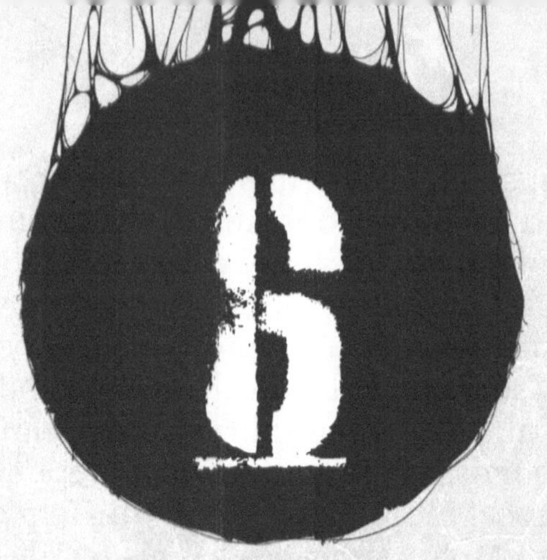

I WAKE UP TO THE SUN FILTERING THROUGH the window. The glare through the white gossamer curtains reveals the tiny particles of dust swirling like a miniature tornado in the air. It's a thin veil of dirt extending from the window to the foot of my bed; like a filthy finger pointing at me, giving me a weird ghostly guilt trip. I'm guessing it's around 8 am, but who knows. There isn't a clock in the room. I sit up in the bed and rub the scruff on my cheeks and chin. I didn't sleep well last night. Never mind the uncomfortable hospital bed I knew would come with the territory, but the dreams were unnerving. Not really sure if they were actual dreams or more like memories. It's only been a few days since I've been back to reality, and I'm still having difficulty separating the two.

I've been cleaned up by these doctors and everything, but I have this sudden need to take a shower, to get clean, to feel cleansed. *If only a shower could cleanse your soul.* I could only be so lucky.

The shower is compact, tiny, not like the large walk-in my parents have at home. No, this is typical hospital size. I undress, remove the god-awful bandage from around my head, step in, and turn on the faucet. The cold-water rains down upon me, and I shiver at first from the coldness. It soon warms up and I roll my head from side to side letting the water pound against my face. I grab the bar of soap on the ledge and lather up. The suds against my arms feel comforting, and I try to memorize the way the soap feels sliding across my chest because if I somehow change again, I'll want to remember this last shower. When everything went down, no one knew it would be their last anything, so I don't want to forget, *I don't want to forget, I don't want to forget...* but then I remember something else. I tilt my head a little too far to the left and water seeps into my ear creating a "whooshing" tunnel sound. I remember that sound all too well. When the world was underwater and the muffled sounds of my own moaning and groaning echoed in my head. I shudder again at the memory, the thought, the reality, and the word "zombie" involuntarily escapes my mouth.

Zombie.

Graves said it. "For lack of a better word."

But I didn't die.

I look down at my chest and run the soap over it one last time. My rib cage is protruding and my stomach sort of caves into itself, like how my mother looked when she would suck in her stomach. She was thin to begin with, but had a little belly pooch, I guess an after effect of having two children. Except I'm not sucking anything in. I've eaten—*had been eating*—up until they changed me back and captured me, but maybe man cannot live on blood and guts alone? I have to remember to ask Graves what month it is so I can better gauge how long my body has been deprived of proper nutrients and stuff.

Shortly after I get out of the shower, Dr. Holston comes in to give me a quick physical. He says my vitals are looking good, and everything seems to be normal. Operative word being seems. He doesn't say it, but I know by the tone in his voice. I can tell by the tone in everyone's voices—how they speak to me, how they walk tentatively around me, how they look at me like they expect me to lurch after them and bite into their shoulder or face. Everyone is jittery and on edge around me, and either it's completely obvious, or my senses have been permanently heightened. The orderlies, the doctors, the guards, all of them, nervous like mice in a cat cage, or whatever the stupid expression is.

But not Graves. I notice he's not nervous around me. Not one bit. He's more like guarded and prepared although I can't make sense of those two words right now.

Dr. Holston (and two armed guards) walks me down to Graves's office after my physical. I sit in the same chair. Holston and Graves have a brief exchange before the guards and the doc leave. Graves saunters over to his leather chair and motions to the blue tray on the end table next to me. Breakfast, I guess. I take a look, and sure enough there's a plate of scrambled eggs and a plain bagel with butter. I attempt to eat the bagel. One bite. Two bites. Three bites. It's going down okay enough, but after the fourth bite, I start to get that sickening feeling again, so I put it down. The smell of the eggs is starting to make me nauseas, and I cover the tray to block the scent. There's a glass of water on the table. I suck it down without a problem. It's tasteless, and that's good.

"Sleep well?" Graves asks in his unfriendly, fake voice. He's wearing a gray shirt with a black silk tie and dark gray slacks, and his black hair is gelled back again. He has a Mediterranean look to him, like Italian or Greek or something. The room is dimly lit. There's a small window, but it's covered by thick white blinds, and it gives the people within the room a sense of timelessness, not knowing whether it is truly day or night out there. Even in the semi-darkness I see Graves's face is chiseled, like a Roman or Greek god statue. *He must get a lot of chics*, I think.

I shake my head back and forth to answer "no." A grin spreads across Graves's face like peanut butter smearing on a fresh piece of white bread, but it's not that phony fake grin he gave me yesterday. This one is outright malicious, like he's happy I slept like crap. Then I suddenly realize, through his demeanor, facial expressions, and hand gestures, the nicey-nice pretense of our first meeting is over. He places the clipboard in his lap and begins flipping through the pages. He's not wearing his reading glasses today. Maybe he has contacts in? He reaches over and presses the record button again on the recorder. "This is Doctor Warren J. Graves at the Mount Sinai Re-Assimilation Center. I am here with Patient Number 024, who has been identified as Griffin King. This is session two. Dr. Holston, Patient's primary care physician, reports this morning that 024's vitals are all normal. No signs of relapse or re-infection. The virus appears to be in remission. Blood pressure was slightly elevated at 140 over 90, but it doesn't seem to be too much of a concern at present time. We're about to pick up where we left off from yesterday's session. You may begin," he concludes as he looks at me.

"What month is it?" I blurt out because if I don't ask him right now, I know I'll forget once I've started talking about the events.

His black eyes darken, and I don't think I can even see any of the sclera, the white part. *Oh man, I amazed myself again that I remembered that from Ms. Snyder's Biology class!*

"May," he answers flatly.

"About six months," I say out loud, but it was really supposed to be an inside thought. Six months from start to start. I can't believe I'd been gone for that long. Sydney's tenth birthday will be coming up, and I bet she'll have some big sleepover party with all her annoying little, teeny bopper friends. I'll probably sleep over at Josh's house to get away from...

Josh...

Yeah, I'm here with Graves, and yesterday I left off talking about Josh.

"Yesterday," Graves says, ignoring my outburst, "you recounted the incident with the bus driver and the other children on the bus."

I nod.

"I think it's safe to assume the bus driver was somehow infected and attacked the other children on the bus."

No duh, I feel like saying to him, but instead I nod again.

"What happened next?" he asks exhaling loudly.

"We ran," I answer, "and it gets a little blurry, but I lost Josh. We got separated. I don't know what happened, but I found a car and went home."

He knows I'm lying. He dips his head forward and cocks his eyebrow as if to say, "do you really expect me to believe that, kid?" But I don't budge, I don't respond, I don't even move. He licks his thick lips again when he realizes that's all I'm saying about Josh. His cheekbones twitch from his grinding teeth, and there's a sudden flash of anger behind his eyes. I get the sense he wants to leap over the coffee table and strangle the story out of me. Thank God for that coffee table—it's saved my life a few times these last two days!

Knowing this validates my decision to be silent about Josh even more. Graves has an obvious hatred for me; it doesn't take a freaking rocket scientist to figure that one out. If I told him about Josh, the guys who picked us up, the infected dude who ate my best friend, and how I drove away without helping, Graves will hate me even more. He hates me because of the things I did when I was a zombie; I don't need to give him any more reason to hate me for the things I did—or didn't do—*before* I was changed.

"So..." he urges like a little kid begging their parents for something, "let's get on with it!" and for the first time, on tape, I hear truth in his voice. He wants this over with. So do I. I don't hesitate anymore and give us what we both want.

I made it home, back to our development. The car ran out of gas before I could make it down the main drag, so I pulled it over to the side of the road and walked the rest of the way. It wasn't too far of a walk. It was pitch black out. No streetlights, no signals or signs lit up, nothing. And there was this weird silence in the air. No, not silence, it was like whispers. I kept telling myself it was only the wind blowing on this chilly November evening, but as I got closer and closer to the houses in our development, the whispers seemed to grow louder, like moaning, or howling.

I needed to get home. Badly. There was this ache in my chest only my mother's embrace could take away. I remembered being a kid and waking up from a horrible nightmare and rushing down the hall to climb onto bed in between my parents because the only thing in the world that could settle my mind was my mother patting my hair or rubbing my back. That's the overwhelming feeling and need that I had as I turned the corner of our cul-de-sac. The moans maintained their volume of being somewhere in the distance. I couldn't tell from which direction they were coming, but I knew they were somewhat close, and I wasn't going to take the chance of letting them get closer. I picked up the pace and headed straight for my house.

As I got closer to the rotunda of the cul-de-sac, I could make out figures in the darkness. Two bodies mulled about aimlessly around the circle, their moans echoing in the cool autumn air. Sitting on the curb of the roundabout was Ashlyn, Stuart, and Debbie Marshall's daughter with something in her hands. I could see she was bringing it feverishly up to her lips and making garg-ly slurping noises. I instantly thought back to the night of the first blackout when Ashlyn and Sydney were sitting on the curb with gallons of ice cream in their laps. As I got closer to the Marshall girl, I realized the sight was much different. Instead of ice cream, Ashlyn was slurping hungrily on something long and stringy with protruding ridges—intestines, probably. I didn't get too close to see well enough. I took a few steps closer and the people who were ambling about stopped in unison and stared straight at me. Ashlyn looked up from the entrails in her lap and met my gaze. Her face was covered with chunks of gore; her dress stained in blood. And every-thing stopped for a split second. No sounds. No moans. I stared at them, and they stared at me, and I wanted to say, "Do you need help?" but even through my own con-fusion, that sounded dumb.

Then they charged me. I let out a scream right before it felt like my heart stopped. They were chasing me, and I thought I was going to end up like Josh, with little Ashlyn Marshall hovering over me, pulling out my bowels as if she were pulling out a jump rope from a toy box. I dou-bled back through the neighbor's yard and cut across the lawn. In my mind, I could hear my father yelling at me for trampling through Mrs. Wren's flower garden. I could also hear the moans of those people getting closer to me. Those sounds weren't in my head, and I knew if I didn't get to safety soon, I would be dead. If I could just reach my back lanai, just reach the back lanai, just reach the...

Sydney's outline manifested behind the screened patio. She stood by the door with a flashlight in hand. "Hurry!" she anxiously whispered, and I increased my speed. I reached her and she opened the door slightly so I could squeeze through, and we both danced around the inground pool to the sliding glass doors where my mother was waiting with an expression of terror on her face.

Ashlyn and her crew were literally on my heels. Even though Sydney had shut the door behind us, the three bodies came barreling through the screen. We were safely in the house as we watched them tear through the black mesh and tumble over each other into the pool. My mother quickly repositioned the blinds and moved the sectional couch back in front of the glass doors. She pushed Sydney gently aside, stood on her toes, and grabbed on to me in the biggest bear hug she could physically give. Her hot tears fell onto my neck, and she stifled her cries in my armpit. I squeezed her back and looked over at Sydney who was in tears as well.

"Mom, I," I began to say, but she looked up at me and quickly shook her head back and forth, silencing me, her eyes darting back and forth, registering the sounds of the splashes and moans from my pursuers now trapped in our swimming pool.

"No, not by the windows," she whispered as she led me to the center of the living room. Sydney followed us with her flashlight, and as we all sat on the shag rug, Syd crept into my mother's Indian-style lap. My head swam. Sydney's flashlight made a glowing orb on the ceiling and my mother frantically forced her palm over the lens to silence that as well.

"Where's Dad?" I whispered.

"We're hoping right behind you," Mom answered with a tiny smile.

"Any ideas?" I asked.

"No," she answered, "Dad at work, you at school, me and Syd watching a movie in the bedroom, and the power goes out again."

"Yeah, but what about the Marshall girl, and those other people, and… and," and I don't have the heart to say the bus driver, and the other kids, and Rob, and Doug, and Josh…

"I don't know," she said shrugging her shoulders. "Me and Syd were hanging around waiting for the power to come back on. I tried to call TECO again, but my cell was out. Stu came knocking on the door a little while after everything went dark and said he was on his way home from work when he saw a major commotion going on at the mall. He said he was going to pick Ashlyn up from school and wanted to know if he should sign Syd out, too. But I told him she was already home and he said "okay" and left."

"And Dad?" I persisted.

"No word," she answered, and Sydney tensed up. "But there was no word from you and look where you are now!" She forced a small smile again and began petting Sydney's hair to calm her down. Sydney curled up against my mother's chest. She looked so fragile, and so young.

"What about those other people? What happened to them?" I continued.

My mother sighed heavily and gripped Sydney a little tighter. "Sydney and I kept checking the windows to see, ya know, if you or Dad were on the way home. I don't know what happened, but this one time, somewhere around 3 pm, we both went to the front window to look, and it... it..."

"It was a horror movie, Griff," Sydney mumbled into my mother's chest.

"People were just... just..." Mom stammered.

"Eating each other," Sydney finished for her.

Eating each other.

They didn't have to say much more about it because I had seen it firsthand. Seen what happens to the human body when another human decides to take a bite.

"Who else is okay? Who else in the neighborhood is okay?"

My mother looked at me puzzled. "How would I know that? When Debbie Marshall came screaming off her front porch and was attacked by her daughter and husband, well, that's when I started to shut things up real tight *ova hea*," she said, her head bobbing back and forth and her New York accent getting thicker.

I looked around the house. Mom had the front door blocked off with the dining room table, and all the wooden shutters were closed tightly. "If those people don't realize we're in here, then maybe they'll leave us alone, and we can figure things out when your dad gets home."

"Mom, I don't think..."

"Shut up! Don't say it!" she snapped, her voice getting a little louder than her required whisper. "I refused to say it about you, and look, you're here. How did you get home anyway?"

"It's a long story, Ma. I just..."

Suddenly we heard some more splashing from the pool, and more moaning from the people. Sydney jumped up and was about to go to the window to see what was happening, but my mother grabbed her arm and dragged her back to the carpet. "Don't!" she ordered and clasped her hand around Sydney's mouth. The moaning got louder, and it came from every direction.

"There's more of them," I whispered. "I think they're surrounding the house."

Zombies, I thought.

I'd seen way too many horror movies to spot the signs. Mom's blue eyes flashed at me. She suspected too, but we never outright said the word "zombie" to each other. It was preposterous, ridiculous. Zombies? Really?

"Just be quiet and sit still!" Mom insisted as she huddled with me and Sydney in the center of the room.

"Shoot 'em in the head, right?" I whispered, trying to make a joke, trying to lessen the enormous fear gripping me from the inside out.

Mom punched my arm lightly and told me to shut up, but it was playful, and I could tell by the timbre of her voice that she found my comment mildly amusing. Sydney, however, was not amused. With her head tucked between her legs, she tried desperately to fight back her sobs. I thought she was going to hyperventilate! Mom whispered gently in her ear and patted her back. With her other hand, she patted my back as well, trying to make both her children feel comforted and safe. I thought I would wake up from the bad dream, and Mom would be lying next to me, coaxing me out of the fear, but there was no waking up. This was no dream.

Some time passed, and the sounds outside got softer. It was apparent they were no longer circling our house. Sydney was curled up in a ball asleep on the floor. I wondered how the hell she could sleep when all this was going on? Mom lifted her upper body and perched her ears to the side. "I think they're gone," she mumbled.

I nodded.

"It's probably okay to get up and move around, but remember to stay quiet," she instructed as she stood up.

"You got it," I said sarcastically as I gave her a salute. She rolled her eyes. I snuffed out a chuckle.

My stomach rumbled as I stood up. "What about her?" I asked, thumbing at Sydney.

"Oh, let her rest, she deserves to sleep."

"What about you?" I asked.

"What about me? You know I can't sleep unless I know everyone is in bed and safe," and there was a faraway look in her eyes that let me know she was thinking about my dad. "You tired?"

"Yeah," I replied, "but I'm too anxious to sleep."

My stomach rumbled again; this time loud enough for her to hear. She raised her eyebrows. "Hungry much?" She smiled.

I shrugged my shoulders as she grabbed my hand and led me to the kitchen.

"How about some spaghetti and meatball pasta-like product from a can?" she asked as she placed the flashlight onto the kitchen island and disappeared into the darkness of the pantry.

"Okay, I guess," I replied politely.

She meant well. Even in the confusion and uncertainty of the events unfolding like a movie before our eyes, my mother meant well. She had that need and desire to comfort her children, let them rest, feed them, and keep them safe. I wasn't hungry, but the look on my mother's face as she happily scooped out the processed pasta product into a bowl told me I couldn't tell her that. So, I let her take care of me the best way she knew how under these bizarre circumstances.

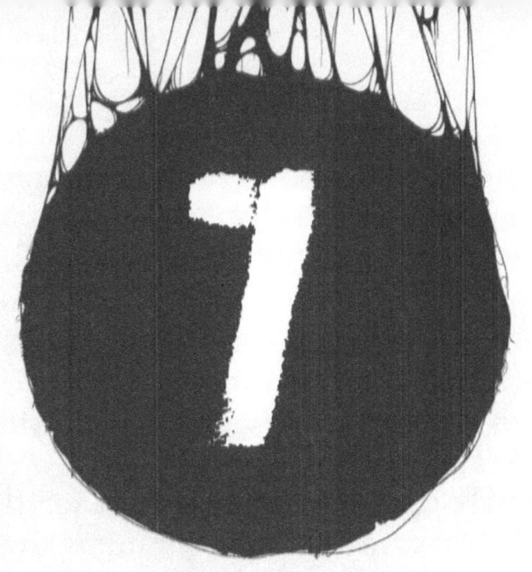

HUNDER RATTLES THE SMALL WINDOW IN the room, and it shakes me from my thoughts. I was almost able to taste the food processed pasta and dogmeat meatballs when the thunder made me shudder. Early afternoon storm. Typical for Florida in May. I stretch my arms above my head and yawn heartily. Graves hasn't acknowledged I've stopped talking. He's scribbling, scribbling, scribbling on that godforsaken clipboard. My back cracks, and it feels so good, like a huge pressure release in my bones. *I need to stretch all the kinks out of my body, and I'll be back to normal.*

I could only be so lucky.

I stand up and Graves shoots me a cautious glance. I ignore him as I continue to stretch my arms high in the air and contort my hips in a way that makes my ribs and back go *pop pop pop*. A sound escapes my mouth, one that's half roar and half yawn. It's a human sound. One I'd made many times stretching out my body out in the same way on most mornings. Before I sit back down, I catch a glance of my ribcage through my white t-shirt. My bones protrude against the cotton fabric, and I shake my head bewildered. I know I need to eat something, but I'm not hungry.

"Have a seat," Graves instructs as he motions to my chair.

"No," I reply, "I need to walk around a little. I've been laying or sitting for a long time."

His eyes narrow as he vigilantly watches me walk around the room.

It's a fairly ordinary office except for the two-way mirror. I go over to the small window and draw the blinds to one side. The rain has stopped. I guess it was one loud rattle of thunder and a few drops of rain. I can tell because the screen of the window has droplets on it, and it kinda upsets me because I like the rain, and we need it.

We need it?

My dad always said that in the summers. "Goddamn grass needs the rain!" he would always complain. St. Augustine grass, the kind we had on our front and side lawn, is a rich, crunchy type of grass that looks gorgeous when it's healthy and green, but it's a "water sucker" as my dad would say; it needs a lot of water, and when it doesn't get it, brown patches develop quickly. I remember a cold front had come in the year before the world shook and our grass, our beautiful, beautiful grass my father worked so hard to maintain, died. He was devastated. Cost him a lot of money to replace the whole yard. He bitched about it for a few months. Drove my mother crazy. But then the world shook, and none of that mattered anymore. None of the everyday nonsense mattered anymore. I guess nothing matters when your life has changed like mine has. Nothing matters when *you've* changed like I have.

"You mention your father," he says not taking an eye off me.

I nod.

"Did he ever come home?"

I pause. I think of my dad. I can remember snippets of images, like burnt up photographs. He had light brown hair, blue eyes, and a beard and mustache, but his face isn't registering in my memory. And it seems the harder I try to remember him, the faster those images fade, like trying to follow a rainbow and it disappears before you can meet its end. I can hear his voice, the way it boomed when he yelled, and his distinct laughter (because he never really laughed, not the way Mom cackled and hyperventilated in hysterics) was more of a sly undertone of a chuckle.

I shake my head from side to side, feeling the length of my hair rub up against the tips of my ears. I probably shouldn't have shaken my head as fiercely as I did because the back starts to throb a little and a wave of dizziness comes over me. I can't inspect the room anymore; I have to sit down.

"So, you suspect your father was killed?" Graves asks.

I nod again and mumble, "Mmhmm. My mother was pretty much in denial, but it was a foregone conclusion. He went to work that day, my mother and sister said goodbye to him that morning, and they didn't hear from him from then on. He worked in the city about forty-five minutes away from our home. We don't know what happened to him, but he's dead." I try to remember if I said goodbye to him that morning, and I can't.

"Do you think he could have been changed?" The question makes my stomach do a violent turn.

"No," I answer abruptly, "my father is dead." I don't know if that's really the truth, and there's no way to be certain of it, but I have to believe he is dead. In my mind, it will be easier if he is.

"How does that make you feel?" he asks, and I swear he's got that malicious grin on his face again.

How *does* it make me feel? I think about this for a split second and reply, "Good. I'm glad he's dead."

Graves tenses for a moment and narrows his eyes. He puts a big checkmark on his paper like a teacher grading a test and asks, "What makes you say that?"

"I'd rather he be dead than changed, that's all. I wouldn't wish that on anyone."

He smirks, and no, I'm not imagining it. My sense of perception may be heightened a little too much, but this is not my imagination. He's smirking, giving me that snarky, 'I'll-show-you' grin. What kind of psychiatrist is this guy, anyway?

"How long were you and your family holed up in your house?" Graves's questions continue.

He's mighty chatty today, isn't he?

"I'm not sure," I answer truthfully, "not longer than a month, maybe a little less, I... I don't know, it's all fuzzy," I say rubbing my temples, "a few weeks, and then Toby came and that was about..."

"Who's Toby?" he interrupts with heightened anticipation.

"Toby. I rescued her," I answer.

"You rescued a dog?" he asks a little confused.

I shake my head, "No, Toby's a girl. A very, very lost girl..."

My sister liked to stay in the crawlspace underneath the staircase. There was a little door that opened to a small storage room. Florida houses don't have basements and every square inch of available space was used for storage. Mom kept her Christmas tree and ornaments all boxed up in that crawlspace. She was afraid the climate in the garage would eventually destroy her sacred treasures. Now, all those boxes and bags were used as window and door reinforcements to keep out the maniacs who wandered the streets, and Sydney spent most of her time in the dark crawlspace with a flashlight and a book.

Mom was smart. When the electricity went out that afternoon, she had been more than a little freaked out. Her over-sensitive motherly instincts went peeling into overdrive, and she filled both of the bathtubs in the house with water. She said, "Just in case." Weird how she thought to do that because after a few days, the water stopped working. She said we always had the water from the pool, but after those people had bopped around in there, I think she was looking at the pool water as a last resort.

After about a week, things were starting to get funky. We took all the garbage out to the attached garage. Without a car parked in there, we would be able to store quite a lot, but already the smell was starting to permeate into the front area of the house. We changed into clean clothes every other day and only flushed the toilets in "emergency" situations. We had to use water from the bathtubs to refill the toilet tanks every once in a while. Mom and I went through the pantry and took inventory of all the food we had. Of course, we cleaned out the fridge first. The food in there that didn't get eaten in twenty-four hours got thrown out. The list Mom and I came up with said the three of us would have enough food for a few months if we rationed it properly. So, we produced a system. Thank God my sister and I liked to drink box-drinks and eat factory canned food over drinking fresh orange juice and eating my mother's homemade meals. Not that there's was anything wrong with Mom's cooking; it's just healthy stuff doesn't usually taste as good as the junky stuff. For once, Mom was actually grateful Sydney and I ate crap.

We were also grateful it was November and not August. We dared not open the windows in fear of attracting attention, and had it been mid-to-late summer, we would have probably suffocated from the oppressive Florida heat. If there was any month to be trapped in your home without any power, November was the best bet.

Besides being careful with our food rations and trying hard to keep everything clean, there wasn't much else to do. I played a lot of solitaire, Mom read a lot, and Sydney pretty much kept to herself under the staircase. The three of us interacted with each other minimally, and we each had our own reasons for doing so.

None of us had gone up into the bonus room upstairs, and eventually I decided to "set up camp" up there. My parents had the room set up with a couch and pool table in hopes that Sydney and I would use it to entertain friends or have parties up there, but we never used it. It was wasted space in the house, and I remember thinking I would have liked for the pool table to be downstairs as it would have been an excellent reinforcement for the front door. Anyway, I brought up some blankets, a pillow, a flashlight, a mini-battery-powered radio, my deck of cards, and a bottled water. I had to do something, keep myself occupied and entertained while feeling like I was helping the family at the same time. In my head, I was playing "look-out," and I was in charge of this grand fort and its protection. Every hour or so, I would kneel in front of one of the windows and crack open the shutter. I could see the street below me, and if I looked from side to side, I had an amazing view of most of the block. At first I was cautious about peeking out, but I soon realized the moaning people in the streets never tilted their heads to the sky. I knew I wouldn't draw any attention if there was any movement or motions from the upstairs room. Still, I was careful at first, trying hard not to make a sound or be suspicious.

I watched them every day from the window. I even brought a notebook upstairs and started taking notes on their movements and patterns, like a war general making notations on the enemy's weaknesses and location. There weren't many of them in our neighborhood, and I started to see the same people over and over. Mrs. Dunbar, Mr. Jameson, Ashlyn Marshall. Sometimes there would be people that I had no idea who they were, but it was always the same: they either moved in that herky-jerky way, like their bodies were barely working, or they ran wildly and aimlessly. Sometimes they went up onto various porches, trying to get into the houses. Most of the time they walked. And moaned. The moaning was the most disturbing part of it all. It was always deep and guttural, and I thought it sounded almost painful. One day, old Mrs. Dunbar sprinted after a squirrel, caught it, and bit its head off. Ashlyn Marshall ignored the birds that pecked at her opened wounds as she sat quietly on the curb in front of her house. I realized there didn't seem to be a rhyme or reason to how they acted. They seemed to avoid our house, though, and that was a good thing. Every now and then I would hear a "splash" from the backyard and knew one had fallen into the pool. The screened lanai was destroyed the night I was chased, and the aimless wanderers didn't take notice of the 5-foot gaping hole filled with water in the ground. Eventually they would pull themselves out of the water, but that's when their moaning would get louder and more somber.

One thing was for sure, there weren't any normal people around. If there were, they were doing a helluva job hiding out. I guess like us. But I had to know. I had to know if someone else out there knew what was happening or if anyone else was alive. As the nights progressed, I got more brazen. I knew the wanderers didn't bother looking up at the top level of our house, so I began opening the shutters a little wider. I took my flashlight and started flashing the on/off button in what I thought I remembered to be the signal for S.O.S.

No luck.

Nothing.

I did that for a few nights. On what must have been the fourth night or so, I opened the window like I usually did and surveyed the area. Down the block were a few runners. Nothing out of the ordinary. But then I saw *her* running toward the cul-de-sac, and I knew in an instant she wasn't infected. I knew she wasn't one of them. She wasn't moaning like them. She was screaming for help, running for her life. There was a small pack of them chasing after her. Their moans got louder and louder, and I knew she would definitely be caught. And while there was something inside of me that wanted to see her get overtaken, I felt an overwhelming need to help her, like the war general that I was.

I quickly raced down the stairs and headed to the sliding glass doors. I must have frightened poor Sydney because she came out of the guest room with a pale look of terror on her face. My mother sat on the recliner chair in the living room like she usually did before she went to sleep.

"What? What happened?" she mumbled in her half-asleep voice.

"Shhh," I snapped, "there's somebody out there!" and I unlocked the latch of the door and pulled the vertical blinds back so I could get a good view of the backyard and side street.

"Griffin! What are you doing?" my mother yelled as she stood up and raced by my side.

"Is it Daddy?" Sydney whimpered.

"Griffin Patrick King!" my mother recited, as if using my full name was going to somehow stop what I was doing. "Are you crazy? Do you want us to get killed?"

I ignored her and slid the door open enough so that my body eased out onto the brick pavers of the lanai.

"Get back..." she yelled, but I "shhh"-ed her again into silence.

The girl stopped and slinked behind a palm tree in the neighbor's backyard. I could hear her panting as she held her hands on her knees. She had a fairly good head start from wherever they had started chasing her, but they would be closing in soon. I had to act fast.

"Hey," I whispered into the darkness and her body stiffened up.

"Please, help me!" she cried.

"Straight across. The downed screen. Hurry!" I answered and she immediately raced across the neighbor's lawn, weaved in and out of the damaged screen, and danced around the pool. I grabbed her hand when she came in full sight of me and dragged her into the sliding glass door of our house. The infected raced alongside the street, never even seeing her duck into the depths of our home.

She breathed heavily and said, "Thank you, thank you, thank you," over and over again. Sydney went into the pantry and brought out a bottled water for her. My mother shook my shoulders and yelled in my face, "Are you crazy! What are you doing? What if she's one of them? What if she becomes one of them? We can't have this, Griffin! We can't have her in here!"

I turned to the girl. "Are you hurt?" I asked.

She shook her head.

"Are you bitten or cut or infected already?"

She shook her head again and wiped the water from her mouth with the back of her hand. I turned to my mother, "See, she's fine, Ma."

Mom stamped her foot on the floor and rolled her eyes, "She can't stay *hea*!"

I ignored her. I turned to the girl again, "What's your name?" I asked.

"Toby," she replied, "my friends call me Toby."

Toby Youngblood. October Youngblood. Graduated last year. Voted "Most Likely to Marry a Rich Old Man."

"I park in your parking spot now," I said dumbly.

"What?" she asked almost choking on a sip of water.

"Ya know, at school. You drove a Trans Am. I took your spot."

"Oh," she replied, still confused.

"Toby can stay with me in my room," Sydney declared before I could mindlessly make the claim myself.

"Toby can stay in the guest room!" my mother corrected, giving in to the new change in situation. Then she looked at me and pointed her finger in my chest. "Whatever she eats comes out of your rations." And for the first time in my entire life, I felt real anger in my mother's words.

Mom stomped away and went into her bedroom.

Sydney sat down next to Toby on the couch.

"I'm Griffin," I finally said to her.

"Yeah," she said still sipping her bottle, "I know who you are."

Sydney pet Toby's long blonde hair and gazed at her like she was a shiny new doll. "I'm Sydney, and you know you can stay with me if you want to."

"Thank you. Thank you so much for saving me," she said, as her eyes pierced right through my heart. But in my head, they weren't *her* eyes, they were Josh's. Josh looking straight at me, straight through me. And it was then that I felt I was able to do for her what I couldn't do for him.

As if saving her was making up for losing him.

Josh...

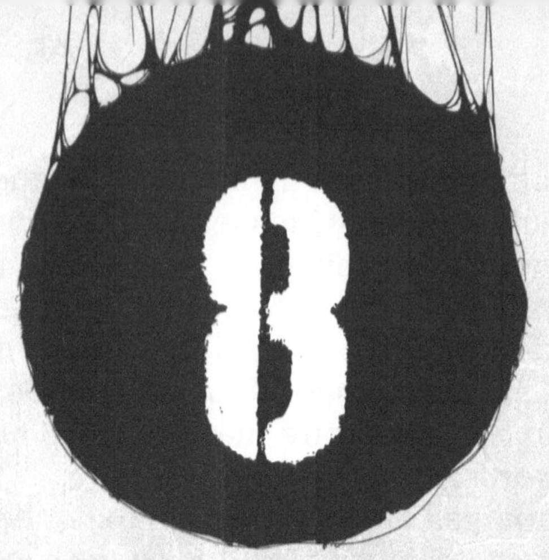

THERE ARE THREE DIFFERENT VERSIONS OF me. The Before. The After. The Now. I wonder what the rest of the world is going through. Does everyone else have their Befores and Afters and Nows? Does Graves?

It's hard to tell with him. For professional reasons, he's tried hard at being emotionless and stoic, but I'm not a moron; I see the contempt in his eyes, in his smirk. He hates me. I know why he does, and at the same time, I have no clue. With each instance I relay concerning what happened to me, *my story*, he gets more vocal and, what's that word, *snarky*? I don't think I'm using that word correctly. Miss Dougherty would be disappointed, but she's probably dead, too, so why should I care?

Graves is trying his best to hold back his feelings, but eventually he'll explode. I know it. I've seen it. Like how my dad used to try so hard to contain and control his anger around my mom and sister. It would work for maybe a day or two, and he'd end up exploding some-thing awful. Dad used to tell my mom to let him get it all out when it was inside him 'cause if he let the anger and rage build up, it would explode ten times worse.

Graves is holding it in. The anger. The pain. The hate. I don't want to be anywhere near him when he finally does explode.

"So, you took this Toby girl in, you say?" he says, his voice booming in the silence of the room.

"Yeah," I answer, "it was the least I could do." I want to palm my forehead with a Homer Simpson "d'oh" because what I said must sound so stupid to him. It does. He raises his eyebrows, and I kind of shuffle in my seat. "Ya know," I stammer, desperately trying to cover up, "the least I could do to help another person. I'd want someone to help me, ya know?" Again, I sound idiotic, but I guess it pleases Graves enough for him to stop looking at me all twisted. It was the least I could do. In my mind, helping Toby was my reprieve from what I did to Josh. It was my penance, my makeup, my do-over. If I helped this girl, then maybe I would be forgiven for leaving Josh the way I did?

"How did your mother feel about Toby being in the house?" he continues.

"Um, she wasn't too happy about it. She was afraid it would draw more attention to us, and we were pretty well holed up, ya know? She was concerned about the food and water situation as well. Mom was always sus-picious of everyone. Toby was no exception."

"How did *you* feel about Toby?"

Good question, Graves. Let me get back to you on that one, I want to say, but all I manage is a shoulder shrug.

"You said you knew her from school?"

"Yeah, she graduated a year ahead of me. She was popular, and I guess everyone knew her."

I didn't particularly like Toby from when I knew her in school. She was one of those loud, phony girls who had bleached blonde hair and wore way too much makeup. She wasn't like Lana, who was soft and natural and pretty. Toby was rude and sarcastic and knew exactly how to get what she wanted. She didn't get an "A" in Mr. Henning's Economics class because she was the best student, if you catch my drift. Her father was a plastic surgeon, and Toby had no qualms about showing off her augmented chest during her senior year. "A present from my daddy!" she had gushed as she let the entire football team "feel how natural they were" after the homecoming game. Now, I'm not gonna lie, if given the opportunity, I certainly would have been first in line to feel Toby's new boobs, but for me, that's about as far as I would go. Like, she wasn't the type of girl I'd want to bring home to introduce to my mother...

But circumstances had proven otherwise and here we were, in my house, with my mother, trying to survive.

"What happened to her? Why was she running from the infected that particular night?"

"Her house got attacked. She lived a few subdivisions over from me. She and her older sister escaped the initial attack. Her mother got infected and tried to kill them, too, but they got away from her. Toby and her sister went from block to block hiding in abandoned homes, cars, trees, wherever they could lay low until help came. They were sleeping in a car when some of those people found them. They killed her sister, and she ran. That's when I rescued her."

"And you're sure she wasn't cut or bitten or injured when she came to you?"

"I'm sure," I answer.

"One hundred percent positive?" he presses, his voice getting slightly louder.

I pause for a second and give him a hard look. "Yes, I'm positive," I insist.

Graves nods his head and writes OCTOBER YOUNGBLOOD at the top of a clean sheet of paper.

"Oh, no no no," I protest, "she's not a person of interest."

"No? Why's that?" he inquires. "Because she's dead," I say flatly. Graves gives a questioning look.

I pause and say, "I killed her."

He maintains his composure, but I saw for a split second he had tensed up. I said that rather matter-of-factly, very coolly, and emotionless. I know that bothered him, but like I said, there are so many versions of me that are disconnected from each other that the feelings *need* to be removed. I still have this mishmash of the Before, the After, and the Now, and I need to find a way to sort all that out.

He doesn't scratch out her name, though. I thought for sure he would have put a big "X" through the words, torn out the page, and crumpled it up. But no. He keeps it there and continues his line of questioning. "How did the dynamic change with Toby now in the household?"

"Well, things got, um, interesting to say the least..."

Toby stayed in the guest room. I stopped playing war general in the bonus room and decided to come back to the ladies downstairs. I felt I had to regulate what was going on. I knew Mom was not happy about Toby being with us. She had good enough reasons that I completely understood, and I guess I was afraid of the two of them butting heads. I knew how Toby could be. She was a mean pit-bull when she wanted to be. I knew how Mom could be, too. Her Italian/Irish blood made her a fiery debater, and her New Yorker instincts often made her come off as a bitch. For Sydney's sake, my mother avoided confrontation with Toby at all costs. Sydney took a real liking to Toby. Looked at her like a big sister of sorts, and of course, Toby openly welcomed Sydney's adoring eyes and affection.

Mom wasn't kidding when she had declared Toby's food would come from my rations. I made it very clear to our new guest that she and I would split everything evenly, and to be honest, I watched her like a hawk when it came time for meals and snacks. Every now and then, I would see Sydney sharing her pack of crackers with Toby or letting Toby have sips from her juice box, and it drove me crazy because no matter how sweet or personable she was, Toby Youngblood was ultimately looking out for one person—herself.

But as the days passed on, I found myself spending more time with Toby. I mean, really, when you're locked up in a house with someone, there really isn't much to do. We started out with small talk here and there, and then kinda got into more serious things, like speculation about what happened and how we were gonna get through it all. Still, it was hard for me to see past my preconceived notions about her. She was a natural flirt, and while I never got the sense that she was flirting with me directly, I always kept her at arm's length. She said raunchy things. Weird things. Things that a girl shouldn't say. Things that Lana Anderson wouldn't even think! Toby was very touchy-feely, too. Always wanted to put her hand on my shoulder, or touch my arm, or put her hands in my lap. And I noticed while my mother and I would be going over food supply numbers, Toby would call from my mother's bathroom asking to borrow her concealer and lipstick. Shows you where her priorities were. Never mind the wandering people outside waiting to eat us, never mind the dwindling water and food supply, never mind that there were now four of us living in this increasingly noxious house—as long as Toby Youngblood had her full mask of makeup on and was dressed to the nines, the world was a slightly better place (in her head, of course). To be honest, she was kind of a repulsive human being, and I had, many times, questioned why I had brought her into the fold. But then I remembered Josh and realized I had to deal with Toby, for the sake of my soul...

This one night, we all gathered in the center of the living room. We sat in a circle like some weird kind of séance; a plate was in the middle of us with a yellow candle burning. We each had a small box of raisins. Sydney and Mom shared a juice box, and Toby and I shared a bottled water. And that's exactly what the topic of conversation was: Water! I'll be the first to admit it; things were pretty grimy in the house. The bathtubs my mom had filled up when everything happened were pretty much depleted. There was water in the toilet tanks, and we only flushed when absolutely necessary, but with the tub water gone, we would run into problems very soon. I was surprised we made it almost a month the way we did, but once Toby joined the mix, our resources were noticeably strained. Once our juice boxes and sodas and Yoo-Hoos and any other form of liquid nutrients ran out, we would die without water. There was no getting around that. And honestly, if I didn't brush my teeth soon, I thought I might die from that as well!

"The water heater," my mom said. "We need to tap into that. There's 40 gallons of water sitting in there, and we can use maybe 30 of it. I say we drain it and use it to restore the toilet situation. This way we don't have to purify it. Besides, it's getting colder, and I don't want it to freeze up in there."

"How are we gonna purify water anyway when we don't have electricity?" Toby said, challenging my mom.

"We can't boil water, *obviously*," my mother snapped back, putting a firm emphasis on the word "obviously", "but if we ever needed to, we could use some bleach. I have an eyedropper and we would have to let the water sit for a while before we could drink it."

"Bleach? Like, to wash your clothes with?" Toby said sticking out her tongue and making an "ick" sound.

Mom rolled her eyes. I did too.

"But that's only 30 gallons," I interjected.

"Yeah, and..." my mother questioned my point.

"You and I both know it's not enough," I declared.

My mother shook her head back and forth, knowing and disagreeing with what I was about to say. "No freakin' way, Griffin!" she said through gritted teeth. "We're so not going to go there!"

"You know it's the only way!" I insisted, but she continued shaking her head wildly.

"What is?" Sydney asked. "What are you guys talking about?"

"We'll be okay," my mother said to me, ignoring Sydney's question.

"For what, another month? Then what?" I barked.

"No!" Mom repeated.

"'No' what?" Sydney continued, confused.

"Ma," I began, "there's at least 12,000 gallons of water right there, maybe more! We would be okay if we had access to that!"

"The pool?" Sydney blurted. "Griffin wants to get water from the pool?"

"Sydney, shush!" Mom ordered. "Griffin, those things have been in the pool, wading in it, *bleeding* in it!" Her face contorted with real fear. She didn't have to say what she was thinking. I had thought the same thing: it would contaminate us, change us.

Toby made another "ick" noise.

"No way, I'm not drinking..." Sydney started, and both my mother and I yelled "shut up!" at the exact same time. Poor Sydney winced and curled up in Toby's lap like a wounded puppy looking for shelter and comfort.

"We can bleach it," I pressed. "Just like we'll bleach up the tank water."

Mom wasn't convinced. She was scared. We were all scared.

"I don't want to talk about this anymore," she said as she stood up. "I'm going to sleep. We're going to empty out the water heater tomorrow. We'll discuss the *cess-pool* water if it becomes an absolute essential. *Only* if it's an absolute essential."

"Fine," I mumbled under my breath. Toby still made the "ick" face, but no sound came from her mouth.

"Momma, can Toby sleep with me tonight?" Sydney whined.

Mom looked down at her with a pained expression and then a flush of jealousy burned in her cheeks. The pink in her face turned red as the glowing candle cast dark shadows around her eyes. She looked old. Tired. My mother expected Sydney to want to curl up in the bed with her. "Do what you want," she said as she waved a defeated hand in the air, "I don't care anymore." And for the first time since everything happened, I got the sense that my mother was starting to give up.

"Wanna play sleepover party?" Toby asked me as soon as my mother left the room. There was a sly grin across her face, and something about the way she said it made me think for a second she was coming on to me. I wasn't attracted to her, and I didn't think I'd had ever given her the impression that I was. I can't be attracted to a person physically if I don't like the *kind* of person they are, ya know? I gave her a puzzled look.

"No! No! No! Girls only!" Sydney squawked as she jumped up from Toby's lap and outstretched her hands. She was clueless to Toby's innuendo.

Toby reached for Sydney who hoisted her up and the two bopped away to Sydney's bedroom. I blew the candle out and went to my room as well. A thin ray of the moonlight seeped in from a small crack in the wood shutters. The girls giggled through the walls of the house and some of the straggling wanderers moaned outside. I put my pillow over my head to block out the sounds and thought about Lana Anderson: the Lana I knew as a kid, and the Lana I would never know as a man. I'll never smell that intoxicating perfume of hers in 5th period anymore, never get to watch her twirl her long blonde hair around the eraser part of her pencil again, never know if she would have gone to the prom with me, *never know what was going on between her and Josh*. And I thought "I'm going to die in this house with my sister, my mother, and *Toby Youngblood?*" I shuddered. The thought of spending my last days on earth with trash like that was like a mental kick in the ass to the memory and thoughts of Lana Anderson. My heart raced, and the more I thought, the more difficulty I had catching my breath. With my pillow over my ears, I could hear the blood rushing on the inside of my body, and I started to feel wave after wave of panic and depression.

This can't be the end. This can't be the end. This can't be...

"I'm not my father! What was I thinking!? I can't take care of them; I can barely take care of myself!" I half-screamed into the pillow.

This can't be all that's left. This can't be all that's left. This can't be...

My heart pounded faster, heavier. My chest swelled up to my chin with every deep inhale, and a tight lump was forming in my throat. And like an idiot, like a coward, like a little stupid kid, I cried. No. I bawled. For the first time since this all began, I cried. I flipped onto my stomach in fear that Toby or Sydney or the mindless wanderers outside would hear me and laugh at me. I felt completely ridiculous as big puppy dog tears flooded my pillowcase, but in a way, it felt good to get all of it out. I guess I'd been letting it build up for far too long, but instead of exploding into screams and throwing things like my father used to do, I exploded into tears. I guess I'm like my mother in that way.

My mother. My poor, sweet mother was going to die in this house never giving up hope my father would come stumbling home (infected or not) someday. My mother, who just wanted her family to be together and safe and happy and fed, and for her kids to be independent and functioning members of society. And Sydney. Poor sweet Sydney. Nine years old and never going to have her first date, her first kiss, experience high school. She'll never have to worry if the boy version of her Lana Anderson will ask her to the prom, and she'll never have to worry if the girl version of her Josh was being sneaky behind her back. She'll never know what it's like to have a forbidden beer at a party and get buzzed, or to drive a car, or to...

Then it hit me.

Drive a car.

My car.

My tears stopped immediately, and I sat up at attention as if some great unseen force had picked me up and propped me on all fours on my bed.

My car. It's fixed. It's at the shop.

I knew exactly where the shop was. I knew exactly how to get there. I knew exactly how long it would take to get me there.

My car. My wonderful, beautiful, black Chevrolet Monte Carlo with the red racing stripes on the hood, and now, a new transmission. 2006. One of the last of a dead breed. I called her "Suzie" because the last three letters on my license plate were "SZY" and because I heard somewhere, you're supposed to give your car a name. I knew Suzie was my only and last resort. Help was not on the way. I was in a do-or-die situation, and the last thing I wanted to do was die... in this house... with my mother... with Sydney... and with Toby Youngblood.

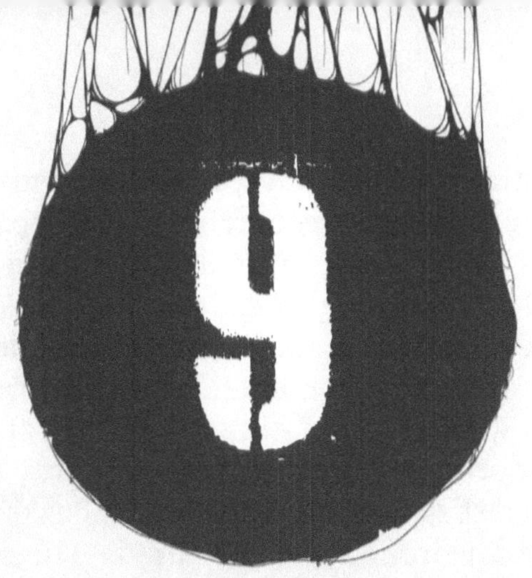

9

THE PHONE ON GRAVES'S DESK CHIRPS, STARtling the both of us. He runs his fingers through his hair and gets up to answer it. He grunts a few times, says a few "uh-huh's", then hangs up. "We're done for now. You need to go back to your dorm," he says to me.

"Oh, okay," I reply, surprised.

The door opens immediately, and there is an unfamiliar doctor with those two brooding guards (armed, might I add) who signals for me to get up and join him. I go. I kinda feel like I should say "goodbye" to Graves, but I stop myself from doing so. I walk out without even looking at him.

They escort me down the hallway and back to my room. The doctor says nothing to me as I enter. I turn around to ask him when I'll be having another session, but the door immediately slams closed behind me. And locked.

Locked in. Again.

I'm starting to get the feeling I'm not a patient here at this Re-Assimilation Center. I'm more like a prisoner. No, more like an animal at the zoo. This is what they must feel like, poor things. Locked in cages, poked and prodded, studied and analyzed, and all under the guise that it's for "valuable research" or it's because "we're saving you." And those animals must want to go back home, back to their jungles and swamps and deserts, but instead they're stuck in their cages and enclosures with their fabricated environments. I remember going to the Bronx Zoo when I was a kid and staring at all the animals, wondering if they knew any better, wondering if they realized they weren't really home. I asked my father about it, and he huffed and answered, "They're animals; they don't know any better." But then when we walked to the chimpanzee enclosure, I watched this old-timer chimp hanging out by himself in the corner. I watched his slow shuffled movements. He lazily scratched at his chest and swatted away some of the younger chimps who tried to play with him, but what I remember most was his eyes. There was a distinct sadness in his eyes. And I thought, "No, Dad, you're wrong. He knows. He remembers." Now I know how that chimp felt. I'm locked in this room, this fabrication of real life, life before, and I'm poked and prodded, studied and analyzed like some wild animal.

And I want to go home.

I look in the mirror on the wall above the clothes dresser, and I look like a wild animal. My hair is disheveled; my beard is getting too thick. It doesn't look like me, like the *me* that I remember. The faces of the people in the pictures smile, but I know they're really laughing—laughing at me, laughing at the shell of my former self, laughing at the mockery I've become. I walk over to the bed, ignoring the new blue food tray on the nightstand because I'm not hungry, and press the button on the wall to connect to the nurse's station.

"Go ahead," a voice immediately responds.

"Um," I stammer, taken off guard at the promptness of the response. "Um, can I get a razor and some shaving cream?"

"What for?" the voice asks.

"Um," I answer, puzzled. "Because I'd like to shave?"

D'uh. Why else would I ask for a razor and shaving cream?

There's a pause, like someone hit a mute button or something, and then the voice comes back and says, "A nurse will be in shortly."

While I'm waiting, I open up the blue food tray. It looks like chicken parmesan and spaghetti, and I laugh out loud at the cook's choice of lunch. Spaghetti. Red sauce. Gooey white mozzarella cheese planted on a piece of white meat. Looks like lunch, alright! Looks like Stu Marshall's entrails swirled up next to Mrs. Dunbar's lacerated back fat and drenched in gallons of blood. No thank you. I wasn't hungry before—I'm really not hungry now! I cover the tray back up and push it away. Maybe the cook will get a complex when he sees I'm not interested in the food he's preparing for me. Maybe then he'll stop making food that reminds me of the time when I ate people.

The door opens and in walks a female nurse. She wears a white nurse's uniform, and her dark brown hair is tied back in a tight ponytail. "Come sit on this chair over here," she instructs and points to the small metal chair at the desk. She has a small black kit in one hand, and a key ring and a pair of handcuffs in the other.

I narrow my eyes. *Really? Handcuffs?*

I walk over to her and sit in the chair.

"Put your hands behind your back," she says.

"Those aren't necessary," I protest as I glance at the cuffs. "I'm not gonna…"

"It's procedure," she says, cutting me off, her voice indicating a slight quiver. "I have to."

She's afraid of me like everyone else. I roll my eyes and comply, because really, what else can I do? Fight her? Attack her? I've been on my best behavior since I woke up here, and I'm not sure I want to find out what they'll do to me if I start acting out. So, I put my hands behind my back, and she clamps the handcuffs tightly in place. Too tight.

"Thanks," I say sarcastically and smile wide, "I really needed that."

She ignores me and places the kit on the desk. The metal latch rattles against the hard casing as she opens it up. Her hands shake something awful, and I smirk a "Graves" smirk in spite of myself.

"What do you want?" she asks as she takes out an electric razor.

I think about that for a second. What *do* I want? Kinda seems pointless to go back to the way I used to style my head and facial hair because that's not me anymore. *The Before.* And the way I look now only reminds me of my brief five month or so stint as a flesh-eating zombie. *The After.* So, who am I now that I've changed back? *The Now.* What happens *now*? Do I want to make a statement like so many teenagers do with their choice of dress and hairstyle? What possibly could make the statement "Hey, look at me, the ex-killer!"? The *me* during *The Before* just went with how he felt. "I feel like being comfortable today, so I'll wear nylon mesh shorts and a t-shirt. I feel like being a little more casual, but nice-looking, today, so I'll wear my khakis and a polo."

I went with my emotions and dressed accordingly. How do I feel *Now? The Now.*

I need to feel clean.

"Get rid of it all," I say confidently. "All off."

Her face twists slightly in confusion. She's cute. She has these huge brown eyes that aren't really brown. They're more like amber, and she can't be more than twenty-five years old. She's new at this; I can tell. Under the circumstances, though, I assume this is new for about everyone.

"Beard, hair, everything. Skin me down. Bald," I emphasize.

"Ok," she answers with uncertainty. "If that's what you want."

"Yes, that's what I want."

She turns the buzzer on and begins shaving down my head. Clumps of hair descend at my feet.

After a few minutes, it registers with the nurse that I'm really of no harm to her, either that or she's just zoning out 'cause she seems much more relaxed as she goes to work on my face and hair. The buzzing of the razor seems to distance her from me, and I get a sense that she's daydreaming about something amidst the electric din. I use this as an opportunity for something, anything—information, clarification. Maybe I can use my wily charms to get free of these annoying handcuffs. I doubt she'll bite, given the way I look, cause I look pretty damn awful right now. Not the dashing and debonair Griffin who could charm the panties off any woman in my fantasy world, but it's worth a shot. "Can you loosen up the cuffs," I say as I wince my face in mock pain, "you put them on kinda tight."

She stops the razor, her trance broken from the hypnotic sound, and looks hard at me. "I... I don't know," she mutters hesitantly.

I cock my head to the side and dip my shoulders down a bit, "C'mon. I'm totally cured. Call Holston if you want to!"

"I can't," she snaps. "I could get into a lot of trouble."

I exhale loudly and obnoxiously to emphasize my discontent. "Is that what you tell all your patients?" I joke.

She snorts a little laugh out. "No, just the *Altered* ones."

"Oh, is that what you're calling me?" I continue in my light hearted voice, but it gives me cause to wonder. *The Altered?*

She smiles, and it lights up her amber eyes and olive colored skin. She really is cute. She smells good, too. Like summer rain. "You and the twenty-nine other patients stationed at this center," she says with a little chuckle at the end, but her smile quickly clamps up when she realizes she's said too much.

"So," I continue to probe. "There are thirty of us?"

"I... I can't say," she mumbles as she turns the razor back on and continues the assault on my hair.

"Why not?" I ask above the noise of the razor. "It's nice to know there are others like me," and I give her the cheesiest, most depressing pout I can muster.

She stops the razor again and sighs heavily. "They're not all like you." And as she turns it back on and raises her arm up to complete her job, I notice her forearms are riddled with scratch and bite marks. A slight gasp unintentionally rises from my throat as she moves the razor down onto my face.

"All done," she says as she rolls the desk chair over to the mirror.

I look at myself, freshly shaved, no hair to be found anywhere, and I realize I look ghastly. Worse than before. The facial hair at least gave me the appearance of a full face, but with that mask now gone, it's obvious how much weight I've lost. My cheeks are sunken in, and my cheekbones are practically jutting out of my face.

Zombie.

"Wow," I joke. "This is worse than before."

The nurse smiles. "You asked for it."

I continue to look at my reflection, and I notice there's a scar under my right eye. It's circular and raised like a mosquito bite that kept getting picked at and will now never go away. I run my finger back and forth over the bump. My mind scrambles to all the deep files of my memory to try and remember where this unusual mark came from. The nurse watches me in the mirror intently as my face contorts in confusion. She wriggles her nose. Her nostrils flare outward, and she says, "You all have that."

I swivel my head to look at her directly. "What do you mean?"

"All of you," she repeats, and fear flares up in her eyes. "It's the same scar from where they injected you."

"Injected me?" I repeat and suddenly I remember the white suit CDC guys.

"Yeah," she says, her voice one notch above a whisper. "They gave you the serum, just like they gave the others. Listen, I..."

I lurch forward, my hands bucking against the cuffs, the chair jerking toward her. She steps back defensively and gasps.

"Please!" I beg her. "I swear, I'm not going to hurt you. I'm not like that anymore. No one is telling me anything. Please. Help me figure this all out!"

I guess I struck a nerve in her. Her amber eyes become soft again, sympathetic, and by the expression on her face, I know she *wants* to tell me something. In an instant, there's a connection between us. There was electricity that had sparked when her fingers brushed up against my hands (even if she was putting handcuffs on me). Maybe she knew someone like me, had a similar experience, and maybe even empathized with my case. Even though she is afraid, there's a faint inkling of sadness and pity in her facial expressions. She hesitantly takes a step toward me again and lowers her head so she's closer to my face. That summer rain smell of hers is nice, pleasant. It reminds me of the Fourth of July parties at my parents' house with pitchers of cold lemonade set on the backyard table and chicken being grilled on the barbeque. A nervous line of sweat forms above her dark eyebrows, and I realize what I smell is actually her flesh. Her fear and anxiety smells like grilled chicken, and my stomach growls. "The virus killed a lot of people. That's what it was supposed to do. But some people didn't die, they were transformed," she whispers quickly.

"Like me," I clarify.

She nods. "The virus got into your blood stream, and well, you know what happened."

I nod.

"Anyway, they came up with a cure. They gassed the infected. That killed off a lot of them, but the ones who survived were given the antidote. Only half survived that."

My hand instinctively touches the scar under my eye. She closes her eyes and gives a sharp nod. "You were cured. Altered."

She says that word again and something rumbles inside my brain. It doesn't sound right, like it's a dirty word, an evil word.

"What does that even mean—'altered'?" I ask.

She stares blankly at me, like she wants to respond, but something is preventing her.

"Does it mean, like, we're not human or something?"

"No, no, no!" she quickly answers shaking her head.

"Then what are we like, genetically engineered people? Super humans? More human than human?" I question in rapid fire.

Tears form in her eyes.

"And what about the others?" I ask, referring to the twenty-nine other altered patients who presumably reside at the Re-Assimilation Center.

Her eyes widen and she stands up straight. "I have to go," she says, and she unfastens the cuffs.

"What about the others?!" I repeat, my voice getting louder.

She shakes her head and takes a step back. I reach to grab her arm, but she backs away quickly and escapes through the door, locking it firmly behind her.

Altered.

"Altered," I say to myself out loud.

To adjust, change, modify.

"Re-assimilate."

To reintroduce, reincorporate, re-conform.

All these words are starting to add up—I changed and was altered back. Back into what? I don't know.

And neither do these people who keep me here, locked in this room.

I WAKE UP TO THE SOUND OF BLOOD CURLING screams in the distance. My body jolts from its sleep to that familiar sound, a sound I know all too well. It's a high-pitched scream of absolute terror; one of those uncontrollable this- is-the-final-moment-of-my-life screams. I've heard that sound one too many times, and I anticipate the line of dialog that will soon follow: "No, please! Stop!" I begin counting to five—one, two, three... and as if on cue, there it comes.

"No, please! Stop!" a woman's voice rings throughout the hospital corridor, and while I imagine it could be my hairdresser nurse with the amber eyes, I can't place the voice as hers. When someone's screaming like that, screaming for their life, vocal recognition is hard to pinpoint.

There are some more howls and moans. Familiar sounds to my altered ears, as well, and I think: *My god, here we go again.*

People shuffle outside my locked door, and I'm tempted to make my way to the small window to take a look, but honestly, I just woke up and am still trying to catch my bearings. And besides, if it's starting all over again, what in the world can *I* possibly do about it?

I sit upright in the swivel chair. After the nurse left me, I must have fallen asleep at the desk. There's a creak in my neck, and as I start rubbing it, my hands run all over the back of my neck and feel the new peach fuzz on my head. The new cut feels so alien to me, so strange, but I'm not surprised. Nothing has felt normal. I don't even know what normal is anymore.

It's dark outside. I can only see the blackness of night from my little window, and the only light in the room is the small desk lamp that's been left on. I glance at myself one last time in the mirror. The light from the lamp casts shadows on my sunken-in face, and it makes me look even more ghastly than I already am.

Zombie. Altered.

I make my way to the bed and notice the blue food tray from this afternoon is still there. I guess they forgot about me. Guess there's so much going on with all that screaming and yelling and commotion they forgot about me. Maybe they forgot about the other 29 altered people too? But I'm not hungry. A little thirsty, yes. Hungry, no.

A woman cries outside my locked door, and I close my eyes remembering all the female tears I've had to deal with. Too much for this lifetime! Mom, Syd, Toby. I swear, being in that house with all that estrogen raging was a little too much to handle. At least when my dad was around the boy-girl ratio was even, but with Dad gone and Toby in the mix, I was certainly outnumbered! I stop and find myself smiling. Smiling about Mom and Syd. Smiling about Toby...

●

"No! I'm not letting you do it, Griffin," Mom declared after I told her about my plan. We were all sitting at the kitchen table eating our allotted bowls of dry cereal when I made the big announcement: I was going to walk to the body shop, pick up my newly fixed car, drive back to get the girls, and go get help. My master plan. My epiphany.

"So, you suggest we stay here?" I probed sarcastically, my eyes furrowing as if to say that staying where we were at that time was the most absurd suggestion ever.

Sydney cried silently. Big tears pooled at the base of her eyelids and tumbled down her pale checks like heavy raindrops on concrete sidewalks. Toby's head hung low, and she used her fingers to pick out the marshmallows from her cereal—the only part of her cereal she actually ate. "We're safe here," Sydney whispered through a muffled sob.

"We are?" I challenged, my voice getting louder. Mom shot me a "lower-it!" look, and I took a deep breath. "That's what Toby and her family thought until they were ambushed!" I looked over at Toby who had closed her eyes from the mention of her family.

My mother crossed her arms across her chest and tightened her lips in defiance. "Absolutely not!" she repeated. "I'm not letting you risk your life out there."

Sydney sniffed back the growing sob in her chest.

Toby looked up at me.

"So, you'll let me, and Syd, and Toby, and you die in this house without even trying to get help. Because, you know that's what's going to happen, Ma! We're going to die here. The end game does not look favorable for us!"

"I don't want to die!" Sydney blurted out.

"You're not going to die," my mother retorted with her "don't be so stupid" voice.

"Don't lie to her!" I snapped. "You *are* going to die, Syd," I said calmly, looking deeply into her eyes. "We're all going to die sooner or later. Some of us more sooner than later! Maybe all of us more sooner than later. If you want it to be later, than you have to let me try this." My face was in line with Sydney's, but my eyes were directed at my mother. She knew I was right. In her heart she knew the situation was bad and was only going to get worse. The food would eventually run out. The water would eventually run out. We were always under constant threat of attack. What would happen if one or more of us got sick? And what would happen when the hot summer months rolled by and the four of us roasted in this house?

"I don't want to die," Toby said under her breath.

"None of us do!" my mother asserted. "And for you to even suggest I would let that happen…"

"That's not what I'm saying, Ma!" I whined at her.

"Then what are you saying, Griffin?"

"I'm doing this," I responded firmly. "I'm doing this because it's what Dad would do!" and at the mention of my father, my mother's eyes flashed with pain. "I'm doing this because there isn't any other choice," I continued. "I'm doing this because there has to be other people out there who can help us. Authorities. Feds. Whatever. Someone, somewhere. I don't want us all to die in this house without knowing."

My mother started to cry. Her big blue eyes swelled with tears and her nose reddened. Sydney put her face in her hands and released all she had been holding back.

My mother extended her hand and rubbed the back of Sydney's head to try to calm her down, but upon feeling my mother's touch, Sydney jumped up from the table and ran to her hiding spot underneath the stairs.

"Do you want me to go after her?" Toby asked, but I could tell by the look on her face and the tone of her voice she really didn't mean it, that it was something to say at that moment.

"No, don't," my mother said breathlessly as she wiped her own tears from her face. "Leave her be. She just needs to be alone."

Toby sat back down and continued to play with the marshmallows in her bowl.

"You know I'm right," I said after a few moments of silence.

"No, you're not right," my mother shot back. "This isn't right."

"Yeah, well, none of it is!" Toby interjected and made my mother's eyebrows instinctively rise.

"What was that you said?" my mother asked her coolly. It always irritated her to no end when Toby said anything. She resented Toby. Hated having her in the house. Hated sharing her clothes with her, her food with her, her water supply with her, her makeup and perfume with her.

"Griffin is right, Maggie," Toby continued without looking at either of us, but I could tell she was crying too. "We can't stay here. If those things out there ever get wise to us being in here, I know what will happen."

"Oh? Really? We're boarded up pretty tight up in here, and..."

"So were we. My family," Toby answered somberly.

My mother caught her breath, and I imagine she stopped to really think about what had happened to Toby and exactly why it was she came to join us. Toby's family had been decimated by those things, and she had nowhere else to go. Toby had been lucky to stumble upon us. If we got attacked now, we might not share that same luxury. It surely would be the death of us.

My mother sighed back tears and put her hand gently on top of mine.

"I don't like it, Griffin. I don't like the way this makes me feel. I don't like letting you go out there with those things. I don't want to lose you," and then she placed her other hand on top of Toby's in a gesture that nearly made me choke in amazement. "I don't want to lose *any* of you." Toby looked up from her bowl and gave a soft smile.

That entire afternoon I sat in the living room figuring out how I would make my move. I decided I wasn't going to take any supplies because if anything happened to me, I wouldn't want to waste the girls' rations any. I was, however, going to take a flashlight because it would serve a dual purpose: light and a possible weapon, if needed. I was hoping I wouldn't need a weapon, but that was wishful thinking on my part. I had seen those things. Seen how they moved, and acted, and hunted, and killed. They were so unpredictable I was going to have to be as stealthy as possible. The flashlight was thick and made of metal, heavy, and would prove to be useful if confronted. But if I was overtaken by more than one, well, I didn't want to think about that. I was also going to bring the spare keys to my car. I didn't want to make it all the way to the mechanic's garage, find my car, and have to fumble around the garage office looking for my keys like some stupid kid in one of those stupid horror movies when we all know damn well the keys are always tucked under the visor in the cab. But that's not real life. I don't know of anyone who leaves spare keys *in* their car, and I wasn't about to find out if it was a traditional car mechanic practice.

"Get to the garage. Find the Monte Carlo. Keys already in hand. Fire her up. Get home to you girls. Simple as that," I outlined for Toby and Sydney who were snuggled together on the living room couch. Both girls nodded their heads in agreement with my plan. "Oh, and evade the infected crazy people who want to eat me alive," I added in a joking tone. Syd apparently didn't like that last comment because she tucked her head deep into Toby's chest.

"I'm going to bed!" Sydney said as she realized Toby was not going to offer any head rubs or back rubs or any other form of comfort to her. Then, she came over to me, kissed me on the cheek and said, "Don't leave tomorrow without saying goodbye to me!"

"I won't, I promise," I answered, and gave her a gentle slap across the face.

"I should get to bed too," Toby said as she too got up from the couch and stretched her arms.

"Okay," I responded.

"Thanks, Griffin," she said over her shoulder.

"Mmm hmm," I called back to her. I got up and went into my mother's room. She was lying on her bed above the covers and staring at the ceiling.

"Ma?" I said as I poked my head in.

"Come in," she answered flatly.

"You okay?" I asked as I moved to her bed and knelt down beside her. She turned her head to me and in the soft glow of candlelight I could see she had been crying.

"Yeah, I'm fine," she managed.

"We ready for this?"

She nodded her head. "I'll have our bags ready to go by the front door."

I gave a sharp nod. "Remember, keep Sydney on the lookout upstairs. When I come back with the car, I'll circle the cul-de-sac so you can take your time getting the stuff away from the front door. When you're ready, make Toby move the shutters up and down so I'll know to stop. Once I stop, make a run for it. Give Sydney the lightest bag to carry. Give Toby the heaviest."

Mom rolled her eyes as I smirked and gave her a "Josh-wink."

"If the coast is clear, we can try to pack up the trunk with stuff, ya know?" I suggested.

She shook her head. "No. If we're leaving the house like this, we're *leaving!* I don't wanna waste any time or gas. We're gonna go."

I nodded. "Okay, Ma. I gotcha. I'll see ya in the morning," and I kissed her forehead.

"I love you," she said as I moved to the doorway.

"I love you, too," I answered as I left and went back to my room.

The house was silent, and I lie in bed thinking about what I was about to do and all the possible outcomes. We could be rescued! I could be the hero of the family and drive all four of us to safety! Maybe we could even find my father? Maybe he's hiding out in the city, holed up somewhere just like we are? I thought it would be a good idea to drive by his office to check. Mom would definitely be on board with that idea. And come to think of it, maybe I could drive by Lana's house to see if she's alright? That idea, I know for a fact Mom would be against!

Or the opposite could happen. I could be killed during my mission and the fate of my mother, sister, and Toby would be out of my hands. What if I was infected and became one of those things? I didn't even want to think about it, and when the knock on my door came, I nearly jumped out of my skin.

"Griffin, it's me, Toby," she whispered through the door. "Can I come in?"

Toby? What the hell is she doing here? I thought.

"Yeah, yeah, come in," I whispered back.

Toby gently opened the door. She stood on the threshold wearing a long white t-shirt and holding one of her pillows by her stomach.

"What's up?" I asked.

She stepped in and shut the door behind her. "Sydney's crying. I can hear her. I can't sleep, and I have way too much on my mind. Think I can stay in here?"

There was a sad look in her eyes, and I immediately got up and went over to the door.

"Um, I guess," I answered, a little confused. "I'll go to your room. Sydney's crying won't bother me."

"No!" she exclaimed. "I can't kick you out of your own room, especially when, ya know, you're leaving tomorrow and everything."

"Um, okay, I'll sleep on the floor?"

Toby walked up to me and put her hands on my shoulders. "I don't want to be alone."

She threw her pillow on the floor and jumped into my bed. She shimmied her body to the spot closest to the wall and patted the bed next to her. "Here," she said motioning for me to join her.

I hesitated. My head swam. I had all these thoughts about being chased by infected people, trying to save my family, trying to find my father, possibly dying, and here was Trashy Toby whose dark brown roots were growing at least two inches against her bleached blonde hair. Who slept with teachers for good grades, and who aspired to marry a rich old man who would kick the bucket after a few months and leave all his money to her. Self-centered Toby, who wore my mother's sundresses and painted her face with garish makeup while the Apocalypse was happening outside our door. Who wouldn't even pet my sister's head when she needed comforting. Loud and obnoxious Toby, who said crude and disgusting things to guys to get them to like her. Who was sprawled out, right then, on my bed, smoothing out a spot on the covers for me to join her. Damaged Toby, who watched her entire family get slaughtered and...

I looked down at her with a look of confusion, but she patted the bed again. "Keep me safe," she purred, and I guess I had no other choice but to get into the bed next to her.

Once I lay down, she cocked her body in a sideways position and nuzzled her head in my armpit. In this position I had no other choice but to wrap my arm around her shoulder. She drew in closer and threw one arm across my chest and one leg across my waist, lifting up my shirt so the bare skin of her thigh was in direct contact with my bare stomach. I tensed up a bit when I felt the coldness of her leg on my flesh, and I could feel in the crook of my arm, through my shirt, a smile curl up on her face. "Am I hurting you?" she cooed.

"No, no, you're fine," I answered softly, but my heart was beating so fast and so loud, I thought for sure she'd be able to feel it and hear it being so close to my chest.

See, I'd had girlfriends before in my short 17 years of life, but nothing ever got too serious with any of them. I would take girls out, and stuff like that, but my relationships never lasted more than a few months. I got bored easily. Lost interest fast. Always was holding out for the "big one." Lana. And yeah, I had girlfriends, and ya know, I messed around and stuff, but right then, with Toby's half naked body intertwined with mine...

I sighed.

"Nervous about tomorrow?" she whispered and her warm breath against my ear gave me shivering goose bumps.

"You could say that" I answered, which wasn't a complete lie.

"You're really brave for doing what you're doing, ya know," she said as she ran her finger across my cheek.

"Nah. It's kinda like, instinct, ya know?" Her soft touch made my eyes flutter into the back of my head for a second or two.

"I guess so," she agreed, "but you were really brave for saving my ass, too."

"It was the right thing to do," I said with Josh's face popping into my head, "I would have helped anyone who needed it."

"Mmmm," she exhaled as she moved her finger to gently outline my lips.

Her touch was maddening. I was starting to lose focus, starting to forget about playing war general and saving my family, starting to forget about the moaning infected wanderers outside my window. I couldn't think straight. Toby was not my type at all. I would have never given her a second thought if this was the real world. But this certainly wasn't the real world. And I don't know why, but for as much as I wasn't attracted to her, something was stirring inside of me, making me fall prey to her warm smoke-like breath and feathery caresses.

"You know, I never really thanked you for what you did for me."

"Sure, you did," I answered like a dummy.

She let out a soft chuckle. "No, silly! Not *really*," and she grabbed the side of my head, tilted it to reach her lips, and gave me a sweet, partial open-mouth kiss.

I pulled my head back, breaking the kiss, and looked deeply into her eyes. "You're welcome," I said, and she pressed her lips together in a sensuous sneer. I turned my head to look back at the ceiling, assuming a kiss was just a kiss, and I needed to collect my thoughts and refocus, but Toby quickly grabbed my face again and turned me back toward her.

"I'm seriously not done thanking you," she whispered as she latched her lips back onto mine, this time kissing me so deeply and passionately that it sent shivers throughout my entire body.

It was then I succumbed. My mind switched off and in one quick motion, I swept Toby's body underneath me and fell into her arms.

That's the last memory I have, the last memory I can stand, before I close my eyes and drift to sleep...

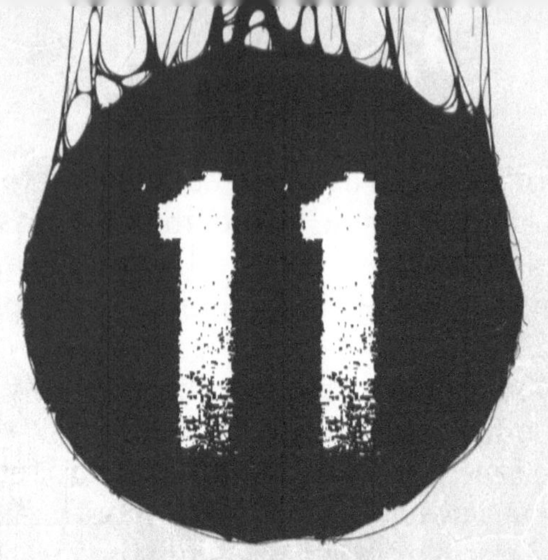

1HE WORLD SHOOK. VIOLENT AND JARRING. *It felt as if the ground beneath me was going to split wide open and suck me down to the deepest parts of Hell itself. The sounds filled the city street and penetrated my ears as if I were underwater. But that could have been the fluid from my decomposing brain, or blood—or both. They were clogged sounds of screams and moans, and I wanted so desperately to tilt my head to the side and let whatever was filling my eardrums to be released. Infected bodies around me fell to the ground, and I soon realized the ground was not shaking, not moving, not splintering to usher me to my death, rather it was the collective force of bodies plummeting to the ground. Falling. Moaning. Screaming a scream I had never thought capable from their mouths.*

I didn't fall, but I was stuck. Paralyzed in mid-shuffle. An aircraft flew overhead. Or maybe it was a UFO. My eyesight had been getting increasingly worse as the days and nights sauntered by, and everything looked cloudy and gray and shadowy, like a curtain with tiny holes had descended over my pupils and was slowly rotting my vision away. But, really, vision had all but become secondary when the instinct kicked in. All my bodily functions and senses had been shutting down, shutting off, but my sense of smell had remained intact. Heightened, in fact. It was all about the smells. So, the aircraft, plane, helicopter, UFO, whatever, hovered above for a little bit, and then the cloud came and blanketed us.

Then the world shook, and around me they all fell. Body after body, like bags of weighted bones. It was hard to tell how many came crashing down because who knows how many of us there were at that point in time or how long we had been infected. Their distorted faces twisted in agony, and the sounds from their throats was like warbled microphone feedback. When the cloud settled, my veiled eyes witnessed bodies writhing on the ground with their flesh bubbling like runny eggs in a frying pan. And yet, I stood. I was the only one. I didn't fall. I didn't scream. I didn't disintegrate like the body at my left foot did. I was only frozen. Paralyzed in mid-shuffle, mid-moan, mid-step. My thirst and hunger had been getting harder and harder to keep in check, and this cloud, this blanket, stopped me. Stopped me from holding on. Stopped me from running. Stopped me from forcing myself to hold back. Stopped me from shuffling through the day. And I felt nothing.

Time wasn't an issue for the infected. There's light and darkness and hunger. Gnawing hunger. Like your insides are hollowed out and bleeding. Starvation accelerated. How long I had been standing is debatable. It wasn't the amount of time spent being paralyzed; it was the feeling of emptiness, hollowness, and starvation that was driving me crazy. The want, the desire, the ultimate need worked its way throughout my very core and tried to propel me into action, but I couldn't move. I fought and struggled against my frozen position. The body at my left foot had its face completely melted off to the bone, but it was able to move and wriggle and writhe. In its unbearable agony, it reached a rotted-flesh hand up to my ankle. Was it asking for help? Did it seek my help? This only increased my rage, and in my mind I bucked against the unseen shackles. My stomach was hollow, and I wished the body before me to die. Get it over with. Just die. Melt away and die!

Just when I thought I couldn't stand the ravenous hunger coursing through my muddied veins, I smelled the smell. Fresh and tantalizing. The aroma of the gods! Meat! I heard distant voices, but they were muffled too, and I was not sure of how close they were to me. But the scent was maddening! Come closer, come closer. Let me smell you, let me smell you, let me taste you!

Then I realized I was able to move my head. Whatever gaseous poison that made hundreds of others collapse in their tracks and locked me frozen in time was wearing off. I was able to move my head. That was a start! I tilted it back as far as I could and located the source of the sweet smell of flesh. There were people surrounding me. Their white protective suits and spacemen helmets made me think for a split second they actually did come from a UFO in the sky, but one of the white suits turned around, and I noticed a blue circular emblem on the sleeve with the letters CDC in the center.

"There's one standing! I think we got a live one here!" one of the suits said from behind his helmet. It was muffled between his breathing apparatus and the clogging of my ears that I almost didn't understand them. But they were words—actual words! And not the ones I'd *heard so many times daily, "No, please! Stop!" They were actual words to form an actual sentence to create real communication! I cocked my head in interest, half hoping the damn fluid would slide out of my ear and allow me to hear better.*

Another white suit ran up to the other one and frantically yelled, "It moved! It moved!"

It? Me? Are they talking about me?

My hazy eyes, paralysis, and poor hearing made my muddled brain ache with confusion, but when the excited white suit dashed in front of me and his fresh meat scent wafted directly up my nostrils, I was overcome! The hunger rushed back, and I uncontrollably gnashed my teeth in his direction. A deep visceral sound emerged from my mouth.

"Get him! Get him!" one of the white suits screamed.

My upper body swayed from side to side. The other one was upon me in a moment's flash. He clamped my hands behind my back, but he fumbled with whatever device he had to restrain me. I bared my teeth again. I couldn't help it. Sweat beaded off his forehead from underneath his helmet. The heat must have been so uncomfortable for him, but it made his flesh smell gently cooked. I could almost taste his lightly roasted thigh flesh between my teeth. His sweat and blood whetted my appetite, satiated my hunger, calmed my rage. I hissed at him again, and I felt him slightly jerk his hands behind me.

"Hurry up! Get him down!" the other one yelled.

"I... I don't know. This hasn't... what the hell...?"my captor stammered.

"Get him on the ground! I have the serum ready!"

"I... I can't see the lock switch! Damn facegear!"

"Take it off for a second. Lock him up. Get him to the ground."

My captor took off his helmet. I felt him trembling behind me. I smelled his sweat increasing, coating his flesh. I hissed again, but this time, not so menacingly. His helmet fell to the ground brushing up against my leg. My leg. I can feel it again! I took one step forward, heard the chain fall behind me as if something plopped into a pool of water, and swung my body around so I was face to face with that beautiful hunk of flesh. His white suit protected his entire body, hands included, but his face was exposed and gray with fear. There were screams from all sides of me, but those were the same underwater sounds. I think I heard something to the effect of "Don't shoot!" but I couldn't be certain. I stared at the face. Although drained of all color, the cheeks were plump with flesh, and as I had presumed, a thin layer of sweat covered its entire circumference. There was no more control. I was completely lost in the craving. I let go. And I attacked.

His knees buckled when I leapt upon him, and we both crashed to the ground. Not as dramatic a tumbling as when the world shook, but enough to create a marked panic in the now masses of white suits surrounding us. I embraced him as he kicked and screamed and cried and begged the same words over and over again, "No, please! Stop!" He couldn't break free from my hold. My instincts were good, formed, developed. I knew how to hold on tightly to what was mine, even if it meant breaking every bone in his body. In my arms I danced with him for a moment, creating a heightened moment of anticipation before I sank my teeth deep into the side of his face. His screams in my ears were muffled, *and I thought maybe that was a natural defense mechanism my body had created for itself—so the screams of my victims wouldn't completely blow out my eardrums. There was a moment of clarity as his blood filled my mouth. The hunger began to subside as my teeth scraped back and forth, back and forth, back and forth on his face. I knew the satisfaction was merely temporary, but for that moment, I savored. Savored this delectable meal. Savored the lightly roasted apple of his cheek. There was flesh, and then muscle, and then highways of veins erupting against my tongue. Then bone. I ground my teeth against the bone of his cheek as if to sharpen them, to ready them for the jewel of his face—his eye.*

I never got that far.

His body collapsed under my weight, and I knew he'd either passed out or died. There was a small part of me that had somewhat conscious, focused thoughts that needed him to be dead because I knew he would never be like me if he was. A gunshot confirmed my suspicions. One of the other white suits had euthanized my meal. He was dead. He wouldn't change. I could only be so lucky.

Someone came up behind me and forced me onto my stomach. The man I ate was dragged away; his blood scent lingered in the air only a few moments longer. My head was sideways, and my haze-glazed eyes saw the hundreds of bodies on the ground from when the world shook. They were no longer writhing. They were all dead, too. Two white suits flipped me onto my back. One straddled over me, pinning me. Another grabbed my arms and threw them above my head. I was paralyzed again, but this time under the weight and force of these suited men. Although I couldn't see him, a third had taken hold of my ankles and kept my legs in position.

"Hold him! Hold him good!" the one straddling me screamed.

"Get the syringe! Once he's in position, I'll inject!"

There was a needle. In my curiosity, I stopped fidgeting. He held it up high, tapped the side of it a few times and aimed the long thick needle in my direction. Closer and closer to my face. And I was curious— curious to see where he intended to stick me with this thing, curious to see what it was going to do to me. It was inserted right below my right eye, and the thick gloved white suit pressed the plunger down into my face.

"Back up! Back up!" someone yelled. The white suits who held me down scattered like bugs, and I was released.

Released.

I staggered to my feet, unsure, unfazed, but then I was soon proven wrong.

The ground rushed up to meet me, and once again, I was sprawled out next to the decaying bodies that made the world shake. My movements were uncontrollable. I spasmed. Full body shakes that would make the worst epileptic blush. My head thrashed against the pavement, and my skull burst open into a pool of putrid smelling fluid and my own blood. The whooshing sound in my ears opened up like a floodgate and the ocean waters receded in my head replaced by sand in my ears. Crisp and clear sand. Liquid gone and sound amplified. Everyone around me screamed. I tilted my head again to see the gaping mouths of the dead bodies and *skeletons, and I couldn't tell if the sounds of the screams were coming from them or from somewhere else.*

Where am I? I thought.

A wave of heat surged from behind my eyes. I closed them tight to make the feeling stop, but for some reason, it increased in intensity. Like lightning, like shockwaves, like tiny knives whittling their way throughout my veins, cutting me on the inside, tearing me apart, ripping my organs to shreds. Gut me. Like I had done so many times...

My face was on fire! I quickly raised my hands to my face to find it wasn't really on fire. It just felt that way. Blood and liquid seeped from my nose. Dark black goo. The smell was unbearable, and my stomach turned violently. I had to throw up. But I couldn't. I couldn't stop convulsing long enough to vomit. The fire sensation raced down my neck and into my chest. My heart jolted in its cage, and I thought it would surely burst.

What did you do to me!? I tried to scream, but I hadn't used my vocal cords for who knows how long. The only sound that came from me was the familiar groaning and moaning. But it was so damn loud! I wished I could stop it, but I wasn't in control. And the noise filled my ears and head with crisp, clear sand sounds while my heart raced and jolted, and my eyes burned, and my voice was trying to find its way out and my arms and legs shook so badly that I thought the ground beneath me would burst open and swallow me whole.

I rolled onto my stomach face down in a pool of putrid fluid and blood. I gagged. The smell of rotted flesh and metal was all around me and up my nose. Vomit finally forced its way out of my stomach. My chest burned and heaved as clumps of hair mixed with bile and blood spewed into the pool. My head bobbed up and down. My open mouth caught some of the strange brew and I ingested some of my previous stomach contents. I wanted to puke again. I was covered in filth, and all I wanted to do was puke.

The convulsions finally stopped, but my eyes still burned. It felt as if my eyelids were going to weld onto my eyeballs, leaving me blind forever. I attempted to open them in spite of the searing pain. Slowly the lids lifted, and I was blinded by the natural light of the sun. It burns, it burns, it burns! I blinked rapidly in hopes of adjusting to the new sensation. I blinked so fast I finally had both eyes open wide and I saw! The brightness of the day was uncensored by the haze my vision had grown accustomed to. I could see all the pretty colors. The reds, the oranges, the browns, the blacks, smeared on my clothing, festering on my skin. I could see clearly, too. The twisted limbs of the bodies that made the world shake. Hundreds strewn across the open city street. Yellow tape in the distance created some sort of barrier. Remnants of purple gas from the cloud created by the UFO slowly settled in the sewer grates.

I sat up on my knees and tried to pull myself together. I vomited again into my lap. My head spun and itched. I was bleeding. Or oozing. Whatever you call it when infected fluids drain from your body.

"Are we good?" someone screamed a few feet away from me.

"Did it work?" another voice interjected.

Even though I could hear fine, their voices were still muffled. CDC white suits behind face gear helmets. CDC white suits with torn off faces and gunshot wounds to the head. If only I could be so lucky.

No one moved. There was a circle of white suits around me, but no one moved a muscle. Except for me. The knives had stopped their assault on my veins. The lightning had ceased shocking my body. The fire had burned out from behind my eyes. And something else. The gnawing, constant, unrelenting hunger was gone. I looked at my bloodied hands as I forced my body to stand up. Death was everywhere. I surveyed the ground. I surveyed the throng of white suits as they closed in on me yet again. My head itched. The smell of sickness and decay was maddening. All I could do was throw my head back. And then it came to me.

My voice returned as I screamed into the morning air.

The white suits descended upon me, knocking me unconscious.

Y EYES FLUTTER OPEN AGAIN. IT'S morning. These endless days are bleeding together, and I don't seem to have any concept of time, day, week, month, or year. I remember lying in this hospital bed and thinking of my night with Toby right before I fell asleep. One would think that remembering such a significant and enjoyable experience in one's life right before going to sleep would bring upon happy dreams, right? I could only be so lucky. My dreams were filled with moans and screams and blood and gore. The day I was changed back. *Altered*. It wasn't so much a dream as it was a memory. Indescribable. Inescapable. Those thoughts and dreams and memories will never leave me, and I'm not so sure I can stand a lifetime of horrific images burned into my subconscious. I will never be normal again now that I've been altered. There's a deep feeling in me that thinks maybe they should have left me that way... as a zombie. Yea, but that had its own other set of issues as well.

Before I can think about it any further, my door is unlocked with a loud clanking sound. The door pushes open, and Dr. Holston enters pushing a metal tray cart in front of him. His gray hair is frazzled, and he reminds me of some crazy scientist character, like the stock characters from those cheesy B movies.

Dr. Frankenstein. Dr. Holston. They're all the same.

He's smiling when he enters, but his face drops a little when he sees me. It's the hair. My shave-job. He's startled by it. The corners of his smile droop for a second, but he does well to recover from his shocked expression. He continues to smile as he moves closer to me.

"Good morning!" he sings in a hearty tone and rolls the tray to the side of my bed. "How are we feeling today?"

I nod and stretch my arms above my head. A small yawn uncontrollably leaves my mouth.

"I read in the nurses' log you requested a haircut, but I wasn't expecting to see this!"

I smile and rub the top of my head. "Yeah, something different. I think I needed a change," I joke.

Holston smiles back. "Well," he continues, "as soon as you start eating the way you should, you'll put on more weight and start looking healthy again. I'm going to do some normal vital tests," and he takes some of his tools from the cart and starts the probing.

I want to say, "How do you know I ever looked healthy in my life?" but I don't. I know he means well, and I don't want to be a jerk to him. He's afraid of me. They all are. I can see it in their movements when they get close, but with Holston, it's different. He looks at me strangely, almost affectionately. There's a glint of wonder and awe in his eyes, and when he looks at my chart and takes my pulse and pressure and runs all his tests, he seems giddy. Happy. Like a mad scientist successfully figuring out an obscure formula. Like Dr. Frankenstein looking at his monster—"It's alive! Alive!" I hear in my head and laugh out loud. Now, if I were laughing out loud at nothing during one of my psycho-sessions, I'd be getting a death-stare from Graves, but Holston smiles more brightly. He must think I'm laughing at his comment because he remarks, "Glad to see you've got a sense of humor!"

I can't respond because there's a thermometer under my tongue. He takes it out when it starts beeping and looks at it. "97.6," he reads as his face furrows with a hint of concern.

"Is that bad or something?" I ask.

He scratches the side of his head and smooths some strands of hair behind his ear. "No, no, nothing to be concerned with right now. We'll keep watch on it."

Nothing to be concerned with right now. Typical doctor speak for "I don't like this one bit."

"Okay," I mutter as he continues with his exam.

"Everything seems to be on the up and up," he smiles, pleased with the results of the exam. "Like I said, we'll watch your temp, but it's a non-issue right now. Don't worry about it unless I do. Here's your breakfast and some water. I think it's okay if you start drinking juices." He reaches under the metal cart and presents to me another blue food tray, a glass of water, and a glass of orange juice. "Dr. Graves told me about the soda pop he gave you. I knew you weren't ready for that! Tasted like pure sand, didn't it?"

I nod my head. How did he know what it tasted like?

"Hand me your dinner tray. I know you ate nothing on it. You really need to put some nutrients in your body. You're not on the IVs anymore, and we don't want to have to hook you up to those again. Please try to eat some of the breakfast."

"What does it mean?" I ask as I hand him the dinner tray.

He pauses and looks at me funny. "What does what mean?" he repeats.

"My low temperature. You said it wasn't bad, but it's not good, right?"

Holston goes quiet, and his face darkens a little. "Anything that is out of the ordinary could indicate a relapse. I'm sure it's nothing."

I'm not sure if I believe him. *A relapse.* Is that what happened last night with one of the other patients? There were people screaming and moaning and scrambling around at all hours of the night—could that be what happened?

"Are you taking me to see Graves now?" I ask.

"No," he answers shaking his head. "It's Sunday. Graves has the day off. Today is rec-day."

"Rec-day?" I question.

"Yes, as in recreation. It's part of the therapy. You need exercise and fresh air, and the weather looks like it will hold up today, so you'll get to go outside. An escort will be here in an hour, so I suggest you eat your breakfast, wash up, and get dressed."

He's still smiling, still looking at me like I'm some grand prize trophy, and to be honest, it makes me feel uncomfortable.

"There are others. Like me, right?" I ask, but the nurse last night already told me, so it's more like a statement than it is a question.

"Yes, there are," he answers, and there's an honesty in his voice that opens an unseen door for me to go forward with my questions.

"Will I get to see any of them? Talk to any of them?"

Holston rubs his hands together nervously and then starts to straighten his tools out on the metal cart. I struck a nerve because he doesn't answer me. I think my door slammed shut in my face.

"Will I?" I press.

He stops fidgeting and looks up at me. His eyes are narrowed and his demeanor changes to one of solemnity and seriousness. He inhales deeply, the way your parents do when they're about to tell you something they don't want to tell you but know they have to. It's an inhale of near-aggravation and resignation. "You will see them," he breathes out heavily, "but you will be advised not to interact with any of them. This is still a delicate situation, and there is still so much to be explored and examined. The virus you all suffered from is a...," he stumbles for the right words, "...*tricky* one. It's not like anything we've seen before in the medical community. Because of its quickly mutating nature, the affects have been vastly different for many different people. The unpredictability of it is astounding, and *you* have been one of the few who have shown stability in recovery. So, again, I highly *recommend* you ignore the others *should* you come into contact with them."

He stressed the words "recommend" and "should" in such an odd way that I repeat his admonition in my head a few more times. I nod my head, he says a few more things that I don't pay attention to, and he leaves. Holston is not a stupid man, and I know he knows my senses have been heightened... altered.

I remember a time when I was a kid, maybe four or five years old. This was probably one of my earliest memories because it was such a traumatic experience. My mother was ironing my father's clothes for work one morning, and I came bopping into the kitchen to be with her. I was always something of a "Momma's Boy" when I was a little kid, and I always hung around her no matter what she was doing. She was finishing up and set the iron on the countertop next to the stove. "Don't touch that iron!" she warned me. "It's too hot, and you'll get hurt," and she walked into the other room to bring my father his outfit. I remember staring at the iron and becoming entranced with its flat silver surface pockmarked with its many holes. *What could it do to me?* I remember thinking to myself. And as if in slow motion, I stuck my hand out, open-palm, and involuntarily pressed it to the white-hot surface of the iron's face. I remember screaming, the sound of my skin sizzling against the iron, and the smell of burning flesh wafting into my nostrils. My mother raced back into the kitchen, swooped me up and screamed, "Why did you do that? I told you not to do that!" My hand was bandaged up for two weeks with second degree burns. I don't know why I did it.

I don't know why I had the urgency to do the exact opposite of what my mother told me not to do, but I was tempted to go against her will at whatever cost. There was a need inside of me to do what I wanted to do, regardless of the consequence. Most children get those very same urges; the urge to rebel, to see for themselves, to learn right and wrong through experience. It must be part of human nature to be curious and independent. It's in our genetic code to want to do something after we've been told not to because "ain't no one gonna tell me what I can and can't do!" Self-preservation.

And after replaying Holston's words over and over while I take a few nibbles of my pancake breakfast, while I slowly sip the pulp-filled orange juice, and while the hot water beats heavily on my bare head and neck as I take a shower, I start to think maybe he said those words so I would do the exact opposite of what he said not to do. I'm confusing myself! But the way he said "recommend" was weird. And the way he said "should" was so peculiar that the sound of the word has actually bored itself into my brain that I don't think I'll ever forget that sound or be able to say that word normally again. *I should be so lucky. Who am I kidding, I'll never do anything normally ever again.*

As I dress, I come to the conclusion that Holston was using some reverse psycho-psychology on me. I gotta hand it to the old chap; he was slick about it. I would have expected it from Graves, but I don't think Graves is that savvy. He would have come on out and said what he wanted from me, but Holston was a sneaky fellow! He smiled, then ran tests, smiled, got concerned, smiled, got serious. He may be my GP, but he's psychoanalyzing me as well, and I wonder if he knows I know, cause *I* know *he* knows my senses are heightened... altered. He wants me to talk to the others. He wants me to interact with them. And this is how I'm sure: he said, *"You have been one of the few who have shown stability in recovery."* The others haven't been responding like I have, and he wants me to get intel from the inside. I'm not a war general anymore, I'm a super-secret spy, and if I'm captured and questioned, Holston will deny ever giving me my mission, because really, he never told me to do anything. In fact, he told me *not* to do it. Technically.

The way these doctors and nurses barge into my room is criminal. My "escort" arrives, and I want to say, "Hey buddy, I could have been naked in here!" but I don't. I don't say a lot of what I really want to these days. I've talked so much to Graves and Holston since I woke up in that white walled room that I don't have the energy to voice my normal inside quips like I used to.

He takes me down the quiet corridor. My bare feet are freezing against the linoleum, and I'm guessing it must be hot outside for the higher-ups to have the air conditioner jacked up so high. It's not this chilly in my room, but what do I know, I'm a prisoner—I mean patient—here. The man doesn't talk to me, which is fine because I don't feel like talking to him either. He leads me to the elevator, and we get on. Lobby. The doors open with a ding; a ding so familiar it reminds me of the elevator at my dad's office. It's actually the same tone. When Syd was little, Mom used to take us up to Dad's office to meet him for lunch. But as we got older, and my father got higher up in the company, those trips stopped. I think of what must have happened to my father, and a vision pops into my mind: Dad stranded in the elevator at the bank where he worked, trying desperately to get out, to find help, the doors opening wide, a swarm of infected people bum-rushing the elevator, my father being dragged out and bitten and torn apart, his lifeless body stuck in the opening, the doors slamming against his body, confused that they can't shut properly, the sound of the bell dinging over and over as the door slides gracefully through his blood, ding, ding, ding. I shake my head like a dog shaking fleas. I shake that thought from my mind because I know it's not true. That's not what happened. It couldn't have happened because there was no power anywhere at that time, and my dad wouldn't have been so stupid as to attempt escaping via elevator. He watched as many horror movies as I did. He knew elevators were death traps...

"Go play. No talking," my escort commands in a condescending tone as he leads me to an open courtyard. The warm sun makes the top of my bald head feel tingly, and my eyes squint from the light. It's fresh out here, but not clean. The air has an unusual stench to it. Almost metallic. Not the usual Florida summer air that I've taken for granted most of my life. The courtyard isn't much of a courtyard as it is an open concrete field. It reminds me of the grammar school playgrounds of the inner-city schools in New York. Concrete. Hopscotch courses. Chain link fence. There's a basketball hoop and some picnic tables. It's a decent sized area set up into stations. There are hula hoops in one corner, and I see a mesh bag with red vinyl balls, the kind you use to play kickball with in gym class. Each corner of the courtyard has a metal pole with a spotlight attached. Right below the spotlights are surveillance cameras. I roll my eyes. *Figures as much.*

What I'm more concentrated on are the *people* in the courtyard. I look around and see there are two "escorts", big orderly looking guys in blue scrubs positioned at opposite ends of the field. Mine is still hanging around, so I guess that's three escorts. There's me hanging out by the main courtyard entrance. There's a dude playing at the basketball hoop by himself. A woman is sitting on the concrete next to the hoop pole hugging her knees to her chest. It looks like she's rocking back and forth. A younger guy is walking the perimeter of the courtyard, and I think he's talking to himself. It looks like his lips are moving, but I'm not too sure. I take careful notice of him because he stared at me long and hard when my escort practically pushed me through the doors. And there's a little girl playing with a doll at the picnic table. My heart stops because for a second, she looks like Sydney. I shake the fleas away again. It can't be Sydney.

I watched Syd die.

The black dude playing basketball puts the ball down next to the woman and goes to another picnic table. The woman on the floor stays, and I make my move. I bend down to pick up the ball, and she stares at me. She has a smile plastered on her face, and she's quietly giggling to herself. Her hair is matted pretty badly, and she has scratch marks on her cheeks. *She has the scar, too.* She doesn't say anything to me, so I pick up the ball and start shooting hoops.

I'm not the best basketball player, but I could hold my own back in the day. I dribble the ball and extend my arm up for a shot. I miss horribly, the ball veering wildly to the right. My senses may have been heightened, but my coordination leaves something to be desired! Before I can take off to retrieve the ball, I hear someone say "psst." I look up, and the guy who was eyeing me, talking to himself, walking around the edge of the field, is standing with the ball in hand ready to make a pass. I lift my hand up as if to say, "Pass it, I'm open," but he comes toward me quickly.

"Thanks," I whisper as he puts the ball gingerly at my feet.

He looks up at me. His hands twitch and his right eye has a slight tick. A slight twitch to it, as well. His head hovers low, and he stays in a bent position. "Welcome," he mumbles.

I'm not supposed to talk to anyone. No contact whatsoever. But my super-secret spy mission tells me otherwise. I cock my head above the guy's sunken posture and survey the courtyard. The orderlies are not paying attention to us. My guy left, and the other two are browsing through some car magazine. The coast is temporarily clear.

"Get up," I say to him. "They're not watching us."

He straightens up, still twitching and all shifty-like. "What's your name?" he asks.

"Gri..." I start but he waves his hand in front of my face to shut me up.

"Never go by your real name!" he exclaims. "What's your number?"

"My number?" I ask confused.

"You know, your patient number, the one the bully doctor uses."

I roll my eyes. *Graves.*

"24. I'm 24," I answer.

"I'm 16. My number, not my age," he snorts as his face spasms rapidly, uncontrollably. It's obvious he's not sixteen years old. Given what he's gone through and the way things are now, I guess he is in his late twenties. "That's 7," he says as he points to the woman on the ground. I look down at her. She's still giggling.

"You have the scar, too," I say as I point to his face and back at mine.

"We all do," he says as he caresses his. "Yours isn't too bad. Guess they tweaked the dose or something," and as he says this, I look more carefully at his. His is twice the size of mine.

"How long have you been here?" I ask him.

He snorts, and his body makes unnatural jerks with each quick breath he takes in. I think he's laughing. 7 starts to laugh a little louder, too.

"A long time," he answers as he takes both of his hands and vigorously scratches his head of greasy blonde hair. 7 gets a little upset at this action and gasps loudly. "I'm okay," he whispers to her, and she rocks back and forth again. "If you're 24, then..." he lifted up his fingers and started counting some bizarre math that I couldn't make heads or tails of, "...you've probably been here about three months. May, April, March... yeah, I'd say about three months. No, no, no two. Yeah, two months, what am I talking about? I've been here three months, or is it four?"

"Two months?" I exclaim. "That can't be right!"

He's wrong, I think. *It's only been a few days.*

"Oh, oh, oh, yeah," he stutters, "that white room you woke up in..."

"Yeah?"

"You didn't wake up on your own. They woke you up, man. Woke you up cause they thought you were ready."

"Ready? What, like ready to go home?" I ask, and the question sounds so stupid to my ears after I say it. My super-secret spy instincts aren't as good as they should be.

16 does that snort-laugh thing again. Watching his eye bug out is almost painful. I look away at 7 whose body heaves up and down in quick laugh spurts.

"Dude!" he says as he claps my back. "Ready for their experiments! These quacky-quacks are experimenting on us, man!" and 7 stops laughing and lets out a woeful sigh.

"What do you mean? What are you saying?" I question.

16 gets closer to me, putting his hand up to cover his mouth so no one could read his lips, "We're different now, and they don't like it. Don't trust that Graves dude. He'll kill you like he killed 2."

7 lets out a frightened squeal.

He stinks. His breath is so vile I don't think he's brushed his teeth the entire time he's been here, and I try to back away, and as he continues to move forward, I back away. He reminds me of those meth-heads who do nothing but get high all day and don't care about the way they look or smell, and I wonder, was 16 always like this? Was he always this shifty-eyed, twitchy dirtbag? Or did the virus do this to him? Did he suffer from the permanent damage Holston spoke about days ago?

"So, what kind of experiments did they do on you?" I ask in a haughty tone.

His eyes widen with terror. "All kinds," he breathlessly whispers. "Mostly psychological, but sometimes, they did other stuff."

"And her? What kinds of experiments did they do to her?" I say pointing at 7.

"Bad kinds!" he whispers again, and suddenly 7 goes into hysterics. She screams and yells and thrashes her body on the concrete which draws the attention of the orderlies.

"Hey! Hey! What's going on over there?" one yells as they both rush over to us.

16 spasms more violently and quickly walks away, mumbling to himself again. One of the orderlies chases after him while the other one straddles 7's waist and holds her arms in place to calm her down. Her yells are the same ones I heard the last night, and by the scratches on her face, I deduce she's my amber-eyed nurse's assailant.

"Let that one be and help me over here!" the orderly directs the other.

"Do you want me to help?" I stammer, shaken by the sight of this convulsing girl.

He turns his head and snarls, "You stay the hell away from me! Stay the hell away from all of them! Get to that table over there or I'll have you in solitary!"

Solitary? Aren't I already in *solitary!?* His words sound so ridiculous, but it's what he's trained to say. It's what he was used to saying when he dealt with real people from the real world. He still hasn't properly adjusted to the nuances of this new world, and the backgrounds of the new people who now populate it. The altered ones.

I don't argue with him, and I find myself a spot at one of the tables.

Soon my escort is back putting handcuffs on me and dragging me back to the elevator. "I told you no talking!" he barks.

The elevator door opens with a ding. My escort is yelling at me the whole ride up, cursing me out, saying nasty things to me out of hatred and fear, but I'm not listening to him. The only thing I hear in my head is the ding of the elevator as he takes me back to my room.

"**T**ELL ME ABOUT THE INCIDENT IN THE atrium yesterday," Graves says as he opens a bottle of water and takes a gulp.

I don't want to tell him, because honestly, it's none of his business. What happened yesterday is between me and Holston, and after what 16 told me about Graves, my feelings of distrust have only been amplified. I knew from the get-go he carried some deep-seated animosity toward me. I knew from the start there was something "off" about him. And now, after 16 told me what Graves did, I need to watch my every word more closely than I have before. So, I don't answer him, and he continues to take big hulking draughts of his water.

"The nurses say you're barely eating," he says, changing the subject and as if on cue, my stomach rumbles loudly enough for him to hear. He raises an eyebrow like a black rainbow arching over one of his eyes. "My point in case," he remarks.

Still, I don't respond. Really, what does he expect me to say to all this?

"Dr. Holston says your vitals are holding strong," he continues, glancing at his clipboard, changing the subject for a third time. I want to comment on my temperature fluctuation and Dr. Holston's mild concern, but again, it's none of Graves's business. If he's looking at a paper of my vitals report, then it's probably in front of him, and if he's not mentioning it; well, then neither am I. I cross my arms over my chest because another rumble rises from my stomach, and I hope the extra padding will stifle it some.

Graves pauses and puts down his water on the end table next to his leather chair. He's frustrated with me. Again. But what else is new?

"Not talking to me today?" he says as he rubs the bridge of his nose, and he's so sarcastic, so condescending, I want to bite his fingers off so he can't satisfy his itch. I think about his thick fingers on his lunchbox hand. They're meaty. Lots of tissue there. Not so much on the tendons on the tops of the hands—they're mostly pink stringy meat like excess gristle on a steak, but palm-side is tender, especially at the fingertips, like popcorn chicken. Graves's fingers are so beefy they would probably prove to be more than a tasty late-night snack.

My stomach growls again. Loud. Ferocious.

My face gets hot. I'm mad at myself for having those thoughts because those days should be behind me. I'm even madder that my face got red because Graves must think I'm embarrassed from the noise my stomach made, and really, I'm not.

I'm not embarrassed. I'm not hungry.

Third time is supposed to be the charm, but when you don't succeed, try and try again, right? Graves flips the pages on his clipboard and says, "What happened when you told your mother you were going to get the car?"

Now he's talking my language. I'm not interested in talking to him about the Now. His whole purpose is to evaluate the Before, right? So, why is he insisting on making small talk with me? Sure, I'll talk about the Before if that's what he wants, and if that's what he thinks will get me to an acceptable re-Assimilated state to have me released, then I'll play his game. I decided the other night I was going to leave out the part of the story where I was seduced by Toby. That certainly is none of his business, and it really has no bearing on my evaluation either which way, right? Josh. Toby. The less Graves has to judge about my decision-making process or my morality, the less he has to pass judgment on me as a person. Lord knows he's certainly passing judgment on me as a zombie. And if he really did kill 2 like 16 said, well...

"She wasn't happy at all," I reply, not allowing anymore quiet time to brew between us.

"But..." he presses me.

"But she knew it was the only plan we had. She knew the protected time in our house was limited, borrowed actually, and she knew we needed to have some sort of communication with other people in order to survive this, so she ultimately   gave in   and let   me go."

"And where were you planning on going?" he asks.

It's such a stupid question because he knows damn well where I planned on going. Then I look over at his desk and notice something I hadn't before. There's a video camera perched on a mini tripod. Its red-light blinks, indicating a recording is in progress. It's watching me, watching my movements and my facial expressions, listening to my voice and how I respond to everything going on around me like a predator stalking its prey, sizing it up, lying in wait to make its final judgment of when to pounce. I'm being watched. Stalked. And Graves is hoping to be the one to chew me up and spit me out.

"Ed's Garage. The mechanic," I answer as I look dead into the camera, but there's an uncontrollable nervousness in my voice.

Graves realizes I've noticed it and glances over his shoulder. He smirks and lets out a slight huff of a laugh.

I hate him.

"And how far was this garage from your home?"

My face gets hot again, and I shift in my chair. I don't want to answer because now I *am* embarrassed.

He raises both eyebrows and nods his head slightly toward me, signaling me to answer. "You're on camera, kid!" his eyes say to me with urgency.

"About two miles," I say softly, almost incoherently.

Two miles. That was all it was. Two miles and I could have had the car. Two miles and we could have made a break for it. Two miles and we could have found shelter and safety and an explanation. *Two miles.*

I could only have been so lucky...

I put on my black, oversized hoodie, zippered it up and stuffed the flashlight in the front pocket. The metal of the handle made a clanging sound against the car keys that were already there.

Car keys, check. Flashlight, check.

Ed's Garage was two miles away, and if I walked at a brisk pace, I could probably make it there in a little under an hour. I certainly wasn't the athletic type but in this life-or-death situation, I was certain my natural instinct to survive would help guide me on my journey. It was night time. I'd eaten a bowl of dry cereal, a bag of Swedish Fish, a bag of mini-chocolate chip cookies, and I drank a full can of warm Pepsi. I told the girls I would need the energy, and the rush of the sugar and caffeine would help me stay focused. It was kind of a partial lie, though. See, we had been conserving food a little bit more the last week or so, and to be honest, I was starving. The three of them didn't protest my large meal.

My mother and Sydney cried. I'm not sure if Toby did, but I'm guessing no. She really didn't speak to me at all the entire day, and I could kinda figure out why. Toby went immediately upstairs to her watch point without saying goodbye.

Right before I was about to set foot outside, Sydney went into hysterics. She threw her body to the floor and clutched her arms tightly around my ankles so I couldn't move. My mother scolded her and yelled at her to stand up through her own agonizing tears. I bent down and rubbed the top of her head to calm her down. "It'll be fine," I coaxed, "I'll be okay." She stood up and ran sobbing into her room.

I had decided to leave out the front door. Even though we would have to move all the furniture barricading it, I figured it would draw less attention. Going out the back sliders and having to dance around the pool and the damaged screen would have slowed me down. If I went out the front, I could turn the corner quietly and quickly and evade being spotted by those infected things.

I breathed in and sighed out. My mom fastened the zipper more firmly at my neck and kissed me on the cheek. "I'm giving you three hours," she teased with a forced smile, "and then I'm coming after you!"

I gave her a hug. "No, you're not," I answered back. "It really is going to be okay. I've been watching them all day, and the ones who like to run don't seem to be around. They're less active during the night, too, so that'll work in my favor."

"Just be careful!" she insisted. "And don't be a cowboy or nothin'. If you don't have to fight, don't fight!"

I nodded my head swiftly, "Roger that, Captain!"

Mom rolled her eyes.

"Okay, stick to the plan," I reiterated. "Stay at the lookout points. Reinforce the door behind me just in case. Don't come after me! Understand?"

"10-4," Mom replied weakly and gave me another kiss on the cheek.

I rolled my eyes back at her which made her smile. "Wish me luck," I said with some hesitance. Inside I was freaking out. I'm not gonna lie, I was downright scared to death, but I was convinced it was the only way.

"I love you, Griffin," she cried.

"I love you too, Ma," I said and walked out the front door.

What happened next is still a blur because it happened so fast but in slow motion at the same time, if that makes any sense. I remember when I was twelve, my dad got rear ended by some drunk driver. I remember I was sitting in the front seat, looking at myself in the visor mirror, and I glanced at the traffic behind me when I saw this car careening toward us. I knew the light was red because my father had stopped, but this car, this crazy fast car wasn't stopping. He plowed right into us, sent us into a tailspin, and drove us right into a ditch. When I saw the car coming, I never said anything. I knew it was coming at us; I knew he wasn't stopping, but I was frozen solid. I didn't scream or warn my dad. It happened in slow-motion in my mind, but too fast for me to react.

When I stepped out into the cold December night air, there wasn't enough reaction time for me again, either. I slinked around the side of the house opposite from the street side so as to be covered in the foliage of the yard. The plan was to cut through the backyards until I got to the entrance of the development and hit the main road. I heard some moaning off in the distance and figured I was in the clear, for now at least.

I had anticipated the slow ones, the fast ones, the runners, the hunters, the kids, and the old people. I had been observing them since the day this all went down, so I thought I had my bases covered. Besides, I had seen so many horror movies in my day I knew one swift shot to the head would be enough to stop 'em.

What I hadn't anticipated was Sydney.

I had reached our back lanai and was making my way through the debris of a screen when suddenly the back sliding doors flew open, and Sydney came rushing out into the darkness hysterically crying.

"Get back here!" I heard my mother screaming, trying to whisper, but trying to assert the authority in her voice through her own hysterical tears.

"Griffin!" Sydney screamed as she ran toward me. "Don't go! Don't go!"

I was stunned. Frozen. No time to react. She raced up to me, jumped up and latched her arms and legs around my body. She wailed and practically strangled me. She held on so tight, I felt as if her body would have incorporated itself within mine.

"No, no, no, no, no," I frantically whispered in her ear as I tried to desperately pry her off me, but her cries were so loud, and her force was so strong all my attempts were futile.

Maybe my senses were always acute? Maybe my sense of awareness was always heightened because above all the commotion, above the blood chilling, high pitched bawls of my sister, and the grating yells of my mother, I heard them. I heard their moans.

"Syd, Syd, Syd!" I exclaimed. "Get back in the house! Now! Go!" But she wouldn't release me. I saw over Sydney's shoulder that my mother was standing at the back door, and Toby had joined her.

Toby. Stupid, selfish, Toby. She had a flashlight pointing right at us.

The moans got louder and closer, and then something in the sound of it all changed, transformed. I guess I hadn't noticed it before, but *they* were screaming. It was a high-pitched screech that sang an agonizing song of desperation. It was frenzied, like a rabid animal panting while suffering crippling pain throughout its entire body. The cacophony grew louder, and amidst the disjointed din of moans and howls and screeches, there was a real melody to it all that made me stop fidgeting with my sister and listen to their mournful opera.

Then in an instant, in a slow-motion-yet-too-fast-to-react-instant, the song of the infected filled my backyard, and they were upon us. Sydney was ripped from my arms with a strength and power so forceful and unhuman that it felt as if a mechanical crane had snatched her from my arms. She screamed as her body rose into the air; a flimsy ragdoll tossed against the purple clouds of the black sky. There were four of them there waiting for her.

She fell down onto the grass with a thud and a snap, and they lurched on top of her, their mouths ready to devour what little meat she had to offer. I didn't know if she had died from the impact of the fall or was knocked unconscious. Either way, there were no screams from Sydney, just the squishing and gurgling from those who ate her.

My mother was still at the door. She had crumbled into a ball on the concrete patio and screamed uncontrollably for Sydney. When the four wanderers were finished with my sister, they went after Mom, who in the mental state she was in, was easy prey.

I felt someone at my neck and a set of teeth clamped down on my shoulder. I jerked forward, not feeling any pain at first, but when I reached my hand up to where the bite was and pulled it back to see, my stomach turned with a nauseating sickness that almost made me puke. "Have you ever seen blood in the moonlight? It looks quite black," so said Hannibal Lecter somewhere, sometime long ago. But no. Not this. Not now. My blood was a deep cherry red against those purple clouds in the black night.

I tried to run back to the front of the house, but I couldn't move. The pain crept up on me. A hot, stinging, not-quite-burning sensation ran up my neck and down my arm. I stumbled forward. The one thought going through my mind was that I had to get to a mirror to evaluate how badly I was hurt. I glanced at my mother's lifeless body and watched as the infected feasted on her. Their voices continued to sing that haunting melody of sweet pain as they worked their teeth across her exposed bones. She no longer screamed, and I assumed she was dead.

In an instant every muscle in my body seized, like they were being clamped down in an oversized vice. My lungs and diaphragm contracted sharply in quick rhythmic spurts. I gasped, and as I tried to take in air, tried to breath in full satisfying breaths, the spasms in my chest only doled out more pain. I fell backwards, my head bounced off the crunchy grass in uncontrollable convulsions. I thought: *I'm going to die! This is what it's like to die!*

But I didn't die.

Pulsating waves shocked every nerve ending within me, and I jerked around violently. My head thrashed against the grass and the force of my head-snap filled my ears with a fuzzy sound that wasn't quite water-like and wasn't quite ringing-like, but somewhere in between. My breathing became quicker, more labored, and I could see my chest rising high with every breath I took. The gash on my shoulder felt as if it were on fire, and I could almost hear the poison in my blood being carried through my veins, pumped through my heart, and filtered out through the rest of my body, creating a fiery effect on every limb, in every orifice.

My stomach lurched upward right to the bottom of my esophagus, so I rolled onto my knees and buried my face in the grass. I gagged. The putrid smell of rusty metal was all around me. Vomit finally forced its way out of my stomach. My chest burned and heaved as everything I ate that day came hurling forth onto the ground. I thought again: *Now, I'm really dying! This is what death feels like!* But my lungs kept moving up and down and in and out and my heart kept beating its rabbit rhythm beats and my veins and arteries were still constricting and pumping my now infected blood, and nothing was shutting down like a dying body should. In fact, everything felt like it was speeding up. On overdrive. Acceleration. Slow-motion but not slow-motion. I couldn't catch my breath because my stomach was constricting, and I could taste the sweet Swedish Fish I had eaten about an hour earlier mixed with the acidic flavor of belly bile and I couldn't stop it from making its way out of my mouth. I puked again, and the convulsions stopped. I sat up on my butt.

Next, there was a wave of paralyzing heat that surged from behind my eyes. I closed them tight to make the feeling stop, but for some reason, it only increased the intensity. Like lightning flashed through every inch of my body. Blood and liquid seeped from my facial orifices—nose, mouth, ears, and eyes. I panicked and thought: *No, this is it! This is really it! I'm going to bleed out and die.* The heat sensation that started in my eyes slowly worked its way throughout the rest of my body, like a blanket being gently drawn to cover a sleeping baby. It was everywhere. It stung me. It burned me. I opened my eyes and there was a cloudy veil that encompassed the world. It was like looking through a piece of sheer white fabric. There was a slight distortion to the way things appeared. Like a foggy windshield, or a gray mist haze.

I breathed in again, hoping the burning blanket feeling would pass, hoping my heart would ease its pace. And it did. My body relaxed and my muscles eased up. The blood stopped pouring from my nose and mouth. I looked around with my new eyes and saw my sister and mother's dead bodies strewn across the backyard. Or should I say, body parts? I wanted to throw up again at the sight of it, at the smell of it. It made me ache with a gutted feeling in my stomach. It made me feel hollow, and empty, and...

...hungry.

I stood up and my first instinct was to run, and to chase, and to *hunt*, but I was well aware of my movements and did everything in my power to keep from losing control. *What did you do to me!?* I wanted to scream, but when I opened my mouth, a soft moan was released from my vocal chords. Knowing that strange and familiar sound, I quickly clamped my hand over my mouth to muffle it.

The growing hunger began to overtake me, consume me. It spread from the pit of my stomach to the back of my throat. It made my head hurt. I needed to eat, I needed to eat, I needed to...

I heard something fall inside the house, but it sounded like it was underwater. It was muffled, but I was drawn to it, nonetheless. My legs wanted to run, to charge, to race to the sound, and I had to struggle with the conscious decision to walk slowly. My mind fought against the instinct to take off at a sprint, like my mind and body were two separate entities functioning independently, and that fight was so difficult that my gait became short and shifty jerk-like movements. Something else fell inside the house, and I heard someone scream.

Toby.

I walked into the dark house, stepping over gloppy wet body parts, looking for Toby. I had to see her. Had to talk to her. Had to let her know Sydney and Mom were dead, and I was changed into one of them. Had to tell her to run away for help. Had to see her. Had to touch her. Had to smell her.

Had to eat her...

I tried to call her name, but my mouth could only produce that indescribable groan. I didn't want to scare her, frighten her away, perhaps into the arms of one of my new kinsmen, so I stumbled into the house, my nose in the air like a bloodhound searching for a lost kid or drugs at the airport. Immediately, I knew my senses were changed. *I was changed.* The sounds of the house that I had grown so accustomed to and loved so much were like booming echoes in a stone-walled cathedral. I heard every creak and shift of the house settling as though it was coming through over an amplified speaker. I could hear the last of the water trickling through the barren pipes in the floor. I could hear large palmetto bugs scurrying inside the walls scavenging for scraps of insulation. I could hear the muffled pants of Toby coming from the storage space underneath the steps. Sydney's favorite place. My rendezvous spot.

I ambled through the living room and into the guest room. Like I said, my mind and body were seemingly acting like two separate beings, and I struggled with control. I said to myself: *Don't run! Don't run!* But with every few steps, my legs would lurch out from beneath me, and I would do this weird hop-like movement. Control was so hard. It was like I had to learn all over again how to walk normally. If I really wanted to, I could have let the instinct overtake me and went screeching and running all over the place, but I really needed to find Toby, and I knew if I went charging toward her, it would scare her half to death, and of course, I didn't want that to happen.

It felt like it took forever to get to the guest room. She was still there, though. I could tell because her breathing got louder in my head and a sweet smell wafted in the air. It was like warm strawberry jam on roasted chicken;

the kind of chicken that's plump and oozes with juices when you dig your fork into it. I guessed the strawberry smell was a hint of my mother's perfume. Either way, I inhaled deeply. It was intoxicating and my stomach growled with such ferociousness I was sure the whole world heard it. Well, the world didn't hear my stomach roar, but it did hear Toby screaming as I tore the door to the crawl space off its hinges.

Shhhh! It's okay! I have to tell you what happened, my brain wanted to say to her, but I didn't even try because the only sounds I was capable of producing were ghoulish and terrifying. She stood there, tears of fear streaming down her face, hands tightly clamped over her mouth. Her eyes widened when she saw me. "Griffin!" she exclaimed. "Are you okay?"

I figured she didn't see what had happened to me. Poor, scared Toby must have run into the house before she could witness the massacre of Sydney and Mom and the transformation of Griffin. I stared at her with so many sentences swirling inside my mind. She reached out her arms and wrapped them around my neck. "Oh God, Griffin!" she sobbed into my unbitten shoulder. "They killed Sydney and Maggie! I thought they got you, too! I thought they were coming in here to get me!" and she leached on so tightly my opened shoulder oozed blood and pus onto her arm. She must have felt it too because she suddenly took a step back with a look of shock on her face. "Griffin!" she panted with fear. "You're hurt! Oh my God, you're bleeding everywhere!"

I'm fine, I'm fine. The pain's gone now, I wanted to reply. But the pain wasn't gone, in fact, it was getting worse.

"Let's get to the bathroom, c'mon!" she ordered as she pulled hard on my hand.

I didn't budge. I didn't move. I stayed stationery in one place, fighting against the inner instinct to run and chase and pounce.

She quickly let go of my hand and cocked her head to the side staring at me. "Griffin!" she sang. "C'mon. You're gonna bleed all over my rug!" and she let out a little nervous laugh.

You can't do this! You can't do this! I said to myself over and over again. But the heat was returning in my arms, radiating its way up into my shoulder and down to my fingertips. My heart quickened, and the smell of warm strawberry jam spread over juicy cooked chicken made the hollow feeling in my gut throb something awful.

I'm so hungry. I'm so hungry. I'm so hungry. I'm so...

My teeth flashed at her as I let out that high pitched screeching sound. She too let out a scream and fell backward into the door.

You can't do this! You can't do this! I thought as I descended upon her, absorbing her strawberry smell, teeth sinking into her juicy bicep chicken meat. I easily pinned her down with one hand, realizing my strength had almost doubled. I gnawed at her skin, the thick fleshy meat of her upper arm. The toughness of it took some time to get through, but once I did, once I had ripped it open, her blood exploded in my mouth like a warm coppery deluge. I lapped at the fluid, suckled the muscle underneath, and savagely scraped the meat between my teeth. Her flavor filled me, cooled the burning sensation to a comfortably warm tingle, and quelled the beast of hunger in my stomach.

Pain and fear were written all over her face, and I understood, too, because I didn't want to hurt her, didn't want to eat her. *Stop! Stop! Stop!* I yelled at myself, but it was no use, I had no control. The mind and body were acting independently, and my body needed satisfaction from this unholy meal.

Her eyes were distraught, wild with uncertainty in the face of her certain death. She was screaming something, but my head was too consumed with the blood swoon I couldn't truly make out the words. "No, please! Stop!" it sounded like, but I couldn't be sure.

She wiggled... *I don't want...* writhed under my massive weight... *to hurt you...* and yet paralyzed... *but I can't stop...* by the agony I inflicted on her. Like, she tried to break free from my grasp, but she didn't try hard enough. Maybe she had lost too much blood? Maybe she was really that weak of a girl? Maybe she wanted to die?

Die.

Then I thought about how I had changed, and I started to panic. I let out another one of those horrifying screeches that rang in my ears. It had happened so fast for me, and I knew if I let Toby sit there much longer, she would become infected from my bites, and this vicious movie-come-true-cycle would continue. I had to kill her. Had to make sure she wasn't going to come back. Make sure she wasn't going to become infected. See, in the movies, only the dead come back. This isn't the movies. Dead is dead. My heightened senses gave me that inside knowledge. That's why I didn't want to finish consuming Sydney's or my mother's corpse. They were dead meat. Dead flesh. I had no use for that. No desire or hunger for something that had expired and begun to rot.

Toby.

After last night, I kinda *knew* her. Knew her body. I knew her slender calves and her toned thighs. I hungrily looked her over, and inside I was shaking and trying so hard to hold back from my impulses. I wanted to kiss her right then and there, to say I was sorry because I knew I had no control. I wanted her to taste the hot-spring blood in my mouth and say to her, "See, you're so delicious," but I didn't have time to express my true feelings. Swiftly, I lifted up her shirt and touched the smooth outline of her stomach. Her muscles rippled beneath my fingers, and I spied a quick quiver of fat rise up gently underneath her belly button. I had my mark.

Without hesitation I dove in, tore through, saturated my face with her insides until I no longer heard her screams.

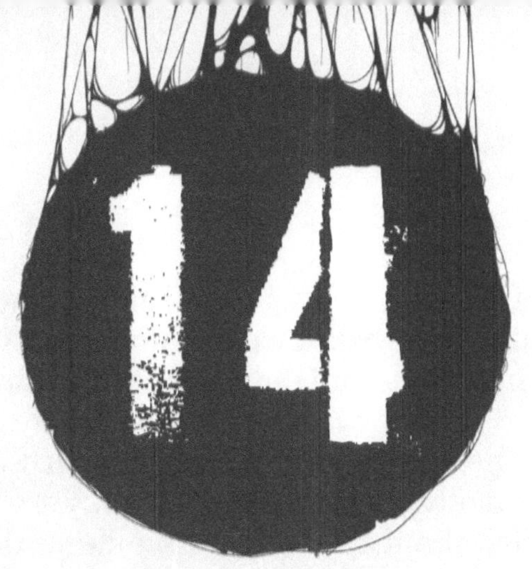

WHEN IT WAS OVER, I STOOD UP OVER Toby's mutilated body, sick to my stomach I could ever do something like that to another human being. Around her neck was a line of red bubbles, like liquid rubies, majestically adorning the outskirts of her collarbone. I soon realized they were imprints from my fingers from where I had viciously held her down. She looked stunning in death, even with her entrails strewn across the carpet, and I thought, *Look who bled all over the rug, for sure*! I wanted to throw up again but couldn't because there no longer was a sick feeling in my stomach, and since my mind and body were not in sync with each other, the biological aspect of my being was no longer hungry, no longer sick, no longer craving. My mind hurt, though. My brain hurt. Because feeling full-belly happiness, like after you've eaten the best gourmet meal ever, and then looking down upon the mangled body of your friend doesn't quite jive with one's soul. If I even still had a soul...

●

I didn't want to kill Toby. I really didn't. She was brash and uncouth and a wicked witch seductress with bleached blonde stringy hair, but I didn't want her to be dead—and certainly not by my own hands. I definitely didn't want to eat her the way I did. And yes, after it was said and done, I felt badly about it, felt sick to my stomach about it, felt guilty about it. I swore I wouldn't do that ever again. I swore I would learn how to control whatever it was that had taken over my body. I was better than all those other infected wanderers. I was more intelligent and superior and had stronger will power. I was determined to beat this sickness and to be right again.

I could have only been so lucky.

I examined Toby one last time to make sure she was really dead before I left the house.

She was dead. Really dead.

She wasn't going to convulse on the floor and open her eyes to greet a new and terrible hunger. That I was sure of.

Time must have passed quickly because by the time I actually left the house, it was daylight. I may have spent too much time practicing walking, but even so, my motions were awkward and jerky. Every step I took wanted to be a dart, a dash, but I kept saying to myself, "One foot forward, next foot follows."

The morning air felt tingly on my skin, and the gash on my shoulder where I had been bitten itched. I rubbed my chin to my shoulder because my hands refused to touch the opening. The dried crusted blood crumbled against my bottom lip. Everything was new and fresh from behind my new smoky glazed eyesight. And my hearing, even though the sounds came through like being underwater, was sharpened.

There were a few infected others on the street wandering aimlessly around without function or purpose. They left each other alone. Didn't interact with one another and didn't get in each other's way. I figured that was the way things were around here. I opened my mouth to get someone's attention. I wanted to say, "Hey, what's going on?" but when I did, the low toned moan was the only thing my vocal cords could produce. One woman stopped in her tracks and swiveled her head around to look at me. Mrs. Flynn. She was wearing a blood-splattered house dress, and her face was badly torn up. She stared at me with her cloudy eyes for a moment, then swiveled herself back around and continued to amble through the streets.

Loners. We're loners, I thought. *But we hunt together and eat together. Like wolves.*

Well, not me, that's for sure. I was determined to be different. I knew I needed help and the only place I could think to go for medical attention was the urgent care center up in town, but as the minutes passed by, I could feel my grip on my own consciousness beginning to fade away. I could feel my thought patterns getting jumbled, and before I knew it, I was running around the cul-de-sac like a crazed predator. When I realized what I was doing, I stopped myself and tried to straighten out my thoughts. *Walk,* I thought, *one foot in front of the other*, I thought, *get to urgent care,* I thought. It worked well for a little bit, and then, from out of nowhere, my stomach felt like it was heaved up into my throat and the hunger was making its way back.

No, no, no, I thought as I remembered Toby, *not again*! I didn't want to hurt anybody. I didn't want to kill anybody else, but I had that feeling when the hunger came on full force; I might not be able to control it. I might not have any other choice. I kept walking because that's what my body wanted to do, and I passed the community lake inside the entrance gates of our subdivision. There were some infected people who had fallen into the water and were flailing their arms around for help. Mindlessly, I walked toward them when some ospreys landed on their heads and started pecking away at the rotted flesh of their backs. And that's when I remembered that before I was changed I had watched birds cleaning out Ashlyn Marshall's open wounds and Mrs. Dunbar biting the head off a squirrel, and I got a brilliant idea! I wouldn't have to hurt another living human because I could eat animals! Squirrels, armadillos, lizards, whatever! It didn't matter! I was sure there were plenty of orphaned dogs and cats roaming about now their masters were dead or infected. Animals do anything and eat anything to survive. There would be plenty to go around! With my new sense of purpose and the growing hunger rising within my stomach, I gave up on my "walking lessons" and ran screeching through the streets, hoping to find something suitable to feast upon.

It wasn't long before I was able to pin down one of the neighborhood stray sewer-cats. He was fast, but my newly changed body was faster! I gripped the black fur of his neck, the part where the momma cat is supposed to drag them around by, and held him up high in the air, examining the scratches on his nose and his yellow eyes. He hissed at me, and I instinctively hissed back, surprising even myself that I had such a similar feral reaction. He hissed at me again when my stomach growled, but that time I could only answer him with a low groan. The hunger was coming on fast and furious, and that heat sensation starting to burn throughout my body like it had before. It was like a spark that turned into a flame that turned into a stovetop-fire that turned into a blazing inferno consuming acres and acres of forest woodland. Before the fire within me got out of control, I lifted the cat to the sky, and plunged his neck onto my mouth where I brutally tore open his throat hoping his warm blood would cool the proverbial flames and satisfy my hunger much like Toby's blood did. The cat's blood was warm and sticky and made my teeth click like I had drank liquid peanut butter. There was a foul aftertaste, too, a sour flavor like expired milk. I immediately dropped the cat to the ground and stomped on its face, ensuring it was dead and would stay dead. It was bad enough we had infected people populating the streets, we didn't need infected animals, too. Afterwards, I did feel a little better. The heat and hunger were suppressed minimally. Eureka! This was my answer! This would be the way. I had forgotten all about going to the urgent care center because now my mind was focused on the hunt.

And hunt I did. I went wild. Anything with four legs that was alive became my prey. It worked for a while. It eased my hunger pains temporarily, but I was constantly on the move—searching and hunting. Squirrels and ospreys and cats and lizards and hard-shelled armadillos and raccoons. I even tried crickets and wolf spiders, but soon found out insects and arachnids were useless to me. I extended my search beyond the boundaries of my community, ran out the front gates and onto the main drag in search of my next quick fix, because that's exactly what it was. No animal had given me the full-belly satisfaction like my first human kill, but it was enough to get me past the pain and burning sensations. It was enough to drive me to find another animal and start the cycle over again because I didn't want to hurt anybody else. I swore I wouldn't, and animals don't have feelings, they don't have souls, so it's okay to kill them, right?

This constant animal chase must have gone on for days, maybe weeks, I don't know. But I knew I was losing the battle because my grip on reality was not quite stable. It was all about food food food food. I had lost track of time. Time didn't exist. I was still on the main road when I thought I was on the trail of something big—a deer or a wild boar—because the smell I started to smell was glorious. The smell of the gods! It was fresh and pure and had the scent of a Fourth of July cookout where my dad would have hot dogs and burgers and fresh chicken flaming on the grill. Succulent chicken that had lightly roasted skin and that dripped its fatty juices when you stuck your fork into it. It was that smell! And it made my hunger scream up from my stomach and out of my mouth in a high-pitched wail. Then I saw them scamper from the ravine off the main road and race into the woods.

People.

Through my cloudy glaze eyes, they looked like swirls of chocolate and vanilla wrapping together in one of those Ice Cream Man double ice cream cones, but it was only the blondes and browns of their hair blowing furiously in the wind. And the hunger overtook me. Made me see red and black and gray, like I was completely detached from myself. A little voice cried on the inside to not pursue them, to not attack them, but the loudness of the hunger voice drowned that out and propelled me to stalk, to race, to hunt. I'm not sure what happened next, but I was soon upon the brown-haired boy, gnawing at the chicken meat of his tender calf.

●

"Alright! Alright!" Graves yells, interrupting me, yet again. He stands up and moves behind the desk to shut the video camera off. "I think I've had about enough of this for today!" He picks up the phone, presses a few buttons and barks, "Patient ready for pick up!" He slams the phone down, and I nearly jump from the boom.

"What? What's going on?" I stupidly ask.

"You're done. We're done today. You need to go back to your room," he says quickly, waving his arms back and forth in the air.

"I... I don't understand," I stammer because I truly don't.

He looks at me with narrowed eyes. Wild eyes. Eyes that are killing me at this very moment. I apparently struck a nerve. *So, Graves does have a breaking point...*

"Your little narrative is all fine and good," he exclaims, "but I'm having a hard time believing what's real and what's not."

What's there not to believe? Graves must be so married to the idea that we altered people were mindless, soulless, heartless zombies when we were infected, that he can't comprehend that maybe, just maybe, there was some inkling of sentience in us. That, or he wants to go home.

"I'm sorry," I mutter because I don't know what else to say, but he just shoots me another dagger laden look. 16's little singsong comes to my mind: *He'll kill you like he killed 2*. I'm confused now. Is Graves trying to help me avoid a life of imprisonment, or is he trying to send me to certain execution for my crimes? Are all of these taped sessions my sworn testimony to be used against me in a court of law, or are they really for observational and medical purposes? I realize I know nothing about this place or these people or their intentions, and I'm scared. Legitimately scared. There's only one way I can be sure if I can trust Graves or not...

When I was a kid, my mother used to tell me and Sydney about Santa Claus. I was about eight, and it was Sydney's first Christmas when I found out the truth, but my mother made me swear to protect that secret so Sydney could grow up with the same excitement as I did. I honored her promise, and Christmas was always a big event at our house. Sydney was about six when she figured it out. Damn kid was too smart for her own good, but my mother still insisted on us "believing." We spoke about Santa Claus like he was an actual entity, and my mother would even threaten us with "Santa's watching you!" when we would get out of line. To a teenager, it's kinda silly to keep up the charade when you know the truth, but there was something innocent and sweet about it. Something magical. Even though we knew the truth, we all *believed*, and there was something in that belief that was almost god-like. Mom once told me, "Never trust anyone who doesn't believe in Santa Claus," and at the time, it didn't make sense to me because I knew that Josh was Jewish and because of his religious beliefs, Santa was never a figure in his holiday lore. But Mom was such a free thinker and a free spirit, that in hindsight, she was using Santa Claus as a metaphor for something much larger and much grander than this concrete world we live in.

The guards and doctor come to get me. The guards grip their weapons a little tighter than normally, and the doctor holds a syringe, probably because of the urgency in Graves's voice when he made the call for them to come get me. I get up and walk to the door, but before I leave with them I turn my head around and ask Graves, "Do you believe in Santa Claus?"

He looks up from the papers at his desk and shakes his head. "What?" he exclaims with a harsh emphasis on the "w" sound of the word.

"Do you believe in Santa Claus?" I flatly repeat.

He glares at me hard. He must think I'm crazy. "Are you serious?" he says with a deep sigh. His shoulders collapse like he's completely given up for the day.

"Yes, I am," I respond.

He tries to run his fingers through his stiff black hair. "No, I don't. I don't know what you're getting at, and I don't know why you're asking, but the answer is no. I never in all my life have believed in the fairy tale that is Santa Claus."

"Why? Cause you're Jewish?" I had to confirm.

He looks at me with a pained expression of a wrinkled nose and squinted eyes. He stutters for a second and mutters, "I'm not Jewish! Get him out of here, he clearly needs some rest! And something to eat!" And he waves his hands in the air to shoo us out.

One of the guards pushes me forward and closes the door behind me, and I'm smiling now.

I have my answer.

And I'm still not hungry.

15

IGHTNING FILLS UP THE ROOM LIKE A strobe light in a cheap nightclub, and deep rolling thunder rattles the family pictures against the walls waking me from my drug-induced sleep. I can't tell which came first, the lightning or the thunder, but I don't think it matters much anyway because a storm is making its presence known regardless. Graves must have been very upset with me yesterday. When I got back to my dorm, the doctor stuck that stupid syringe in my arm and the only other thing I remember was being dragged to my bed. He's a powerful one, that Graves. When he speaks, people do exactly as he says, and I wonder how high up on the food chain he is? I already know where Holston stands. He's the mad scientist. The Dr. Frankenstein. They say he's my general practitioner, but he's more than that—he's the one who displays the least fear of me. No. That's wrong. Graves shows little if any fear, too. Maybe they're the most experienced with my kind?

My kind.

The Altered.

My new moniker gnaws at me constantly because I still haven't figured out what that means. Altered? The thirty of us. Or twenty-nine of us if I believe what 16 said about 2. But I'm not alone because there are others who have gone through something similar to me. Twenty-eight other people were bitten and infected and *changed*. Twenty-eight other people who did what they had to do to survive, and by survive I mean kill others. Twenty-eight other people who maybe infected twenty-eight other people (well, twenty-seven because I can't speak for the others, but I know I made damn sure not to pass on the infection to anyone else. Dead is dead). Twenty-eight other people inhaled that purple gas cloud and got paralyzed. Twenty-eight other people who got injected with an antidote in their faces. Twenty-eight other people were cured. Altered. Twenty-eight other people who are currently living in this Re-Assimilation Center trying to be rehabilitated. Reformed. Re-assimilated back into a society that probably fears them. Or hates them. Hates them just as much as Graves hates me.

"All patients be ready for pickup at 9 AM," a voice booms over a crackly loudspeaker.

I'm mildly curious at the change of routine. Usually, my day consists of a morning physical, breakfast (*but I'm not hungry*), shower, and meeting with Graves. I wonder why the change-up. Thunder rumbles loudly, and I'm guessing the sudden change in weather could be a contributing factor.

I'm picked up by my nurse with the amber eyes. *Madeline.* That's what her name tag says, and it's the first time I notice it. I wonder if she pronounces her name Mad-duh-lyn, or Mad-duh-line, or if she prefers Maddie, or Mads, or Madge, or Lyn, or Lynnie, or any one of those cutesy nicknames. She looks to me like she's a Mad-duh- line, so that's how I'll say it if I ever need to.

She smells like rain again, raindrops on roses. Wet and sweet. She doesn't speak to me as she leads me down the hall. I don't really want to talk either because I'm rather enjoying paying close attention to her smell and glancing at the way her white nurses' uniform skirt crinkles against her thigh as she walks, but my brain is working overtime, and I have this need to know what's going on.

When we reach the elevator, I break the uncomfortable silence and ask, "Where are we going?"

"The day room," she answers as she presses the button; her voice is soft and almost melodic.

"Why?"

"The rain," she replies as the door opens with that ding-sound. "Some of you were scheduled for rec-time outside, but because of the weather, he thought it would be best for you to go to the day room to do some activities." *Activities*. Like we're mental patients in an insane asylum or something.

I huff and shake my head as I enter, but it dawns on me I'll at least get a break from Graves.

She presses the number five, the doors close, and we descend. She's playing with her hands, cracking her fingers, and picking at her short finger nails, but she's definitely more relaxed. Not scared. I try to put her at ease a little more by making some small talk.

"Ya know, you're gonna have to come back and shave me again soon," I say as I touch the scruff on my cheek.

"No, I think you're okay for now," she says without looking at me.

"No!" I insist with a smile. I reach for her hand and pull it up to my face, forcing her to feel the thin layer of scratchy hair growing in. She jumps and instinctively pulls her hand away at first, but when our eyes meet and she sees I'm smiling, she eases up and goes with the motion of my hand guiding hers across my face and over the dome of my head.

"Whiskers on kittens," she says, and her smile grows so wide on her face that I notice a cut on her bottom lip opens up and a dark red bubble of blood blooms up like a succulent berry ripe on the vine. When she feels the small wound oozing, she quickly darts her tongue to stop the bleeding. My stomach growls uncontrollably, and I pray to God she thinks it's thunder coming from outside. A flash of fear streaking across her amber eyes tells me she knows it wasn't. I release her hand as the elevator door springs open. "This way," she directs as she hurriedly steps out into the brightly lit hallway. I follow her. I have nothing else to say as she leads me to the double doors and types in a four-digit code on the keypad. She has nothing else to say to me too, but as I enter the day room, she taps my shoulder, and I swivel my head to look at her. "I'll come with my kit when they bring you dinner, but you have to eat something first before I give you my beauty treatment." She smiles again. This time it's a controlled and contorted smile. She's probably trying to avoid another lip bleed.

"That would be great," I reply as she walks away, and the smell of wet roses follows her.

Madeline.

The day room is a cozy space with many couches and lounge chairs. There's a card table and a game table with boxes of checkers and dominos. There are handmade pictures taped to the wall like a child's artwork display. Everything is bright and friendly. Like, for mental patients at an insane asylum. There are other patients in the room as well. They don't stop to look at me; actually,

I don't think they realize the door even opened up, but Dr. Holston, who is standing at the front desk talking to a female doctor, notices I've entered the room. He quickly walks over to me, and I notice he has a limp. I never realized that before. I mean, he's a little overweight and has a fat man's wobble, but for the first time, I notice he has something wrong with him that's causing him to favor his right side a little too much. I guess this is really the first time I'm looking at him from a distance. Maybe that's why I didn't pick up on it before.

He slaps my back with a hearty *thud* that's right in time with a clap of thunder outside and gives me his usual awe-struck smile. "How are you feeling today?" he asks gaily. I say *gaily* because that's really the only word I can use to describe his tone. He's giddy. Jolly. Not Santa Claus jolly, but more like Richard Attenborough jolly in the beginning of *Jurassic Park*. Yeah, I know, I watch too many movies.

I nod my head. "I'm okay, I guess," I mumble.

"Good, good," he says in a rushed voice. "Feel free to walk around, play some games, read a book, relax. We're waiting on one more patient before I call in Dr. Graves for group."

A lump forms in my throat, and I swallow hard. Dr. Holston gives me two more quick pats on my shoulder and goes back to the front desk.

Group. As in: group session. As in: group therapy. As in: insane asylum observation. All kinds of doorbells and sleigh bells are ding ding dinging in my head, and I suddenly don't like the way this feels.

After a few minutes, the door flies open and in struts Graves dressed in a black button-down shirt and black suit pants. Again, no tie, but he's much more formal than he was yesterday. There are rain spots on his shoulders, and I guess he must have just gotten here. Following behind him are three nurses escorting 7. Her hair falls onto her face in thick dreadlock-like chunks and she's wearing an oversized t-shirt. When the nurses sit her down in one of the lounge chairs, 16 races across from the other side of the room and sits down in the chair next to her. I hadn't even noticed he was here. He grabs her hand and starts petting her like a kitten. She pulls her legs to her chest and rests her chin on the tops of her knees. Her face is even more badly scratched up than the other day, and that insane smile she had on her face is completely gone. She looks sad. And tired.

"Thank you, ladies," Graves says with a condescending tone and the nurses leave. "Dr. O'Hare," he calls across the room, "we're ready now."

Dr. O'Hare is the woman Holston was speaking to before. She comes over with a video camera and sets it up on a tripod. Graves arranges the lounge chairs into a circle and O'Hare rounds up all the patients. Group is in session.

Geometrically, it's impossible for there to be a "head" of a circle, but somehow, Graves manages to pull it off. O'Hare is next to him on his right side. Then, there's 16 and 7, a middle-aged man who Graves introduces as 10, a teenage girl identified as 15, a young Hispanic man who is 20, and me, 24, at the left hand of Graves.

I could only be so lucky.

"Okay, everyone," O'Hare begins with her deep southern drawl, "I'm Dr. Wendy O'Hare, and we're here today to talk about some of the things that happened to you. We know y'all have had your time with Dr. Graves here, but this is one of the first times we're getting y'all together to share with each other. We think this is good for the healing process and getting y'all on the right road to recovery." It's so painfully obvious she's trying so hard to mask her accent. Maybe she thinks it sounds unprofessional? Who knows? I personally find her covering of it to be irritating. Why can't people be who they are? My mother was a New Yorker through and through, and she never found the need to change her speech pattern. She didn't care that her consonants blended together or that she often dropped the syllables at the ends of her words: "How are ya doin'?" or "Get outta hea!" or the stereotypical "Fuhgettaboutit!"

O'Hare smiles. Her teeth illuminate, they're so white. And against her red lipstick it makes them look freakishly like white Chicklets. My mother would call that shade of red "hooker-red" whenever we watched a movie or saw celebrities on TV. O'Hare is just as fake as Graves; the only difference between them is she's actually scared.

Everyone kind of shuffles in their seats. I don't think 16 is paying too much attention. His sole focus seems to be on 7, who is totally gone. Out of it. I see it in her eyes. There's a glare, a glaze, like she's completely detached, completely removed. I doubt she has any idea about what's going on.

"That's right," Graves adds, his deep voice eerily echoing in time with another blast of thunder. 16 twitches. 15 lets out a small squeal. 7 stares with her vacant lot eyes.

"So, would anyone like to open up and talk about how they're feeling?" O'Hare asks as she narrows her eyes and pouts out her lower lip. No one says a word. "Ya, know," she continues when she sees she's not getting anywhere with us, "y'all are in the same boat. It's good to share your experiences with people who have gone through similar situations. Look around," and she waves her hand in a semi-circle in the center of us, "y'all are from different walks of life. Different ages, different races. But you've all had the same thing happen to you. Y'all had the same horrible, debilitating infec-shun. Wouldn't it be nice to go through this ordeal with people who can truly understand you?"

I swear, if there were crickets in the room, you'd be able to hear them right about now. The only audible sound is the rain pounding ferociously against the building and the occasional crash of thunder. This is seriously laughable. She has absolutely no clue what we went through. When no one gives any indication they're going to play into her psycho-analyzing babble share session, she gets flustered and uncomfortable. She eagerly looks to Graves for help, and when he notices she's floundering and begging him with her eyes, he licks his lips and sits himself straight up in his chair.

"Okay, let's start at the beginning?" he asks the group. "How did you become infected?"

The group stays quiet for a moment, but the question is completely innocuous that the hesitation to share sort of eases up. Graves is good.

"I got attacked at the mall," 15 speaks in a low voice as she tugs at her hair. "I was skipping school. No one knew I was there. They came at me…"

"My wife," 20 says interrupting 15. "I thought I had her chained up real good in the garage, but she got out and bit me before I killed her."

"My office was attacked," 10 says. "They came charging up the stairs, and I got swept along in the throng."

Graves turns his head and glares at me, waiting for my response.

"I was trying to get help for my mother and sister and was attacked in my backyard," I say, altering the truth.

Graves shakes his head at me in disgust. O'Hare puts her hand out and touches 16's knee. "What about you? How did you get the infec-shun, dear?"

He shudders at her touch, I guess 'cause his trance of 7 has been broken. "Me?" he answers in his shifty shaky voice, his head jerking side to side like someone with Tourette's. "Uh... yeah ... I... uh... my dog! Damn little fella! Bit me right here, right in the ass!" and he stands up and slaps his backside with a strong whack that even makes a zombified 7 shake.

We Altered let out a collective giggle at 16's maniacal display, but are silenced when Graves's commanding voice yells out, "Alright! Alright! That's enough!"

He balls one hand into a fist, and it's like a control switch violently shifting into the off position. I look around the circle at the others and can see they are a little fearful of Graves. I'll admit it, I am a little, too. I mean, the man is very large in the muscular sense, and he has a very domineering presence for sure. He can do real damage to someone. I wonder if the others heard of the *Tale of 2*? Probably.

Graves glances quickly at me, and I see that grin of his. That sneaky snakey grin that says he's up to no good or delighting in someone else's misery. That fake phony grin that makes the hairs on my arms stand at attention. "Tell me, does anyone remember what it was like *being* infected?" and his voice sounds so syrupy sweet that I want to vomit into his lap.

Here we go, I think, and I look over at 16 whose eyes are bug-wide, and his head is shaking slightly back and forth so that I can't tell if he's spasm-ing out or if he's trying to get a message to me. Everyone is quiet again until I call out an emphatic "yes!" 16's head slumps forward and everyone else's eyes are plastered on me. O'Hare feverishly writes something in her notepad. Graves turns to my direction and cocks his eyebrow.

"Oh, really?" he questions smoothly.

"Yeah," I answer with a hint of defiance, "I remember not wanting to do the things I did."

"Oh," he blurts out with a sharp head nod, "is that a fact?"

My blood boils. My face gets hotter and hotter. I know he's antagonizing me, and like a dummy, I'm falling right into his trap, his sneaky snakey snake pit. 15's mouth opens in disbelief. 20 looks directly at the floor. 10 drums his fingers against his leg pretending not to hear.

"Yes," I answer with such certainty that there's no backing down now, even if I tried.

"So," he continues as his voice rises.

O'Hare crosses and re-crosses her legs nervously. "You're going to go on record, in front of everyone here, on tape, that you're the only one who had remorse, who was aware, who felt guilt?" Graves goads.

"I never said I was the only..."

"But you must be!" he interrupts.

"No, I said ..."

"Patient 24, I have had others before and after you in my care. I think you're being a little bit holier-than-thou when you claim to have been the only sentient *zombie* on the planet!" and he spits the word zombie out like it left a foul taste in his mouth.

"You're putting words in my mouth!" I shoot back, and from the corner of my eye, I see 16 tighten his grip on 7's hand.

"Well, let's see!" he booms. "Let's see what everyone else here sees!" and he stands up from his chair lurking in the group circle like a demonic statue dressed in black. This is the first time I've ever seen Graves so animated, so angry, so upset. *He'll kill you like he killed 2* plays over and over in my mind, and as I look around at the faces of the other Altered, I can almost hear it playing in their heads too.

Graves saunters over to 20 and points his meaty finger into his chest. "Do you remember what it was like?" he demands. "Do you remember *feeling*?"

"Of course he does!" I want to scream, but don't. 20 looks to his side and over at me. He closes his eyes and shakes his head "no."

"No. He doesn't. Do you see, Patient 24? He doesn't!" Graves barks.

He moves over to 10 and does the same thing. 10 responds in the same exact way. Frightened, intimidated, bullied.

7 cries. Her muffled sobs pour out from behind her bent legs. 16 rubs her back, trying to calm her down.

"Warren, I think that's enough," O'Hare says, but her voice is so low, and Graves is so fired up, I don't think he hears her.

Graves goes to 15, the young teenage girl with dark hair and blue eyes. She's trying so hard to hold back tears. Her face is all twisted and struggling, but she's losing the fight, and Graves knows it. He gets down, nose to nose with her and through gritted teeth says, "Do you remember? Did you *feel?* Did you hurt? Did you ache?"

Her eyes open up like a faucet and her breathing becomes a dog-like pant. "N... n... no," she stammers, and he backs away and slithers over to 7.

"Leave her alone!" 16 shouts, but Graves ignores him and knocks her legs off the side of the chair.

"You! You hear me in there? Have you ever heard me in there?" he yells at her as she rocks wildly back and forth.

16 stands up to confront Graves, but all Graves has to do is *look* at him, and immediately, 16 is back in the chair. O'Hare gets on a walkie-talkie that's attached to her belt and radios for help. She stands up and puts her hand on Graves's shoulder, and he looks back at her, not through her, and eyeballs me. Nurses rush in and swoop up 7. She thrashes and flails about. Her oversized t-shirt brushes up against her stomach, and I notice the outline of a pot-belly, a pooch that's too pronounced to be over-weight, but they whisk her away before I can get a better look.

16 is on his feet and following them. "Where are you taking her? Where are you taking her?" he screams desperately. "Where are you taking her? Where are you taking her?"

15 sobs in her hands. 10 and 20 get up and quietly move to the game table, and I can't understand why they didn't tell him the truth. I can't understand why he doesn't believe me. Why he doesn't want to believe me.

Graves and I lock eyes for what seems like an eternity, and the storm outside continues to rage.

Soon Madeline is behind me telling me to come with her back to my dorm.

W E MUST REALLY BE ON GRAVES'S NAUGHTY List because I haven't had a session in what seems like forever. A few days have passed, and I've been pretty much confined to my room. Dr. Holston has seemed to have abandoned me as well. The doctor who's been coming to give me my morning physicals is Dr. Eisenberg. I don't like him at all. He barely looks at me and doesn't respond well to my jokes. Well, let's be honest; I'm not really a funny-by-nature guy, not like Josh was, anyhow, so I guess I can understand why he doesn't laugh when I try to be. Funny, that is. He certainly didn't laugh when he poked me with a needle to draw some blood, and I hissed at him. That seems to happen less frequently, but sometimes I can't control it. When it happened with Eisenberg, though, I kinda knew it was going to come on, and I had that feeling that I probably could have controlled it if I really wanted to. But I gave into it and even embellished a little. Like, I consciously curled my upper lip a little too dramatically and bared my teeth. I really can be so dumb sometimes because after I did that, and after he recoiled for a second, he took the needle and jabbed it so deep into the crook of my arm that I literally let out a yelp. Like a dog. Like an animal. And I know he kinda liked it because that's how he sees me. As an animal. I guess if they all look at me as an animal, it can reconcile their animosity toward me. I probably would do the same thing, unfortunately.

Anyway, my vitals are still the same, and I don't think the doctors are concerned about me relapsing or anything, but they are insisting on running some kinds of tests. I don't really know what for, but for the last two days, they've taken my blood. A lot of it, actually. And my temperature hasn't been stable at all, either, like I can't naturally keep it in check. It'll get really low one hour, and then shoot up real high the next. I don't feel sick and can't tell when it happens, but they say they're keeping an eye on it. Oh, and my weight seems to be a thing with them, too. I told Eisenberg I'm seriously not hungry, but he wasn't hearing it. He threatened me with IVs and forced supplements. Whatever.

All I've been doing these last few days is sitting. It's truly been uneventful. I don't even have the desire to turn on the TV. I tried to read some of *Catch-22* but had a bad flashback of my AP English class and decided to put it down. I couldn't get passed the title: *Catch-22*. I felt like I was in my own little Catch-22. Changed, but not dead. Cured, but not normal. I seriously don't know whether I'm coming or going. I'm a medical miracle and public enemy number one at the very same time. Like God and the Devil rolled into one person! Alright, alright, that might be taking it a little too far. I should know better than that. I get carried away in my own thoughts sometimes. I really should know better because right now, it really feels like *both* of those guys have forsaken me.

Yeah, so I'm constantly looking at those scary pictures on my walls. I want to take them down and hide their happy eyes. How could they be so perky and fun-loving when the world around them is in shambles. Guess they didn't get the memo, eh? Guess they're locked forever in those poses, in that one last happy moment of their lives. Guess their eyes will never see body-littered streets and infected people with half torn off faces racing toward them screeching in agony.

That screech! That high-pitched screech that came so easily out of my mouth! When I attacked someone, when I mutilated them, ripped out their tongues, ripped their limbs from their sockets, I always tried to hold back and to say I was sorry, but all that would come out was the screech. The wail. The deafening high-pitched tones of guilt and sorrow. Among their cries of "No, please! Stop!" I shrieked above their words: *I'm sorry. I'm sorry. I'm sorry. I'm sorry*...But as those days and weeks passed on for me, I knew I was losing myself. I was losing myself to the infection, to the hunger. As people became scarcer and I actually found myself having to hunt to pacify the torment of the *need,* it got easier, and I somehow began to justify it to myself: Survival. Survival. Survival. But that screech was always a constant, regardless of what it was saying. The screech and the moans and the wails and the groans. If I close my eyes right now and sway my head back and forth, I can almost hear the mournful symphony echoing in my mind, the melodic sounds bouncing off the walls of my room, the opera pulsating throughout the halls of this Re-Assimilation Center.

I bend my limbs, rock my body gently back and forth, nod my head in time to the ominous music. The familiarity of it is haunting and beautiful, and for a brief second I'm at peace with myself and with the world. The music washes over me, lifts me up, carries me away. I'm lost in the song, lost in my movements, and an instinct within me wants to howl in harmony with the song that I hear in my head.

Only, I realize, it's not in my head.

I stop and break out of my trance. And it comes to me, so loud and clear. Reverberating its chilling din throughout the confines of the rooms.

The song.

They're singing. All of them. Some are offering up deep howls and moans, while others are interspersing the melody with the high-pitched shrieks. We're scattered throughout the hospital, but my fine-tuned hearing, my heightened senses are picking up even the gentlest of lulls and groans. I smile as the disharmony of the ballad rises, and it fills me with such a twisted sense of pride that I want to burst! I want to lift my voice for all to hear! I want to howl and snarl and sing of my journey, of my discontent, of my brethren! We are The Altered, a mighty breed who will not be ignored! And as I open my mouth to join the chorus, I hear doors slamming open, one by one. Agonizing screams, one by one. Thrashing sounds and pulling sounds and fighting sounds, and then one by one, the voices fall out of the chorus, ending the ominous canticle and starting the barrage of frightened screams.

My door flies open, and I jerk my head to see who has arrived. It's Holston with syringe in hand. The screams fade out a bit when the door shuts behind him.

He looks at me with a glint of hesitation, and there's real fear in the way he sidesteps into the room.

"You okay?" he asks me gently.

"Fine, why?" I sarcastically say above the background noise of chaos.

Holston puts a hand on his hip and sighs. I give him a small smile.

"What's going on out there?" I ask.

He sighs again. Double sigh. He's super-stressed. "I'm not really sure what happened, but we're getting it under control. Nothing to be too alarmed about."

"I'm not," I reply flatly.

He stares at me again and then puts the syringe down on the desk. I guess he must know that I'm somewhat in my right mind and doesn't see me as a threat, but then again, I don't think Holston ever sees me as a threat. He approaches me and takes out his small examination flashlight from his white coat pocket.

"Eat today?" he says as he flashes the light in my eyes.

"A little," I answer. "Nibbled on some of the vegetables and apples."

"Hmmm," he groans with displeasure, "Dr. Eisenberg says you lost a few pounds," and he furrows his gray bushy eyebrows.

I shrug my shoulders. "I don't know what to say. I'm not hungry."

"And then there's this matter of your temperature," he says as if he didn't hear my last statement, "but I have a feeling it's connected to your eating. Get your eating in check and maybe everything else will follow. Your body needs the proper nutrients, and you're more than capable of holding down a full-blown mean at this point."

He puts the stethoscope buds in his ears and lifts my shirt a bit to gain access to the skin of my chest. "See this," he says as he rubs the cold metal disc over my jutting ribs, "I don't want to feel this when I do a chest check!"

I breathe in so he can listen to my lungs. *Listen, and get out, Doc!* "Why did Dr. Eisenberg take so much blood?" I ask nonchalantly.

"Procedure," he replies. "It's standard. They're isolating components in your blood to determine certain factors."

I'm Altered, I think. *More human than human.*

"It's not simple," he continues as if he's read my thoughts. "There are a lot of factors in play here. We're dealing with, first and foremost, the virus, then the effects of the paralytic agent that was introduced into your body, then the antidote. Getting you back in shape is quite a complex undertaking," and he lets out a small chuckle.

"When will I be meeting with Graves again?" I ask.

Holston takes the stethoscope off his ears and tilts my head to one side to get a look into my ear canal. "Soon," he answers. "Dr. Graves had an on-site call he had to attend to, but he'll be back soon."

"Another Re-Assimilation Center?" I probe.

"Hmmm," he mumbles, "something like that, you can say."

"He hates me," I declare matter-of-factly.

"Now what on earth would ever make you say a thing like that?" he says tilting my head the other way.

"I don't know; it's a feeling I have."

"You have a lot of those, don't you?" he sings with a grin.

I can't help but grin back at him. It's oddly infectious and welcoming and warm. He kinda makes me feel comfortable and safe, like I can talk to him. Before I know it, I start babbling, "It's like, the other day, during group session, I felt like he was directing everything at me. Like, to prove me wrong or something. Like he was trying to make me look and feel like an idiot!"

Holston grabs my chin and jerks my head to face his. He runs his thumb over the small bump of scar tissue under my right eye. "This hurt?" he asks, and I shake my head "no". And when I think he's not going to respond to or acknowledge what I've said, he blurts out, "Your new perception of the world is distorting your capacity to reason. You're going to have to train yourself to not be so sensitive. I will admit Dr. Graves's behavior the other day was a little out of line, but you have to understand something. Dr. Graves has been through a lot. We've all been through a lot. And all of this, all of these treatments and therapies and interactions, are new for *all* of us." There's that mad scientist smile on his face again. "Listen, tomorrow we're going to allow you to congregate together again. Depending on the weather, it'll be either in the day room or outside. I've realized you all need more time together, to get to know each other and create bonds. Dr. Graves won't be around, so you won't have to feel uncomfortable. I know, I know, he can be a little intimidating, but you won't have to worry about that. All good now!" he says as he claps his hand. "The nurse will be by to pick you up in the morning, and please, do eat something!"

Holston leaves and locks the door behind him, as usual, and I think: *While the cat's away, The Altered will play.*

The next day, I get dressed and ready and Madeline, my sweet, sweet Madeline, comes to take me to the day room. The thunder and lightning last night told me we wouldn't be able to go outside and play. God forbid we turned into sugar or something. Anyway, I walk into the room and there are some new faces. Not all of us, but a bunch. Enough. The only ones I recognize are 16 and 15. The rest are new to me.

I try not to make eye contact, but 16 spots me immediately and comes walking all shifty-like over to me. At first I pretend I don't notice, so I make my way over to one of the couches and sit down. He sits on a love-seat across from me and stares me down. Through the strands of greasy hairs in his face, his eyes bug out of his head. I look up at him, knowing he wants my attention. He leans forward. "You hear all that last night?" he says in his nervous jumpy voice.

"Yeah," I answer, and the second he opens his mouth, I hear that stock sound byte 'cuckoo, cuckoo' in my head.

"Kinda weird, right?" he says as his eyebrows rise up on each syllable.

"I guess so," I say as I shrug my shoulders.

"7's not here. Don't ya think that's weird, too?"

"Uh, not really," I say, but the last word is almost in the form of a question.

"It is weird, dude!" he exclaims as he slaps the top of his knees, "It's weird because they took her away last night!"

16 is weird. He talks about weird things. Makes weird comments. Smells. Has dirty disgusting hair and bad breath. He reminds me of a meth addict who is constantly scratching himself in hopes of tapping into the next high. He's shifty and ferret-like, and I can't be sure anything he says is true, but right now, he's piqued my interest. "What do you mean, they took her away?" I press.

His breathing gets a little frantic. His breaths come in and out of his nose in short, quick pants. "They did stuff to her!" he says wild eyed.

I crinkle my nose, puzzled.

"Ya know," he whispers, "stuff!" and he motions his hand in a half-bubble over his stomach.

"C'mon!" I reply in disbelief. "How do you know?" "Because, I know. My room was next to hers. I could hear through the walls. Everything sounded so... so... *loud!*" he answers as he cups his hands over his ears as if to block out some imaginary sound.

So, I guess I'm not the only one with enhanced senses?

16 takes his hand and runs it through his greasy hair frantically a few times. He mumbles something I can't make out at first, but then I soon realize, he's counting. Counting the times he ran his hand through his hair. He stops at five, blinks his eyes unnaturally a few times, and then shifts his body forward in his chair as if to get closer to me.

"So, 7 got out?" I ask.

"That's what they want you to believe. But they took her away. Man, there ain't no getting out of here. We have to keep our mouths shut tight, shut tight, shut tight, and tell them what they want to hear or nothing at all."

His words stab me. "What do you mean, we're not getting out of here?"

"Dude, I'm telling ya, man. The first ones who came here, man, 1, 2, 3, 4, they were damaged goods. Bad news. The first batch of serum they got messed them up big time. They relapsed; I think. They got rid of them. Graves killed 2. The others, they got rid of." He nervously darts his head around to make sure no one is watching or listening to us. I do the same, looking over my shoulder and scanning the room behind me. "The serum got straightened out by the time they got to 8."

"What about 5, 6, and 7?" I ask in a low tone, taking 16's cue.

"Still in the working phase. So, they ran experiments on them. 7 was the last of the experiments," and he creepily widens his eyes and makes the bubble motion over his stomach again. "They didn't get it right until 8."

"How the hell do you know all this?" I ask in awe, although, really, I think most of this is crazy BS.

"I *listen!*" he says emphasizing the word and closing his eyes.

He creeps me out. Like, he reminds me of the stoners at school. The kids with the long hair who hung out in the pizzeria parking lot across the street and smoked pot all day and listened to Led Zeppelin or The Doors thinking they were some breed of nu-hippies.

"Did your dog really bite you?" I ask.

16 starts to laugh his snort-filled laughter. "Hee hee," he laughs, and it actually sounds like the way he says it. "Yeah, my dog bit me, but that's not how I got infected!" and he snorts some more. I soon realize 16 is only going to tell you what 16 wants you to know, and any other questions or solicited information will leave you nowhere. He's played this game far too long, but I have to try. He knows something about Graves. Something I need to know as well, and I have no other choice but to come out and ask him. I don't know when I'll get another chance.

"Graves," I start. "What did Graves do?"

16's snorting halts abruptly as if I quickly turned off a switch. There's a loud hitching noise in his throat as he catches his breath from his laughing fit.

"To 2," I say firmly. "What did Graves do to 2?"

He twirls his head around again looking from side to side and leans forward a little more. "Ya see, man," he says, "2 was damaged. Bad news. Didn't talk, didn't eat, nothing. 1, 2, 3, 4. All the same. Well, Graves, ya see, he talked something awful to 2. Said stuff to him. Put thoughts in his head. Made him think. Made him dream. And those thoughts got inside 2 real deep, like burrowed their way into his brain, man. And that was all she wrote. 2 went and killed himself. Took his shaving kit, sliced his whole face up, bled out and died."

I gasp out loud. I hope I didn't, but I know I did. I can't believe him. Maybe he got a bad batch of serum, and maybe everything that comes out of 16's mouth is utter nonsense. Insinuating Graves talked a man into his own death, insinuating the first few Altered relapsed, insinuating 7 was tested on and was pregnant as a result, insinuating his zombie dog bit him and infected him. He spasms a few times, and I realize I seriously need to get away from this lunatic.

"Listen, man," I say, trying to speak to him on his level, "I gotta go take a leak. I'll catch ya later. Sorry to hear about your friend and all," and I stand up. He runs his hand through his hair and mumbles his numbers again. I listen and realize they're not in order from 1-5, or 1-10, or 1-20. He says a bizarre series that has no rhyme or reason. He's so far gone. Trapped in this fantasy world/real world, and I get scared because I don't want to end up like that. Before I get behind him and try to look for the bathroom, I stop to see if he's completely out of it or if there is still some semblance of humanity left in him.

"Dude," I say. "Do you believe in Santa Claus?"

16 turns his head around to look at me. His greasy bangs are stuck together forming jail cell bars over his eyes, but I can see them. His gray eyes lighten with joy and wonder and a smile creeps up on his dirty face.

"Shit," he answers without hesitation, "I was a frickin' *zombie*! How could I *not* believe in the big SC?"

17

GRAVES IS FORMAL AGAIN TODAY: WHITE button-down shirt, dark gray slacks, gray and pink striped tie. His jet-black hair must have extra gel in it because every time he cocks his head to one side to pop his neck bones, the hair doesn't move an inch. His shoes are super shiny, too. They must be new. *He* looks new, refreshed. His bronzed skin is taut against his face, and he seems to be glowing with either happiness or an injection of Botox. Maybe both, I can't be too sure. Even his fingernails look shiny. Manicured hands with a layer of clear nail polish coating the surface. We guys at school would certainly call Graves "metro", as in metro sexual. As in a dude who spends way too much time on his appearance in order to pick up hot chics. He does seem to spend way too much time on the little details. Hell, even the cufflinks on his tailored shirt are bright and shiny, like they've been carefully polished! I guess in Graves's line of work, you can be called away on a job and still have time to pretty yourself up.

He smiles as he presses the record button on his tape machine-thingie. No video today. And just when I think I should maybe change my outlook on Graves, I see that snakey smirk that's hidden underneath his chiseled chin, and I get a feeling in the pit of my stomach that looks truly are deceiving.

I surmise he's going to mention the group session from the other day for sure, but he doesn't. He kicks back in his chair and flips the pages of his clipboard. "Dr. Eisenberg has written some unsettling things here in your file," he comments without looking up at me.

I'm taken aback. "Really?" I respond. "Nobody shares much of anything with me, so I wouldn't really know."

He bites his tongue. His jaw muscles flex against his tight skinned face. He wants to smack the sarcasm right out of my mouth, but he sits tight and breathes in deeply. I don't know why I push his buttons that way, especially when I know what he's capable of doing. Sometimes I can't help myself. Actually, it was either make a smart-ass remark or hiss at him. I didn't think he would have appreciated the hiss.

"He says they're thinking about putting you on IV treatments," he continues.

"Yeah, they actually did tell me that much," I answer.

He continues to ignore me, "Issues with your temperature, and your blood work..." his voice trails, and I stop my silly sarcastic remarks and perk up.

"What about my blood work?" I ask with curiosity. I place my hands on the arms of my leather chair and kind of prop myself up in the seat, as if I were going to leap out at any moment. I'm suddenly afraid my blood test results indicate something bad.

The smirk slithers around his nose into a full-blown Cheshire cat smile. He has perfect teeth that glow an unnatural white like those of Dr. O'Hare's. The smile tells me he's not going to answer the question, at least not the way I want it to be answered, and my heart sinks down into my stomach as my body collapses back down into the chair. He knows I know, and it somehow fuels his vendetta thing he has against me.

"Oh, I really can't discuss that with you," he almost sings in a biting voice. "Just some *abnormalities* in your blood, but you need to talk that over with your GP," and he juts out his lower lip in the most condescending way it makes me want to jump over the coffee table between us and bite it off, but instead I roll my eyes and keep reminding myself I have to be on my best behavior. I have to play it cool like 16 does. I have to only answer his questions, and not incriminate myself any further than I already have. But he said *abnormalities*, and I'm worrying maybe I'm going to relapse. Maybe I'm going to become re-infected and not re-assimilated?

"You started attacking people," he declares as he flips through some more pages. "The last you said you were living off animals and had finally elevated to humans, is that right?"

He makes it sound so matter of fact. He makes it sound so dirty and animalistic. But I guess he's calling a spade a spade. "Yes, that's right," I answer with no emotion because really, I don't have much emotion in me right now.

"You had abandoned the idea of getting to the medical center," he restates keeping his focus on the pages of his clipboard.

I nod. "I had forgotten about it."

"So, what did you remember?" he asks, and I suspect he's goading me into something bigger. This time he looks up at me, curious to see how I'm going to react.

I hold tight to the arms of the chair, gripping the leather for dear life. 16 said to play the game, tell him what he wants to hear. And right now, it would be so easy for me to shrug my shoulders and say I have no idea, that the sickness took over and I had acted on pure instinct. It would be so easy for me to make up a new story for him. One that suits him nicely and neatly and plays into all his pre-conceived notions about my kind. The Altered. My brain gets fuzzy and dizzy, and I want to scream and hiss to feel normal again, but I stop myself and bite my bottom lip so hard that tiny droplets of blood rise to the flesh on the inside of my mouth.

"I remember everything," I answer, and he exhales so hard the sound practically makes me deaf. The look of disgust on his face almost silences me into a lie, but I hold tight, to the chair and to my truth, and tell him what happened next...

●

My eyesight was changed, my hearing was changed, my sense of touch and smell were changed. I still had that sensation of two completely different entities at odds within me, but the one that was the *me*, my human side, was becoming less vocal. Like, it was being drowned out by that whooshing sound that filled my ears. My eyesight was increasingly getting foggier and foggier like a white hazy film had formed over my pupils, and my body seemed to operate more on instinct than reason. I felt like I was being turned into an animal or like I was some crazy animal hybrid from Dr. Moreau's Island. I can't really explain the feeling. The one word that sticks out most is "primal." I was regressing into a primal being. I still had my moments of clarity. Every now and then I could command my body to act and react in a certain way. Every now and then I was able to formulate a cohesive thought. But as the days creeped by, the changes of the sun to moon and moon to sun, my ability to focus singularly and cohesively became less and less.

There was no sleep. Sleep was never an option or even a thought, really. There were lulls of relaxation that would force me to slow down or stop moving altogether. But I had no need to lie down and close my eyes to rest. I rested, but in a different way. No sleep for the wicked, I guess. There were moments of time where I felt tired, but my mind was constantly shifting and moving, and there was no control over the brain waves to shut them down even temporarily. I would sometimes lean my body against a tree or an abandoned building, but there was never any real sleep. Sleep like the way humans know sleep.

The hunger continued to rage throughout my body, and it was always accompanied and intensified by that surging heat sensation. It truly was maddening. It would flare up in the depths of my belly and shoot out like cannonballs to every limb and appendage. It was agonizing. That's why we moaned the way we did. It was a way to try to release the pain.

I fought really hard against the take-over of my conscious self, the *me*. I really did try so hard to be aware, to be in control, to not lose myself, but the rational state of mind was being bent so brutally, and I was never sure of the reality I was a part of. Because once my mind twisted and warped, there were often hallucinations and a bizarre stream of consciousness that continued to detach me from any sense of realism or humanity.

For example, I was at a carnival eating pink cotton candy. I had walked miles and miles to get there just to see the flashing lights of the Ferris wheel and to hear the haunting tune of the calliope. It had started to rain, and the cotton candy I was eating was beginning to melt around the paper cone. It made me so mad. I ate the cotton candy faster and faster, but the granular sugar liquefied onto my fingers and left my hands pink and sticky. That made me mad, too, because I was furiously licking the sugar off my fingers and kept wiping my hands on my shirt, but the sugar was so sticky it wouldn't come off. The music from the calliope got louder, and louder and the flashing lights from the Ferris wheel gave me a dizzying feeling of vertigo that I fell to my knees and took my pink stained hands and ran them through my hair. I wanted to go home, I wanted to go home, I wanted to go... and then in an instant, the carnival had disappeared. I looked down at my hands and saw they were covered in blood and gore. Underneath my knees was a teenage girl with a head of pink hair, except it was now littered with her own skull fragments and bits of brain. I'd cracked her head open somehow and indulged in her gray matter.

Scenarios like that began happening more and more often. Images from my happy childhood, images I had once took comfort in, memories and daydreams, all swarmed into my mind at moments of complete and utter violence, masking the reality of what I was partaking in. My first plane ride with my father turned into the slaughter of an elderly man who was hiding underneath a car. The time I won the spelling bee in elementary school turned into a feast of a little boy who was living in a port-a-potty. My first real kiss with that girl in 7th grade turned into the tongue devouring of some woman I stumbled upon in a shopping center. Whatever soul I had left did this as a defense mechanism to preserve the last traces of humanity that resided in me. Survival. Because at the end of the day, that's what it's all about, right?

And then one day, my mind tapped into one of the most wonderful thoughts and memories I could ever remember having. 5th period. The window of the classroom was opened, and a gentle breeze blew in from the west. I turned my head to the door, and she stood there like a vision of beauty. Her blonde hair caught the breeze and tiny strands of it whipped up around her face. She wore a short denim skirt, and if she bent over even a fraction of an inch, I'd be able to spy the black lace lining of her panties. When she came into the room, her perfume danced in the air. That sweet smell of vanilla, like a bakery making cookies, mixed with the bold erotic scent of musk that drove me wild with desire. Sweet and sexy. Lana Anderson. And that's the last coherent thought I had. Lana Anderson. I finished what was left of the middle-aged woman I had taken down. She must have had the same perfume as Lana for me to generate that thought.

Lana Anderson.

I wanted to keep her forever, wanted to hold that memory, live in it for the rest of my life, bathe in the beauty and smell and taste that was Lana. My humanness was faltering, but I thought that she could save me. Her face, her hair, her scent. *Help me, Lana*, I thought. And I forced my mind to concentrate on her and only her. Lana Anderson. The last human memory I bore.

I had to find her, and in my conscious focus and fix-ated cognition, I was *determined* to find her, to seek her out, to make sure she was okay, to make her mine.

I didn't know where I was. I had no sense of direc-tion. There was no way of knowing where Lana was or if she was even still alive. Maybe I would run into her, and she would be like me, and we would go screeching and running into the night like two zombified lovers. The fact of the matter was, I knew she was dead somewhere. Just knew it. In my bones, in my festering diseased brain. But I had to try.

●

Graves clears his throat and I snap out of my story. "So, you mean to tell me..." His tone is harsh and snobby sounding, but he stops mid-sentence and recollects his thoughts. "What I meant was—you're saying you remem-bered the girl you liked, Lana Anderson, and planned to go to her house?" And when he says it, it really does sound idiotic.

"I guess you could say that," I say, shrugging my shoulders.

"And you were *aware* of wanting to see her?"

"Yes. I had her face and her... her... *essence* in my memory, and I guess that triggered a need to find her."

"Not your father. Not any other of your relatives or friends, but a girl you barely knew from school?" he reiterates. He gets more and more agitated by the second. He's doing a great job of maintaining his com-posure, however.

"Yeah. I told you, my mind worked differently."

"But what did you expect to happen if you did find her?" he asks, but he doesn't believe a word I say. This little Q&A is strictly for the recorder.

I thought about that for a second, and then answered, "I don't really know. I hadn't thought that far ahead. But like I said, there was something inside me that knew she was already dead, that she couldn't be alive, she couldn't have survived it all. I think it was the *thought* of her that gave me a purpose, a focus, something to tangibly attain."

He runs his fingers through his stiff hair. Well, he tries to, at least. They get stuck at the mid-way point of his head, and he wiggles them out. One of his little spiky thingies falls forward like a lone strand in front of his eyes, but he quickly smooths it back into place.

"A purpose to do what?" he asks and this time, I don't detect any sarcasm or patronizing tones in his voice. This question is real, and honest, like he too is trying to make some sort of sense of the journey, the fall and re-rising of man.

And for the first time, he's asked me a decent question. Something real and not scripted. He's listened with great interest to the narrative, and I've been as open and honest with him as I know how. I never once BS'd him or over emphasized certain points like 16 had, and the others for that matter. I may have left parts out for my own sake and sanity, but generally, I was real with him. There have been plenty of opportunities for me to embellish, and if this was Josh's side of the story, you'd find more relish to embellish, I tell ya that one! So, why now would I give Graves less than what I've already been giving him?

But he brought up a question, and I'm left stumped. I don't know how to answer it. Why can't I answer it?

What about the purpose and the meaning and the focus am I having such a difficult time with?

Faces flash before my eyes. Nameless faces. Expressionless faces. Faces that have futile clenched fists, and closed tight eyes, and mouths that scream "No, please! Stop!" Age, sex, race, I discriminated none. The purpose for me was the meal. The blood. The flesh. Raw and warm. Fresh and live. Human and succulent and fleshy and meaty and dripping and wet and warm and satisfying. And...

My stomach rumbles like thunder from a darkened sky. Graves waits patiently for his answer. I still don't have one. I rack my brain for something clever and quirky, but wit was never really my strong point. Nothing is coming to me because I can't put into words how the thought of Lana made me feel human. Thinking of her took me back to Mr. Miller's 5th period class when the world was normal, and I was normal, and Josh was alive and winked at cheerleaders, and I daydreamed about her under my covers until I fell asleep. The brain and body were acting separately, but the thought of Lana seemed to bring them both together, to make them work in congruency. She gave them purpose. She gave me purpose. How do I say that to Graves and leave it there?

"A purpose to do what?" he repeats, getting antsy for an answer. He raises both his eyebrows in a "well, come on!" look.

"But I knew she was dead, and I don't..." I stammer.

"But why? If you had cognizance, if you had true feeling and emotion while you were infected, going to this Lana Anderson's house had to mean *something*!"

I don't know, I don't know, I don't know. I don't know what he wants me to say. I don't know what the right answer is. I don't know if this is a giant trap to get me to say something that will prove him wrong, or prove him right, or set me up for a firing squad. I haven't had such a hard time with the truth until now. 16's skittish gestures and ominous words have poisoned me real deep. *He'll kill you like he killed 2.* But the only way out of here is to be honest. Honesty is the best policy, right?

I just want to get out of here. I just want to get out of here. I just want to...

"My soul," I finally blurt out without further thought. "I needed to preserve my soul. My humanity. Whatever was left of it."

Graves scoffs. On the inside, of course, because he doesn't want to interject his personal feelings onto the recording device. "Well, okay, then," he says as he claps his hands together with finality, "I guess I'll be seeing you tomorrow."

There's a fake smile, and I want to remind him he doesn't need to do that. There's no video camera watching us. But I don't. I don't say another word as I get up from my chair and go to the door to wait for my armed escorts to take me back to my dorm.

TOAST. IT'S THE ONLY THING I CAN STOMACH. It's the only thing I can seem to keep down without any issues. It actually took me some time to figure out the proper combination of bread to toast to butter ratio, but once I got it, I decided to stay with it. White bread, lightly toasted, five slabs of butter on each half. I have to be able to see the butter. Like, it can't be melted into the bread. If the bread is too toasted and melts the butter, I get images of oozing pus from infected wounds, and it seriously is enough to make me hurl. I'll even take six slabs of butter. That's fine with me. It makes me remember the time when I was a kid and my mother stripped me down and let me sit on the tiled floor of the kitchen with a stick in my hand. She had been cooking, and I had begged to eat it. Instead of telling me "no," she allowed me to stuff my face with the greasy substance and learn for myself it wasn't the best of choices. I remember having a horrible stomach ache after I had eaten half a stick. It actually turned me off to butter for quite some time, but it proved once again that my mother had been right. She was always right, somehow. Now the cook knows that toast is the only thing I eat, he gives me extra. But I know—man can't live off toast alone. I don't have it in me to scarf down chicken enchiladas, or micro-portions of lasagna, or chicken noodle soup. Toast is fine for now. Besides, I'm really not hungry.

Graves dismissed me in such an odd way yesterday. Actually, it wasn't odd at all, considering it was the second time he acted like that during a session. I can't put my finger on what it is he's not connecting with, what it is he can't understand or believe, what it is that makes him so hateful of me. Holston had said Graves has been through a lot. Okay. I get it. But isn't the idea of this whole Re-Assimilation Center supposed to be a healing for everyone? Or is that my own romantic vision of it all? I'm really fooling myself, aren't I? But honestly, if I wasn't here getting my daily fill of toast and butter and sleeping on this hard and uncomfortable hospital bed, where would I be? Alone at my parents' house? Out on the streets eating people?

My suspicions grow more and more everyday about this place and the intentions of these people holding me here, and yet I say nothing about it. Maybe because deep down I know the alternative is far worse. Maybe deep down I know there truly is nothing for me beyond these prison cell walls.

Catch-22 stares at me from on top of the nightstand, but I refuse to pick it up because that's how I'm feeling right now, in a catch-22. Damned if I do, damned if I don't. Following orders, continuing the rat-race. Let's face it—I'm screwed either way. Screwed here on the inside and screwed there on the outside. I don't want to read it because the first page talks about the main character being in a hospital on purpose and that infuriates me. I don't want to be in this hospital. But, then again,

I'm not sure if I want to be on the outside, either, and therein lies my catch-22. I throw the book under the bed, so I don't have to look at it anymore.

Next to the lamp on the nightstand is a remote control for the TV. In my former life, I was a TV junkie. I watched everything and anything: TV shows, movies, hell, I even watched some soap operas with my mom on days that I would play hooky from school. I haven't turned the TV on once since I've been here. The doctor who first brought me here said that there were only a few stations that worked, and they played some old sitcoms. Why not? I need some mindless stimulation to get out of my own thoughts. Who knows, I might even catch an old episode of *Three's Company* and have myself a good chuckle. That Jack Tripper was always a funny guy!

Static. Static. Static. Snow and snow and snow. Man, he wasn't kidding! This leaves me wondering, *what really happened to the rest of the world six months ago?* And then, by some grace of a higher power above—call it God, Santa Claus, magical unicorns with rainbow-colored manes—a station flickers to life. The news! The station is somewhat blurry, but I can see there is a blonde anchorwoman and an anchorman of mixed descent. Is he Asian? Is he black? I can't tell, but really, they're the stereotypical racial lineup for an evening newscast. The woman has on a red power-suit, and she's trying to be all professional-like. The fuzziness of the TV screen makes the red hue intensify to a hazy magenta color then to a weird tangerine shade. The man wears a gray suit and red tie, and the color of his tie is also doing that crazy color change. It gives me a headache, and I almost shut it off, but I notice in the video box in the corner of the screen there's a picture of a wasteland city, and what appears to be hundreds of bodies littering the street. The tag below it reads "ZN Halted." And for a split second it looks all too familiar.

My re-birth place?

Can it be? Can I really be watching a newscast that will give me some information, some insight? Are they talking about the same city street I was on when the world shook, and I was reborn? Altered? Is it truly possible I'll get another point of view on the situation and maybe some actual answers for once?

I raise the dinosaur of a remote control and aim at the screen. My heart races in anticipation, and my hands shake. I'm so curious to hear what these two cookie-cutter newscasters have to say. What is ZN, anyway? "C'mon, Gail," I say out loud, reading the name of the anchorwoman as it's flashed across the screen, "tell Daddy what he wants to hear!"

Why does Gail feel like she has to wear red like that? And why are anchorwomen's names always "Gail?" I'm so amped with anxiety I fumble a little to find the volume button.

And wouldn't you know, just as I'm about to make the program louder, the door to my room flies open and Madeline, my nurse, comes racing in. She's flustered with a wild look on her face. She runs over to me and snatches the remote control out of my hands before I even have a second to react. My senses may be heightened, but I'm still kinda weak, so my response time is still a little off. She smashes the off button, and the TV dies away with a crackling fizz.

"What the hell?" I exclaim.

"You can't be watching that!" she answers breathlessly, putting the remote control in the pocket of her nurses' uniform.

My eyes open wide. "What are you talking about? It's the first time I've watched TV!"

She shakes her head wildly back and forth, and I smell her fresh rain smell wafting through the air all around her. "No, no, no!" she insists. "Not that channel."

"What are you talking about?" I ask, confused.

"Yeah, they got that station up and running, and well," she fidgets with her hair. "I'd forgotten to come and take your remote away."

"Forgotten?" I ask with raised eyebrow.

She ignores me. "I noticed on the control board you had the TV on."

"You can tell when I'm watching TV?" I yell in disbelief. Really? They're monitoring me *that* closely?

She nods her head. Strands of loose dark brown hair bounce around her face.

"Really?" I stress. "*Really*?"

This situation is truly aggravating.

"Really," she replies, and her voice is small and almost apologetic.

"Please," I say softly as I extend my hand out to her. "Please, look past it; turn off your control command center station or whatever, and let me watch this one time." My begging routine is getting to her a little bit because her amber eyes glisten. There's a sadness to them.

"I can't," she whispers. "I'll get into a lot of trouble if I don't follow protocol." A tear uncontrollably escapes her eye, and she quickly brings her hand up to brush it away.

"Please!" I insist. "You won't get in trouble. I won't let you get in trouble. Blame me if you get caught. Say I threatened you or something."

"I... I'm sorry," she stammers as she turns around, "I can't."

"No, please! Stop!" I beg, and the words are so hauntingly familiar it actually sends shivers down my spine. Cliché? But so true. There's no other way to describe the goose bumps that blossom on my skin when I say those words. Those words echo the "No, please! Stop!" I heard countless times. They mirror the extreme desperation, the longing, the wanting, the desire to be free, and above all, saved. She stops in mid-walk. Motionless. With her back to me her hand moves up to her face to brush away some more free-flowing tears. She turns her head back and her hand digs deep into the pocket where the remote control rests.

"Fifteen minutes," I beg again. "That's all I need. Fifteen minutes."

Our eyes meet with an intensity that could break glass. She's hurt, too. There's a story there—one that speaks to mine with unspoken words and inferred glances, but with a volume that could pierce even a deaf man's ears. She catches her breath with a soft gasp, stifling the sobs that would surely flow if she allowed them to, and reaches into her pocket. She takes out the remote and looks down at it, almost in a loving way. "Fifteen minutes," she repeats softly. "You deserve some truth." And with that, she tosses it to me and walks out.

Fifteen minutes, I think as I catch it with both hands. Not enough time for full blown answers, but enough to give me some insight, a glimpse, an inkling. I press the on button and once again the TV crackles to life. Gail and her partner are on screen again with their red clothes that magically change color. Gail Waters and Rodney Prescot. Or is that Preston? I can't tell. I don't care, actually. I raise the volume slightly and walk closer to the TV. Gail is in mid-sentence, and I try to piece together the broadcast.

"...of early speculation. But that doesn't seem to be the case. Officials at the CDC have confirmed the airborne virus, named Hz7RNA, is a rare and most likely, bio-engineered hybridization of the flu virus and rabies."

The screen switches to an interview with a man wearing a white suit. There's an emblem on his lapel that says CDC. The same white suit I saw when the world shook. When I was re-born. When I was Altered.

"We cannot deny or confirm this was an act of terrorism," he announces. It looks like he's speaking to a large crowd at a press conference. The name 'Dr. Wilson Jones; Virologist, CDC' pops up on the bottom of the screen. "What we can confirm is we've gotten it under control, and now with the vaccine, Hz7RNA will ultimately be arrested. Our initial attempts at a vaccination failed due to the newness of the virus and the speed at which it spread. The H1N1 flu virus, commonly known as swine flu, and the RNA composition of the rabies virus were put through a process called 'reassortment,' where they were forced to swap genetic code. It made it difficult for us in the beginning to identify the changes and mutations of the two viruses when they had combined and formed something new. However, our team, made up of top virologists and disease pathologists have successfully isolated all the specific components of Hz7RNA and have worked around the clock to ensure that chances of another outbreak are slim to none."

People start shouting their questions at the doctor, but the screen switches back to Rodney. "Initial reports had pointed fingers at a terrorist attack, which the CDC is now neither denying nor confirming. However, widespread power-outages nationwide, and top-government agency websites being hacked days prior to the outbreak of the virus, still have many survivors believing that there was some form of terrorism at work."

There's a shot of a woman with no front teeth. Delia Berry. She looks dirty and disheveled. "Those damn terrorists!" she screams. "What do the gov'ment think, we stupid or something? Who else go'ne want Americans dead, but them terrorists?"

The shot goes back to Gail in the studio. "This tragic event had widespread effects not only nationally, but globally as well." They flash images on the screen that make my stomach do flip-flops. Dead bodies in the streets of Paris, the Ganges River littered with dead animals and people, death, death, death, death, death. Horrible picture after horrible picture, and I think, *yep, give the people what they want!* But it's not what I want. I want something more. I don't want the sensationalism, the Hollywood-*Night-of- the-Living-Dead*-version. I only have ten minutes left. Give me something *real*.

"Those who have responded well to the vaccine have been assigned to various Re-Assimilation Centers across the country," says Rodney in his 'I-have-no-idea-what-ethnicity-I-am' voice. "Cities in Florida, New York, California, and Texas have converted hospitals to harbor those who have successfully received the CDC's vaccination."

"That's right, Rodney," Gail jumps in, "every effort has been made to monitor and rehabilitate the nearly one hundred survivors of the Hz7RNA outbreak. None have been released yet from these detainment centers, but the public seems to already have the verdict out about how these *Altered* people should be dealt with once they are. At a rally outside the Justice Department in San Antonio, many make their voice heard to public officials."

Switch scene. There's a rally outside the government building. People holds signs that say "ZN" with a circle and X through it. ZN. *Zombie Nation?* Someone has a sign that says, "I don't care about your feelings, you still ate my mom!" There's a chant going on, but I can't make out what they're saying. The camera focuses on a young man with a megaphone who's riling up the crowd. "These people aren't human anymore! They're animals! And these animals decimated our families! Killed our children! Mutilated our parents! Destroyed our lives!" and the throng cheers after each sentence. "And the ones who claim to protect us are going to let them walk the streets? I say hell no! I say let them burn! I say do to them what they did to our loved ones! We need justice for our dead!"

The crowd breaks into "Justice for our dead! Justice for our dead!"

Cut scene to two teenage looking girls wearing sunglasses and too much makeup. I think, *how the hell did they survive the initial outbreak?* "They're like, not human anymore!" one says as she pops a large pink bubble from her bubblegum into the news reporter's microphone.

"Yeah!" the other one chimes in. "They like, did lots of bad stuff to people. They should like, be put on trial for murder or something."

"Yeah, murder!" the bubblegum popper parrots.

"Yeah, cause we were, like, driving away from a whole bunch of those *things* and we came to this construction road block," the friend offers.

"Yeah, and we pull over to ask the guy holding the "Slow Down" sign what was going on," the other butts in.

"And he leaps in the car, and like kills our best friend, Jackie!" The two squeal as one of the girls quickly makes the sign of the cross over her chest and kisses her forefingers like some little old Italian lady. I roll my eyes and think instead of poor Jackie getting eaten alive; these two ditzes should have been flayed. It sickens me to think the stupidity gene pool is left untouched while poor sweet Sydney was tossed in the air like a ragdoll.

Cut scene to a group of older women protesters wearing t-shirts with the same X over a 'ZN' logo. "Those people," one starts sympathetically, "they've been through a lot. I get that," and the others pout out their lips and nod their heads in agreement. "But, really? There's no place for them among us. Everyone knows who they are and what they did. They're scared. Marked." At the word "marked," I instinctively touch the scar under my right eye.

"They shouldn't be wasting valuable resources on rehabilitating them; they're damaged goods! Who knows if they'll go back being *zombies* and cause another outbreak?" another piped in. "They should be putting that money toward kids' homes and helping support people like us who actually did survive!"

"Where are they gonna go when they get out? Who will have them? They won't be able to get jobs; they won't be able to be seen in public without being harassed, what's the point for them?" And all three nod and emphatically remark, "Uh-huh!"

My stomach rolls again, and I turn off the TV. I probably have five more minutes left, but I can't stand to watch anymore. It was interesting to say the least. Not as informative as I had hoped, but interesting. It made for good TV, and isn't that the point of the news? Entice your viewers with grotesque and bizarre images, tantalize them with provocative tales, present them sound bites of everyday people saying outrageous things, and then scare them with facts and figures of what might or might not possibly happen.

One thing I do take away from all that is I'm public enemy number one. All of us Altered are. That one lady was right, too. How on earth do I expect to be welcomed back into society with open arms? I can see it now: being at the grocery store getting my change, and saying to the cashier, "Have a nice day. By the way, sorry for eating your sister! My bad!" It's not logical. It's not going to work. Makes for a great horror movie, but this isn't the movies. This is real life. My life. *The Now*. And getting a job? Yeah, I can see how that one's gonna play out. What the hell am I even qualified to do? I'm guessing school is off the table, if schools even exist anymore. And what would I put on a job application? Previous work experience: Professional zombie? No, that's definitely not gonna work, either.

Zombie.

There's that word again. I guess it really is the closest thing to explaining and describe what happened to us infected people. People are so inundated with horror movies and novels and TV shows, and that word gets thrown around so often, I guess it was the natural progression for the world to use that word. To sensationalize us, demonize us, vilify us, make us monsters. A new race to hate. A new group of nu-humans. I can see it now: "Altered Only" water fountains and dining sections at restaurants, "Altered Only" dressing rooms at department stores, "Altered Need Not Apply" signs in local businesses. Yeah, I'm getting ahead of myself. Those things are far from happening. If they happen. When we get out.

If we get out.

Madeline walks back into the room carrying a tray in one hand as she outstretches her other. She turns her face up in confusion when she sees that the TV is off.

"Had enough?" she asks.

"For a very long time," I reply with a defeated tone and hand her the remote.

Another look of sadness sweeps across her face. "Here," she says handing me the blue tray. "More toast. Extra butter."

"Thanks," I reply as I place it on my desk, but after watching that news broadcast, I don't think I can eat anything.

Besides, I'm not hungry anyway.

GUESS I HAVE TO KEEP MY VIEWING OF THE nightly newscast a secret because I don't want to get sweet Madeline in trouble for letting me watch it. I sit back in the leather chair, and across the coffee table is Graves with his condescending remarks and suspicious eyebrow raised. I could have very well seen his face in the crowd at that rally on TV. Is that the business he had to attend to? I have to be conscious of my words today and put on my game face. I can't let *him* know *I* know about the virus and the other centers.

He's formal again today: dark brown suit with a beige shirt and dark brown silk tie. He even has his glasses on today. I like it better when he doesn't though because the way he peers at me over the rims is so unsettling. It gives me the creeps. Makes me feel like I'm in an interrogation or something. Kinda like how he's doing now! The glasses are halfway down the bridge of his nose, and he's staring at me with his dark black eyes. They look darker and blacker set against the ridges of his eyelid folds and the bushels of his thick black eyebrows. His Mediterranean features are really coming through right now, and I want so desperately to ask him, "Are you

Italian? Greek? Maybe a hint of Spanish? Or Gypsy?" Wouldn't that be a hoot! If good ole' Graves over here was Romani! With all the persecution and discrimination those people have faced for centuries, I would think he would have some compassion for me and my new race! Funny, too, that the Gypsies have purposefully gone out of their way to *not* assimilate into the culture of the different lands they settle, and Graves is working at a Re-Assimilation Center. He's probably not a Gypsy, then. I'm still kinda curious, though.

So, he's still staring at me. Hard. He clears his throat and crosses his leg over his knee in a manly way, and the absence of his clipboard makes it easy for him to adjust into a comfortable position.

Wait.

There's no clipboard.

And I realize there's no tape recorder, either. No video camera. Nothing.

A cold feeling sweeps into my chest, and I get a sudden urge to run away. I look to the side wall where the two-sided mirror is, and it seems like Graves is not concerned with that either. He watches me tilt my head toward it, and then he smirks at me. I want to react in some way but can't. I'm frozen in my own fear. *There's no one on the other side.*

I try to hide my nervousness, but I'm failing. I scratch at my shoulders and my palms are coated with a sheen of sweat. I hope he doesn't ask to shake my hand, 'cause then he'll know for sure the extent of my terror.

He clears his throat, and like an idiot I smile and say, "Good morning."

He rolls his eyes. He must have picked that little gesture up from me. I have to be honest; it is an infectious piece of body language.

"So," he begins, his deep voice booming throughout the office, "I'm having a little bit of a difficult time figuring you out."

"I don't understand," I truthfully reply.

"Well, ya see, the thing about it is this: all the others have no recollection of their time when they were infected. I mean, they do in the sense that they can remember the killings and the feeling of the hunger and all that, but as far as actual memories, or feelings, there's none."

"I still don't understand. I told you everything. Like, I'm being honest with you," I respond.

"Yeah, you say you're being honest, but I'm not believing you. I'm not buying the guilt routine. I'm not buying the sad face and the regret," he says as he massages his clean-shaven cheeks and chin with one hand.

I'm still confused. I don't think I like where this conversation is headed. He's awfully confrontational right now, and the absence of any kind of recording device makes me feel unprotected. I shrug my shoulders. "I don't know what you want me to say."

"You're a smart one. I think you're telling me what I want to hear. And I'm not quite sure what your motive is."

"There's no motive!" I blurt out, but recoil as soon as the words leave my mouth. I don't like what he's accusing me of because, like I said, I'm being as honest as I possibly can be.

"Hmmm," he says with his lips pursed together as he gently nods his head.

I hate that. My dad used to do that exact same gesture when he didn't believe what I was saying. It's obnoxious and my ears start to get hot. "I'll tell you what I think," he says calmly licking his lips, "I think you're smart. Really smart. Too smart."

I fold my arms over my chest. *What the hell is he getting at?*

"I think you're trying to play me," he continues. "Telling me you were aware of what you did, is that supposed to make me feel bad for you?"

The heat rushes from my ears to my cheeks. They flush red and burn on the inside.

"Is that supposed to make me like you?" he continues.

I close my eyes tightly and mumble, "No."

"Is that supposed to make me forgive you?"

I open my eyes and glare at him. "Why would I need *you* to forgive *me*?" I say sarcastically, the rage and heat now seeping from my cheeks and peaking in my chest.

He breathes in deeply, his shoulders rise, and his chest puffs out dramatically. "You said you had to do what you had to do in order to survive, right?"

I don't respond, but he acts like I said "yes" or something. "Well, you're not the only one," he coos.

The plot thickens, I think as I inch to the edge of my chair defensively. He's about to strike like a cobra. He's sized me up for weeks and is about to make his move. This is it. *He'll kill you like he killed 2*. There are no Big Brother eyes or ears watching or listening to us right now. It's just me and Graves. Like at the end of one of those movies when the villain reveals his ultimate plan right before he attempts to kill the hero. Except, on the big screen, I'm not the hero, and the audience is rooting for Graves to beat the holy hell out of me.

"Ya see," he says in a conversational tone, "I had a pretty nice life until you came along. I had a pretty ex-wife with whom I got along fabulously, lots of girl-friends, a great son who far surpassed you in looks and intelligence, money that you could only hope to see in the rest of your pathetic existence."

My blood screams.

"Then, it all fell apart in one fell swoop," he continues as he re-crosses his leg. "*You* came into the picture and stole my life away from me. Money is worthless right now, like scraps of paper in a recycling bin. The girl-friends I could care less about. Ex-wife, too. But my boy, my son. Christian. You stole him from me. Ripped his 15-year-old life away. Turned him into a demon. Made him mutilate his own mother. And when all was said and done, when the bodies were still warm and fresh and starting to pile up on the ground, when everything was happening in the chaos and confusion, what do humans need to do?"

I grip the edges of the chair. I'm ready because I have this horrible feeling he is actually going to leap across the coffee table and strangle me to death.

"What do humans need to do?" he shouts at me, his deep voice not only filling the room but my head.

I grit my teeth and close my eyes letting the sound of his voice wash over me. I don't want to answer him. I don't want to answer him. I don't want to answer...

"Well?" he presses forcefully.

He's backed me into a corner. I don't like this feeling. I haven't felt this helpless and hopeless since I was infected. A growl rises up to my throat, and I'm afraid if I try to answer him with the single word he so desper-ately wants me to say I'll only emit a deep gurgling moan. I hate him for making me afraid of my own voice again, but I don't have another choice because he might kill me if I don't answer him.

"Survival," I manage to say quietly.

"Ah, yes!" he exclaims as he claps his lunchbox hands together in mock excitement. "Survival! The very essence of man. So, when the bodies are still warm and fresh, and there's confusion and chaos, and my ex-wife has had her arms and legs torn off by our son, and he's coming at me with the intention of doing to me what he did to her, my vision gets blurred with that one encompassing human emotion. To survive. And I catch my son's neck in the palms of my hands," Graves makes a strangling motion in the air with his two hands, "and before he can bite me or scratch me or tear me up like he did his mother, I squeeze," and his hands tighten up. I see the thick veins on the tops of them jutting out like blue-green ropes running down into his wrists and fingers. His knuckles are like bone white cabinet knobs, and as I glance up at his face, I see a blue-green vein protruding out from the side of his neck like a bubble rising from a tar pit. "I squeeze so hard," he continues, "that he loses consciousness and falls to the floor, but I had seen it in his eyes. They were whitened with disease and rage. When he woke up, he would have surely tried to kill me again. So, I had to survive. My instincts took charge. You wanna know what I did?"

I shake my head back and forth because really, I already know what he's going to say.

"I stomped his face in," he says matter-of-factly. "I stomped his face in until there was no face. I stomped his face in until the pieces of bone and skull were so embedded into the tile floor of my ex-wife's kitchen, that I knew Lupe, the maid, would never be able to scoop them all out. I stomped his face in until there was only a neck and a body left."

My stomach turns as the image of a monstrous Graves bashing his size 13 shoes into the face of his only son paints itself in my mind, but I don't let go of the edges of the chair. Even though a wave of nausea has made me unsettled, I need to remain on guard.

"So, I get to thinking," he goes on, "how am I to believe you? How am I to believe your agonizing narrative of pain and remorse and *wah-wah-wah*? Because if what you say is true, if what you say about the guilt and the "not wanting to" is true, then that makes the relationship with my son a lie. It takes everything that Christian and I had as a father and son and bastardizes it. Don't you see? Cause if *you* felt, then that means *he* must have felt. And if he had no problem with coming at me the way he did, then I really didn't know him, now did I?"

Graves stands up slowly like a massive tower rising from the depths of the ocean. He's said too much, shown me too much, and I should hold my tongue and wait for him to make his next move or say the next part of his diatribe, but of course I don't. I open my mouth like an idiot. "It's not like that," I say under my breath.

A wild look penetrates Graves's face, and he swoops down across that stupid coffee table and gets nose to nose with me. His breath is hot against my mouth, "No?" he says as I back up an inch, "then how is it?"

He's like a rabid dog, and for a split second, I wonder if he himself is infected.

"I didn't hurt your son," I say as I curl my knees up to my chest trying to create some distance between us.

"But you did! You did!" he screams as he points a meaty finger into my shoulder blade.

I see red. He touched me, provoked me, and my mind is still trying to process everything he's said about his son and his life before all this. I pop up and stand on the chair, towering above him. The movement startles him a bit because he seems to take a step back, allowing me the room to step down from the chair.

I'm not in control anymore. I smell his anger, smell the sweat beads forming underneath his armpits, get a slight whiff of a gently roasted chicken scent, and my mouth waters.

I gnash my teeth at him, and immediately he grabs both my arms and turns me around. He's fast, and it seems like he effortlessly got me twisted in an arm lock behind my back. I want to bite him. I want to taste him. I want to eat the flesh of his face and feel the gelatinous texture of his eyeballs between my teeth. I'm so hungry. I'm so hungry. I'm so...

I screech. The hideous sound comes out from my throat and fills the room. And I'm snarling and hissing like a wild animal backed against a wall. I can feel him smiling that snakey smile behind me as I buck like a wild animal against his grip.

Am I reverting? Am I relapsing? I think for a spilt second.

"Go ahead!" he says laughing. "Let's see you try to get at me!"

"If your guys hadn't taken my strength away, you'd be dead on the floor, Graves! And I'd be chomping on your big ole ape hands right about now!" I roar without even thinking about the words that I choose.

The door to the office flies open, and I turn my head to see Holston and a few guards armed with their weapons. Are they aiming at me or at Graves, I can't really tell.

"Let him go, Warren!" Holston shouts.

"No way, Peter!" Graves shouts back as he tightens his grip on me.

"I said, let him go!" Holston reiterates. "You're out of line! You're not following protocol!"

Graves lets go and throws me to the ground. I extend my hand to break my fall, but my wrist snaps back and shoots a horrible pain up my arm.

"*You're* out of line!" Graves screams, pointing his finger at Holston. "You're out of line for even entertaining this idea that these *things* can be helped and put back into society! To think that you could cure them and fix them!" he scoffs.

Holston takes a few steps closer to me and extends his hand to help me up. I grab it and stagger to my feet. "You okay?" he whispers to me, and I nod my head.

"They're dangerous!" Graves continues as he goes over to his desk and starts fiddling with a stack of papers. "They're dangerous, and this is the proof I needed. They're changed, Peter, altered. There's no reform or going back for them. You're a sick man if you can't see that!"

"Warren," Holston says lowering his voice a bit, "you were hired to make your professional observations and..."

"And I have!" Graves interrupts. "And I have all my notes in my official report to the CDC," and he takes some papers from his desk and waves them around in the air like a child taking a temper tantrum. "You're getting shut down, Peter. My report will shut all the centers down if I have anything to say about it. This is a worthless project and a waste of resources. You're delusional if you think you were doing anyone an ounce of good."

Holston's mouth twists in a look of despair and defeat. "Warren, can we please talk about this rationally," he says in a pleading voice.

Graves huffs. "Get him out of here!" He barks, and Holston looks at me with a pained expression.

Holston looks over his shoulder at the armed guards at the entrance. "Take Patient 24 away," he says calmly and callously.

The guards approach me, and I put up my hands, showing them, I'm going to go peacefully and without incident.

"To the dorms, Doctor?" one asks Holston. I look at Holston. Holston looks at Graves. Graves looks at me. I'm in some kind of weird showdown, and in my head I start counting 1, 2, 3, waiting for the 5 when we can all whip out our guns and take each other out.

"No," Holston answers with his eyes still locked on Graves, "take him to solitary."

They both nod, and one of them presses his gun into the small of my back and forces me out of the office. Before the other one closes the door, I look in to see Holston watching me being whisked away, a pained expression etched on his face, and Graves behind him with his phony smile.

I HAD BEEN THREATENED WITH SOLITARY THE first time I was allowed to go into the courtyard with the others, and at the time, I thought the orderly had been kidding around, or trying to scare me. Because, really, the confinement of being locked in my room every day was solitary enough. But now I see what he meant. Where I am right now is *truly* solitary confinement. Not like how you see on the prison shows when an inmate flips out and gets put in a white padded room. That's Hollywood. Strictly made-for- television. *This* is solitary. *True* solitary.

The guards dragged me down to the basement of the hospital. First of all, I didn't know there were basements in Florida, but apparently, this hospital has one. The button on the elevator said "S", and I could only guess it meant "Sub", as in, "subterranean." The word subterranean is a euphemism for this place. I got this weird *Silence of the Lambs* feeling walking down here, like when the chic agent goes to see Hannibal Lecter for the first time. Creepy. Except, there aren't any cells. Just cold cement block rooms with rusty iron doors. It's quite possible they used this area for mental patients. No, I don't think it. I know it. The damp smell barely masks the true odor beneath it. A smell that only someone Altered like me could detect; someone whose sense have been heightened. It smells like death, and mixed with the heavy moisture scent, it not only smells of death, but it *feels* of death, of agony, and dare I say, torture?

Solitary. They certainly weren't kidding because that's exactly what it is here. They closed the iron door behind me and locked it up real good, leaving me in complete and total darkness. No window. No ray of light from a crack in the door. Nothing.

I'm so used to the *click-click-clicking* sound of the turn of the key that I almost didn't notice it. But this one had a hollow sound that reverberated throughout the entire underground facility, an echo that told me I'm alone here. Solitary. There isn't another soul in any of these other rooms. Cells. My heightened senses can tell. No. The only movement or noise being made comes from me and only me. Solitary.

I stay close to the door and try to work my way around the room from that point. I feel the walls. They're cold and hard, not white and padded like in the movies. The ground beneath me is the same texture. I cough. Deliberately. My voice bounces off the cement. There isn't a bed in here, or a chair, or anything. Just cold, hard, cement. And me. I sit down on the floor and prop my head against the wall.

So, Holston is the head cheese. I kinda figured that out from the jump. I mean, he was the only dude in this place who looked at me with wonder and *hope*. Why he chose to put me in here is a mystery. I thought I was his golden boy. I thought he saw something in me he hadn't seen in his other patients. But Graves can be a very intimidating person, and it is quite possible that Holston sent me here to appease Graves. I mean, I did try to eat him and everything, so I guess it's only fair I'm punished.

But did I really want to kill Graves? I'm struggling with that question. Wrestling with it real hard, and I'm even more confused because there's still this little piece of me that wants to say "yes." There's still that little piece of me that wants to indulge in the flesh; that needs to taste the warmth of the blood. Something excited me so much about diving my face into the tender region of a young girl's stomach and ripping out her entrails with my teeth. *Toby*. But the other part of me threw up in my mouth. It's revolting to think of what I did. What I became. And now, to be left with those cravings and those urges?

My brain is still working independently from the rest of my body. Like, I've regained a good portion of the control, but I still have moments of *instinct*. I'm relearning how to live. How to be human. *Re-assimilation*. And there it is, right in front of me. Holston's view and vision. He had anticipated this all along. He had anticipated the struggle of the Altered to relearn life. I don't want to kill Graves. I don't want to eat him or anyone else for that matter. I want to be *Griffin* again. Whoever that was.

I'm marked, too. Forever to be identified as being different from the rest of the people of the world. The rest of the survivors. I bet a plastic surgeon would refuse me cosmetic surgery to hide the scar under my eye. It'll probably be against the law or something because the rest of the world is going to need to identify us, and we surely can't go around wearing bright red "A's" on our chests, now can we?

What is all this? What has my life become? I don't even have a life. I feel like I'm existing in some nightmare, and I'm hoping one day I'll wake up and be in my bed, thinking of Lana, with Sydney banging on my door interrupting my fantasies, urging me to get up and get ready for school because the bus is going to be there soon. Shit, I'd even ride that disgusting germ-filled yellow embarrassment the rest of my life if it meant I could go back to *The Before*. Anything! Because *The Now* ain't looking so hot. This isn't life. This is just existing. And right now, I'm not so sure if I want to exist like this. I'm not sure if I want to relearn everything—dealing with emotions and people, controlling something inside of me I fear is never going to go away for as long as I continue to exist. 'Cause I'm different now. Marked. *Altered*.

Sydney. Mom. Dad. The only time I've thought about or talked about my family was during my sessions with Graves, and I really haven't come to terms with the loss of them. I feel so guilty about it, but maybe that's the selfish teenager in me. *The Before* Griffin. They were the only family that ever mattered to me, and honestly, I tried to avoid them at all costs. When I was little, I was close to my parents because they were my only social outlet. I enjoyed family trips to Disney World and corny family parties, but as I got older, I became disinterested in those types of things. Like, my friends were more important. Girls were more important. Watching baseball and playing video games were more important. Watching Josh make an ass out of himself was more important. Twiddling my thumbs in the privacy of my own room was more important. I guess most teenagers go through that stage because my friends were the same way. Like, you reach a certain point and the whole "family" thing isn't fun or cool anymore. I heard when you reach your mid-twenties, the pendulum is supposed to swing back again, and family takes center stage once more. I'm not afforded that luxury, however. I don't have a family anymore to spend time with, go on Disney vacations with, or have corny family parties with. Mom, Dad, and Sydney were all I had. Both my parents were only children, and all four of my grandparents died years ago. The only family I had is dead, and had I known this was going to happen, I would have acted completely different toward all of them.

I could have only been so lucky.

"*My family is dead.*" I say it out loud to let the words penetrate my sensitive ears.

"*My family is dead.*" I say it again to absorb the gravity of it all.

"*My family is dead.*" I say it one last time as hot tears escape my eyes for the first time in god-knows-how- long.

"*My family is dead!*" I scream as I try desperately to stop the wave of pitiful sobs.

But I can't. It overwhelms me. Overtakes me.

I cry for my mother—the neurotic, angel haired, family oriented, eye-rolling mess that she was. She was a free spirit who let me eat brownies for breakfast and whole sticks of butter. Who let me curse like a sailor because she wanted me to "find my own way in the world" and "be my own person." She only wanted the best for me and my sister and father. She never took any crap from anyone when it came to us. She was fierce. A lioness. My mother. And I watched her crumple on the back patio of our house as a mass of mindless wanderers devoured her perfect flesh...

I cry for Sydney—the pain in the ass, smart-alec, whiner, with the gentle smile and too-wise-for-her-own-good nature. She was such a pest, but I truly enjoyed her wit and wisdom. She would have been a great person had she been able to live, to survive. I want to kill her all over again for racing out to me that night. It's all her fault! But I can't blame her, because, really, it's not. It's not anybody's fault. She was scared and loved me and didn't want me to leave them. Let's face it, I probably would have died or been changed regardless. Sydney was naïve. She was wise beyond her years, but at the end of the day, she was still only a child. Nine years old. That's not a lot of time for a kid to live. You're forever young, Syd. Forever a child. Forever catching the violet twilight moonlight in the strands of your strawberry blonde hair as you're lifted like a ragdoll to your death.

I cry for my father—the hard-ass, hard-working business man with the fiery Italian temper and New York attitude. He was a good man, a good provider for his family. I had hoped to be half the man he was when I grew up. Stand-offish. Didn't laugh much. Yelled a lot. But would do anything for us. He loved my mother more than he loved me and Syd. That's okay. I understand why. I know that now. You can make more kids, but you can't replace your wife. I hope he died quickly even though he was strong-minded, strong-willed, and would fight a horde of zombies to get home to my mother and us kids. He would have never been able to survive the change. I know his own personal anger and rage would have fed the disease and completely consumed him. I hope he's dead. I know he's dead.

And Josh. And Toby. And that brown headed boy. And that old man. And that CDC guy. And the countless,

countless faceless nameless others. Dead. All of them. I hear their voices, see their faces, feel their struggling bodies underneath mine and the "No, please! Stop!" sings over and over like a telephone that won't stop ringing. The reality of what I became, what I did, reaches my heart. It swells up inside me needing to break free. My chest is tight. Gripping me. Strangling me with the memories and realization that, *yes,* I ate people. *I ate people. I ate people. I ate...* My breath comes in quick pants. My chest rises and falls in super-speed- slow-motion, if that makes any sense. Each up and down for each person I killed, or watched die, or wished dead.

I'm not a monster, I'm not a monster, I'm not a monster.

And I don't want to feel that way ever again. I don't want to want the screams, the blood, the flesh between my teeth. I don't want to devour and rip and tear and slash and bite and chew and...

I stifle down a sensation of vomit in my mouth.

I want to be Griffin. I just want to be Griffin. I just want to be Griffin.

And I want my mom.

I remember how Josh had screamed for his mother as he was being torn apart. The last-ditch desperation of his voice filling the night air, coating it with the sounds of death and agony, and pure pathetic-ness. Now I know how he felt. I want my mom to run her hands across my fuzzy head and down my back, patting me like I was a child again, whispering to me that "everything is going to be alright, Griffin." But I can't hear her voice, and I can't feel her comforting touch, because my mother is dead. I watched her die.

Oh, God! I watched my mother die!

I close my eyes and continue to cry, hoping that sleep will envelope me and make me forget.

I'm not out long enough for the dreams to start. I'm not sure how long I drifted off, but it couldn't have been a lengthy amount of time. I've stopped crying, that's for one thing, but my eyes must be swollen and red. What startled me awake was the *click-click-click* of the lock on the door cranking open, and the inside hum of electricity springing to life. A light on the ceiling of my cell flickers on. It's one of those rectangular fluorescent deals that casts unflattering yellow shadows on human faces. I squint my eyes into focus and sit up straight, anticipating the worst, but when Madeline enters pulling a metal cart behind her, I breathe a sigh of relief. Cliché? Yes. But I can't put into other words the way my chest eases with relaxation when I see her dark brown ponytail swishing in the doorway.

"Hey," she says softly as the slamming of the iron door almost drowns out her voice.

But I heard it. My Altered ears pick up sounds that normal people can't, and the gentle nuances of Madeline's vocal pattern are easy for me to detect.

"Hey," I reply as I rub my eyes.

"Are you okay?" she asks, and I realize she's looking at my face—my tear stained, sunken in, swollen eyed face. I must really look like a monster to her. And for the first time in a long while I'm cognizant of my appearance, and I'm embarrassed and wish I could hide somewhere dark and damp and cold. Or maybe stay here and shut off the lights.

"I'm fine," I say. "I'm tired, ya know?"

I'm not really being completely dishonest, but she's not buying it. "I know," she answers as she sits down next to me on the floor.

I move back an inch away from her, startled that she's come this close to me of her own accord. "You're not…" I start.

"Scared?" she interrupts. "No. Not anymore." She takes my hands and holds them in her own and her amber eyes gaze deeply into mine.

I'm kinda confused. I don't know where these gestures are coming from. I mean, this was the girl who put me in handcuffs to give me a haircut!

"I was working the night shift here at the hospital when it happened," she begins. "I stayed in this very room for three days with a few other nurses. We were lucky when help came. There was about ten of us holed up in the hospital for some time until our security was breached by the infected, and I watched a lot of my co-workers die. I don't know how I survived both attacks. You're not like the others. I know that now. Whatever Holston gave you, or whatever you have inside of you, or maybe a combination of both, it makes you… *different*. I see the humanity in you. You have human eyes. You have a soul."

"Why are you saying this to me?" I say and tears come up into my eyes again. I'm fighting so hard for them to stay where they are, stay where they are, stay where they are.

"You remind me of my brother. He was a fighter. A lover of life. And I see that spark in you. I recognize your will. You're not a monster." She clasps my hands together and lifts them up to her mouth and kisses them gently.

Great. I'm crying in front of her, but tears well up in her eyes as well, so I don't feel as stupid.

"Mad-duh-*lyn*? Or Mad-duh-*line*?" I ask as she stands up and walks over to the metal cart by the door. She stops in her tracks and smiles.

"Line," she says as a pink blush sweeps across her face. "But it's Mazzy. That's what everyone used to call me, at least."

Mazzy. I would have never guessed. "I like that. It fits you." I say and think I must sound like such a loser.

"24?" she asks with a touch of sweet sarcasm in her voice and a smirk perched on her lips.

"I guess so," I answer as I shrug my shoulders, "but it's Griffin. That's what everyone used to call *me*, at least."

"Griffin," she repeats out loud, and the sound of a human voice saying my name is probably the nicest sound I've heard in a long while. "I like that."

I smile.

"Well, Griffin," she continues as she brings me over one of those blue food trays, "this is for you. I can only give you ten minutes until I have to shut out the lights again, so eat up, and get some meat on those bones of yours!"

I reach for it. "What is it?" I ask grimacing.

"Roast chicken. Mashed potatoes. Diced carrots. And some toast with butter, of course."

"Thank you, for everything," I say as I take the tray from her.

"Don't mention it," she responds as she leaves the cell with another smile.

I open the tray and survey the food before me. The smells waft into my nose and fill my senses, overpowering the scents of death and decay in this dungeon. My stomach growls. I hesitate. Mazzy said I wasn't a monster, that I had a soul, and the smells of the food continue to fill me, tempt me.

She said I have a soul. She said I'm not a monster. *I'm not a monster. I'm not a monster. I'm not a...*
But what I am, is hungry.

My stomach growls again. I pick up the plastic fork on the tray and devour the food on the plate.

FTER I ATE, I FELL ASLEEP. I MUST HAVE fallen asleep hard because my eyes shift their focus when the light flickers on again. I look around the room. The blue food tray is gone, and I'm not sure what has happened since Mazzy's visit. I remember eating, *no,* devouring my meal, the lights flashing off again, and that's about it. Maybe my food was drugged? Maybe Mazzy drugged me to help me sleep better, and while I was out cold, she came back to take the tray away? It was a dreamless sleep, and that's why I'm having difficulty with the time displacement.

But the lights are on again. The door opens again. I sit up, anxious to see who is coming to visit me this time. I hope it's Mazzy but know I could only be so lucky.

It's Holston.

He does his half waddle, half limp, into the room and shuts the door behind him.

"I'm sorry," he says.

"For what?" I reply with a hint of anger in my voice. I rub my eyes, and he comes into focus. I kinda wish it wasn't him. He's not my favorite person in the world right now.

"Waking you," he answers gently as he moves closer and sits a few feet away from me on the cold floor. It seems to be a bit of a struggle to inch his slightly overweight frame and bum leg onto the ground, but he uses the wall for leverage and eventually gets there. "I'm sorry for having to put you here in the first place."

I wave my hand in front of my face.

"You know I was only following protocol."

"Yeah, yeah," I huff, "protocol."

There's a sadness in Holston's eyes. He lowers his head a bit. "I shouldn't feel badly because I created the guidelines to protect myself and the others working for me. You threatened Graves. It was the only thing I could do. It was the only procedure put in place. Had I known..."

"Don't worry about it," I interrupt which elicits a big tooth smile from him.

Don't worry about it? Wait, did I actually say that out loud? Aren't I mad at him for throwing me in this dark cage? Aren't I raging mad he ordered my solitary confinement without hearing my side of the story? That he sentenced me without a fair trial? Slick bastard just double psycho-ed me with his feigned guilt! Tricky, tricky! I knew Holston was good, but I would have never expected that from him!

"Dr. Graves is gone. He's left the project. I suspect that once his report is written up, he'll present his evidence to the CDC," Holston says.

I'm confused. Isn't that what he's supposed to be doing anyway?

"He never agreed with the program, and I knew he was trying to build a case against me. I knew he would eventually try to have me shut down."

"I gave him that ammunition, didn't I?" I ask.

Holston sighs and fixes the collar on his white lab jacket. "Yes, and no," he answers ambiguously. "He's a very bitter, very callous man—rightfully so. He comes from the school of thought that says your kind needs to be eradicated."

"My kind?" I quickly jump in.

"Yes," he says with a slight nod of his head and a small smile on his lips. "Your kind. The new breed. The new race. The Altered." He says it so matter-of-factly, so coolly, and with a hint of pride.

"I guess it wouldn't shock you too much if I told you I'm not understanding you all that well."

Holston's face twists in confusion. "What do you mean? What's there not to understand?"

"Um," I say, "all of this," and the word "duh" almost ends my sentence, but I stop myself just in time.

He laughs. Out loud. Like, I'm a dummy. Like, I'm supposed to know everything. I guess the expression on my face must be one of pure confusion because he reaches over, puts his hands on my ankles, and blinks his eyes a few times. "Before this center, before all this," and he warbles his head in a circular motion, "I was a top Virologist. I studied human, animal, insect, plant, fungal—all types of viruses—in many different capacities. At the University of Toledo, College of Medicine I helped to organize the American Society for Virology. Viruses have always been my life's work. I had no wife or children and was able to completely immerse myself in it. Shortly after the formation of the Society, I left Ohio, and began working for the Center for Disease Control in Atlanta. I also did research for the government's virus unit which, starting in 1985, began to seriously consider the possibility of biochemical warfare. The Cold War was coming into full swing, and most people's attention was focused on nuclear, nuclear, nuclear. But there were underlying conditions and things happening behind the scenes that pointed fingers at something larger and more dangerous. I worked behind those scenes. I tested numerous strains of the world's deadliest pathogens. I studied countless variations of naturally occurring diseases and calculated the human factor in most all of them. The 'what- if's' were phenomenal. It was something out of a science fiction movie, only the people making those movies could have never fathomed the horrors I faced on a daily basis. I knew if any of them were to get out, or be engineered by a terrorist perhaps, or somehow present themselves naturally, the landscape of the world would be changed forever. You're probably too young to remember, but after 9/11 there was a series of attacks on journalists and government officials by way of anthrax laced letters. And who broke that case? Me!" and he pounds a fist on his chest with a thump. "Who did damage control? Me!" and another thump. "I first encountered a variation of the Hz7RNA strain in 2000."

"That's what infected me, right?" I ask, knowing damn well that the answer is yes.

"Yes," he answers. "The first instance of it was found in a dog. I called it the U Virus, for 'unknown.' I had never seen anything like it before. The dog's owner originally suspected rabies, but things didn't add up in the symptoms. One of my colleagues decided to treat it for bubonic plague. He prescribed a dose of Tetracycline and the animal showed improvement. However, I was not convinced and wanted to order more tests on the animal and hold it for observation before returning it to its owner. To be honest, I was so unnerved by the characteristics of the infection in the animal that I wanted to euthanize it and hold it for further evaluation. My colleague and I butted heads. He disagreed and discredited everything I said. He went behind my back and released the dog back to its owner, and that was the last that I had seen of the U Virus."

"Until now?" I add.

He nods his head. "Knowing what I knew about the nature of viruses, I couldn't rest. The U Virus was something so unlike anything I'd ever come across in my thirty years of research, and I knew from that moment, that procedures needed to be put in place if an outbreak of anything serious were to occur. Natural. Bioengineered. It didn't matter. There needed to be preparation because, quite honestly, there was nothing. This country and other countries of the world had no idea, no clue, about the science-fiction 'what-if's' that lurked in swampy water, or in nuclear contaminated wastelands, or in the saliva of infected animals, or in the bite of a mosquito, or under the ultraviolet lights in a makeshift laboratory in some madman's basement. I needed to act and act fast. From that moment on, I began creating my manifesto, my guidelines, a Bible, if you will, for severe circumstances titled *The Policies for Disaster of a Biological or Biochemical Nature and/or Attack*."

"The Re-Assimilation Centers," I say under my breath as the veil of secrecy and confusion is slowly stripped from my naïve brain.

He nods again. "I contracted a team of doctors, psychologists, specialists, you name it, and formed an emergency committee. I was well-respected in the scientific community and my previous work for the government allowed me a hefty budget with carte blanche. We pulled our resources together, did think-tanks, looked at possible scenarios from all angles. For instance, we discussed the possibility of an Ebola virus outbreak in this country and formulated a plan for what we would do and how we would handle it. We discussed plague, and swine flu, and bird flu, and smallpox, and anthrax, and a mutant strain of the common cold. We even entertained the idea of an airborne strain of cancer. Nothing was off-limits. I particularly piqued their interests when I told them about my findings on the U Virus. I had my detailed records and the few samples left from the animal. There were two other top virologists in the committee, and they were both especially unnerved. On the side, the three of us decided to work on a prototype vaccine, something that could be used if needed in a dire circumstance.

"We were lucky we did that because the outbreak happened. I'm not one to say, "I told you so," but, well, there, I said it. Anyway, the virus spread rapidly over a period of about three months. After the initial chaos and confusion cleared away, we were quick to act. Our first center to open was here in Florida. We were able to obtain a sample of the new virus and determined that it was, in fact, a mutated strain of the U Virus. The team began working right away on a vaccine. While that was in motion, I got desperate. Members of my team developed and organized the first rounds of gassing in Atlanta."

Purple clouds, I think.

"The gas attacks were an attempt at something," he continues, "and the CDC field operators were fortunate enough to capture Patients 1, 2, 3, and 4. While they were in the paralyzed state, I administered the original U Virus Vaccine. I had no other choice. Something needed to be done."

I remember my conversation with 16 a few days ago. He had told me all about this. The failed vaccines. The experiments. He believes in Santa Claus. I don't know why I ever doubted him.

"The results were a disaster," Holston goes on. "It was like giving a patient chemotherapy to fight the common cold. It worked to some degree, but it left the patients nearly non-functioning. I knew time was not on my side, so I worked day and night with my team to create something viable.

"After the second batch of the vaccine was completed, we secured Patients 5, 6, 7, and 8, and gave the new vaccine to them. It was successful in the sense that they were now showing signs of being cured, of being somewhat like their former selves. The government was happy with my results, and we were able to officially open up the other Re-Assimilation Centers, as outlined in my manifesto, with the full support and funding from the government. Gas attacks were implemented throughout the world by the United States and other first world country militaries. Unfortunately, there was not enough of the vaccine to go around in the short amount of time we had. The infected outside of the United States that survived the poison had to be put down. That's why there aren't any Altered people but here in America."

There's a far-away look in his eyes, like he's reminiscing. He snaps back into reality, rubs his temples, and says, "I'm almost ashamed to say it, but I wasn't too concerned with the state of affairs in the rest of the world. I was promised full control over my research, and quite frankly, I was not willing to give up any amount of my vaccine to people in foreign lands. But I was still unhappy with the latest results. I knew the vaccine could be better.

Stronger. So, I tweaked it again. Patients 9–20 showed increased improvements and performance. They exhibited even more signs of their former pre-infected selves. My grant got extended, and I was promised funds to provide my patients with proper after care. A home in a housing development upon completion of their therapy, job opportunities, health insurance. They titled the grant 'Altered-Care,' and would be standard in the likes of government programs like Medicare, Medicaid, and Social Security. That was an exciting venture, but I still wasn't 100 percent thrilled with the results of the vaccine. So, I changed it for a final time, this time for my own sake. I knew I was taking a big risk and was endangering the life of my program, but this last time seemed to prove perfect. 21-30. You. 24. My shining star. My beacon of light. My supreme candidate," his face lights up with pride and happiness. I can't help but smile back. It's infectious.

I think I get it now. This center, this project, this is Holston's baby. *I'm* Holston's baby. He saved me, or so he feels, and is trying to get me and the others to be functioning members of society again because that would be his mark on the world. His gift. His whole life has been spent behind closed doors in laboratories, never getting publicly recognized for his efforts. He probably stopped the world from going to hell a hundred times before the outbreak and was never acknowledged the way he deemed fit. But this! This whole program would be his ticket to immortality. His legacy. This would get his name in the history books once schools were established again. And now Graves was going to have it shut down, and I'm partially responsible for that.

"Dr. Graves is convinced that you and your people are not fully cured, that you'll somehow relapse or revert. I will admit that 1, 3, and 4 will need constant round the clock care for the rest of their lives. 5-20 will need some supervision, but I know in my heart that 21-30 will be okay. The data says so. The results say so. The psycho-analyses say so. My gut says so."

"What about the other centers?" I ask, not caring that I'm not supposed to be privy to that information.

Holston sits upright. "There are between 20 and 30 Patients in each center. Each city has their own 1, and 2, and 3, and so forth." He smiles again.

This time I don't smile back. I get it. Like, I get the technical parts. I understand why Holston would be missing for a few days at a time. He had his other children to check up on at the other centers. I get it. I understand. I'm here in this hospital, this facility, being watched and monitored so that I will make my grand re-introduction into a society that is crying for my head on a silver platter. I get it. I understand. But what I don't get is *The Next*. Is there a *Next*? What happens *Next*?

Holston can read me well. Much like a father can read his son. "Don't worry; everything will be fine," he says gently.

"That's kinda hard to believe though," I answer flatly. "I mean, what happens if the CDC shuts you down? What happens to me and the others?"

This is something Holston is not comfortable with. I can tell. I see the bright light of pride dim in his eyes and the small gentle smile melt off the corners of his upturned mouth.

"I'm not sure," his voice wavers. "If I lose the grant, we will have to abandon the centers." He stands up and offers his hand to me. "Come on," he says as I reach for him and stand on my feet. But even my emaciated frame seems to be too much for his elderly body, and he sways forward a bit as I gain some momentum. "I'm taking you back to your room. With Graves gone, there's no reason for you to be down here any longer."

"You still didn't answer my question," I say, brushing the backs of my legs off.

"Don't worry yourself with that," he replies in a somber voice. "We're going to continue your sessions, continue with treatment and monitoring. Like usual. We'll have to take it day by day."

He opens the door to the room, and I follow behind him. I want to tell him my life has only been about the day by day, and now, that's not enough for me. I need to recreate and rebalance. I need to get up by myself and stand on my own proverbial two feet. Day by day is not going to cut it any more. I need a vision. I need a goal, something to work toward, a plan.

It's time to restart.

I T DOESN'T FEEL LIKE 'BUSINESS AS USUAL' SIT-
ting in this leather chair. I'm in Graves's office.
Everything is the same. The video camera is set up
on the desk and the red-light flashes, letting me know
everything is being taped even before the actual session
starts. Next to the video camera is the tape recorder. The
button has already been pressed to "record."

*Guess they don't want to take any chances with a
wild card like me.*

On the coffee table in front of me is a plastic pitcher
of lemonade and a red plastic cup. It's one of those dis-
posable cups like my dad used to buy for when we would
have barbeques in the backyard, and he didn't feel like
cleaning the glasses. I pour myself a cup and drink it
down. It's cold. And too sweet. My lips pucker, and I
squint my eyes at the first taste but go for another gulp
when the sensation passes. There's never been a nice
homey drink for me before. Then again, I've never had
a formal session with Dr. Wendy O'Hare.

O'Hare refuses to sit in the leather chair across from
me. Well, I'm speculating she refused; I can't be certain of how she's feeling. She sits at the desk, safely

perched behind the tape recorder and the video camera. Her blonde hair is slicked back into one of those French braid things, (like how Sydney used to make my mom do when she wanted curly hair the next morning) and she's wearing her white lab coat. Her lips are as 'hooker-red' as ever, and she pages through Graves's clipboard. I'm guessing she's catching up on all of his comments about me and my sessions with him.

She looks nervous. Like, I can tell she's looked over these notes a hundred times in preparation for this moment, but she's fumbling with the pages as if she's never seen them before. She's stalling for time. Like, she's trying to fill up every conceivable second of our hour together with dead air.

"So," she begins without looking up at me, "Dr. Graves took copious notes on your meet'ns with him."

I shrug my shoulders and mumble a "I-guess-so" under my breath. I sense this is going to be agonizing. What the hell is she going to ask me about? Seriously, what more can I say to this woman that I haven't already said to Graves? Read his copious notes, lady, and let's call it a day!

"Hmmm," she purrs as she looks at me and pouts out her lips, "your whole fam'ly, huh?"

She's trying so hard again to conceal that thick accent of hers, but I can see right through it. My height-ened senses can pick up every Deep South note of her voice pattern.

"Yeah," I reply curtly.

She furrows her brow. Or tries to, at least. There are no wrinkles in her forehead, and I guess she and Graves must see the same Botox administrator.

"Hmmm," she says again, stalling. "I'm not sure what kind of approach Dr. Graves was gettin' at with you, but I want you to know I am here to listen and help. I'm not here to judge nobody or nothing like that, ya understand?"

"Thank you, that's nice," I respond with a fake smile.

She smiles back and almost blinds me with those white Chicklet teeth of hers. "Now," she says flipping over one of the pages, "says here when you last left off with Graves you were telling him how you were trying to get back to that girl's house."

"Lana Anderson," I interject.

"Yes, that's right. Well, did ya ever get there? Let's pick up from there."

I breathe deep and clutch the sides of the chair. This is going to be very tedious; I can tell. But I'm on camera, on tape, and I guess I need to go on with the tail end of the story because it wasn't too long after that that the world shook. "No," I respond flatly, "I never made it to Lana's house."

O'Hare pouts her hooker red lips out again in her fake facial expression of empathy. "Aww," she says as she does this obnoxious click sound in her mouth, "and how does that make you feel?"

How does that make you feel? She did it. She said it. The typical psychiatrist/psychologist mantra. "How does that make you feel" is code for "I have nothing to say to you, so I'll listen to you babble on and on until the timer runs out." I'm not sure who I hate more right now, her or Graves. Maybe O'Hare. Because at least with Graves, he wasn't shy about his voice pattern or facial expressions. At least with Graves I knew where I stood. I knew he would have done anything in his power to kill me. With O'Hare, this façade, this front of hers is sickeningly sweet, and I'm confused as to whether she's using it to hide her own hatred or her own fear, or both.

"It makes me feel like shit," I spit out, and I see her tense up in her seat and her eyes flash wide. She's probably not used to being spoken to like that. She probably never uses cuss words herself. Too unlady-like, I suppose. My cussing makes her even more uncomfortable, and she tries to fake a smile, but it's obvious I've rattled her. It's only a matter of time before she becomes completely unglued. I hold in a chuckle.

O'Hare collects herself and straightens up. She's a professional, so I'm sure she's heard it all in her career, but coming from me, an Altered, maybe shook her up a bit. That's the fear. She twists her mouth into a wicked looking half-smile, and I get a flashback of Graves's snakey smirk in my mind. "But really," she continues without missing a beat, "what did you think you were actually gonna do if you got to that girl's house? I mean, it's not like you was *normal* or anything." She pouts her lips out again.

And there's her hatred.

My cheeks flush hot. She watches wide-eyed, and there's a hint of sadistic satisfaction that sweeps across her face. It takes every ounce of my consciousness to control my raging anger. One side of my brain is telling the rest of my body to leap across the room, jump on top of her, pin her down, and bite off her hooker red lips so she can't pucker them in that irritating way anymore. The other side is screaming at me to "be cool, be calm!"

I find the strength to compose myself. "I know I wasn't *normal*," I coolly say. "There were two parts to me. It's hard to explain. One part of me wanted to reach out to her and have a safe place to go. One part of me wanted to eat her face. It was like a jagged reasoning, ya know?"

She flinches again and in my head I'm kinda keeping score: Griffin - 2, O'Hare - 1.

"Yeah, um," she stammers, "Dr. Graves reports here you claim to have had some type of reasoning. Tell me what that was like."

Now, I seriously want to eat my own face! It would be much more interesting than enduring this nonsensical charade.

"It's hard to describe," I indulge her. "It was like looking through a blanket with tiny holes in it. I could see things clearly at times, and at other times I saw things with a layer of haze. As the days went by, I started to have an alternate sense of reality."

"Hmmm," she responds. "So, the infec-shun was wearin' you down some. Changin' you. Transformin' you." For the first time she's making some sense. There's no way for her to fully understand what I'm talking about, but for the first time I feel like she's taken something that I said and made a true assessment of my situation. Like, she was able to summarize the main idea of a passage in the Florida State Comprehensive Exam. But just when I think she's starting to *get it*, she goes and says, "And how does that make you feel?" and her southern twang grates on my last nerve.

I want to strike my forehead with my palm, but I stop myself from displaying my aggravation and shrug my shoulders. If she keeps asking me that question, this session is going to go nowhere real fast. It already is a bust. She's no Graves, that's for sure. He was a master psychologist. His actions and demeanor blatantly displayed his hatred for me, and yet he was able to get me to talk about anything. O'Hare is an amateur by comparison. Her voice wavers a little. I'm not sure if that's from her accent or her nerves. Or both. And I have absolutely no desire to share anything with her. But maybe she'll share with me? I decide to flip the script and change things up a bit.

"You're not from around here, are you?" I brazenly ask, ignoring her touchy-feely question.

She stiffens in her chair again, not knowing what to say. The tapes on the recorder and camera are still rolling, and she makes a huffing sound in her throat. I caught her off-guard.

"What? Alabama? Georgia? South Carolina?" I press as I slightly smirk.

She looks confused. Bewildered. She doesn't know how to answer me or if she even should.

"Louisiana," she finally answers quietly, probably trying to evade detection on the recording devices. "Naw'lens," and her twang is so clear I know for the first time she's saying something real.

"What was it like for you there? Like, when the outbreak happened."

She's motionless and looks like she's scanning her brain for the memories of what happened. Her eyes get a glazed over, faraway look to them and she's staring at me.

"Dr. O'Hare?" I ask as I wave my arms up and down.

"We scatter'd," she starts in a low voice, "like roaches." Her eyes open wide at the word "roaches", and I know she's talking to me, but she's not looking at me. She's looking through me, like she's looking at a TV behind me that's projecting the events of her memory onto a screen. "It was absolute chaos," she continues. "Those *things* were evr'ywhere, and with the hospital barely func-shun'ing on that back-up generat'r," she pauses and shakes her head side to side. "We stayed at the hospital and tried to help as many people as we could, but we had no idea what was goin' on, or what type of sickness we was facin'. The patients started changin', and soon we were outnumbered in the ER. Rhonda and I locked ourselves in the records room. She had a key. She told me she knew that a cruise ship in port was sched'led to leave the next day. So, we decided to make a run fo'it. We got to her car and drove like wild horses to the port. 'Parently others had the same idea. Luckily, those ships can hold lots of people, and there were three ships waitin' to haul out. Me and Rhonda were lucky enough to get on one."

"How did you get here, to this center?" I ask, the roles having clearly been reversed.

She thinks for about a minute—a minute of silence passes through us, and in that minute I can only imagine the conditions of that cruise ship. Her face darkens, and I assume she's remembering her time spent on the ship, as well. "The boat stayed in the Gulf for about three months," she says, and her body gives a slight shudder of discomfort at the thought. "Then the captain one day comes on the loud speaker and asks if there are any doctors or nurses on the boat, that they had finally received a transmission from the Port of Tampa. Rhonda and I immediately went to the library to meet up with the head officials, and that's when we learned of Dr. Holston and the Centers. A few days later we docked in Florida, and I was picked up and transferred here."

"What about Rhonda, your friend?" I ask with a serious psychologist-like tone.

"She didn't make it," she answers shaking her head again. "Someone on the ship was sick, and he attacked her."

She's sad. Real sad. Not fake sad or fake concerned. Like, she's genuinely sad. O'Hare is like the rest of us. She lost people too. And for a split second, I feel sorry for her, and her chaotic experience in the New Orleans hospital, and her treacherous three months on some luxury liner. A split second. That's the extent of my empathy. Because, regardless of what she's experienced, regardless of her journey, she still has that wall, that barrier or fear and hatred for me and my kind. *The Altered.* There's still a phony hooker red smile that reveals her luminescent pearly whites, coupled with a condescending and biting tone to her voice. Yeah, we've all been through a lot. We've all had our fair share of craziness and confusion, and moments of utter terror and horror. So, yeah. My sympathy for O'Hare only goes so far because she's still the same hateful bitch she was the day of the outbreak.

I look at her and without realizing it, I jut out my lower lip and crinkle my eyebrows in mock concern. "How does that make you feel?" I ask, mocking her and the way she asked me that very same question.

She stands up sharply, like she's been awakened from a trance, and removes her lab coat. She's wearing another one of those power suits underneath it—those power suits that women in business find it so necessary to wear, especially when they work around high-ranking men. It's a navy-blue blazer over a powder blue silk shirt with a navy-blue pencil skirt that matches the jacket. O'Hare slithers around the desk and sits in the leather chair across from me. Like Graves. I may have pushed her too far and have quite possibly unleashed something very dark and very sinister deep within her scared and hateful psyche because she's too smooth right now. Too calm. Like how my mother would get right before losing it on me and Sydney when we did something wrong. She crosses her legs and lifts her right pointer finger to her cheek so that her face is nestled in the "L" shape of her hand.

"Tell me something, Patient 24," she says as she taps her forefinger against her cheek bone. "If you had to make an estimate, about how many people do you think you infected?"

"None," I say with assertive certainty.

"None?" she questions, tilting her head forward an inch or so. "Are you sure about that?"

"Yes," I repeat with the same fervor.

"How can you be so sure?"

"I'm sure. I knew early on if I bit anyone the infection would pass to them."

She re-crosses her legs quickly. The glaze of her blue patent-leather pumps catches a ray of light from the window and shines in my eyes. She did that on purpose. "But you attacked people, did you not?" she urges coyly.

"Yeah," I say.

"So, if you're sure that you didn't infect them, but you attacked people, then the logical conclu-shun is that you kill'd them. Correct?"

I lower my face because she's staring right at me, and it's making me uncomfortable. "Correct," I mutter.

"So, let me re-phrase my 'riginal question. If you had to estimate, about how many people have you kill'd?" she asks as she moves her middle finger to the top of her lip. She's doing that pouty thing again, and the urge to bite her lips off creeps back into my mind.

"A lot," I answer quickly and quietly.

"Can you give me a number? Ya know, just an esti-ma-shun, of course."

I want to punch her in the throat and then strangle the sarcasm right out of her. "I don't know," I repeat, quelling my inner urges, "just 'a lot'."

"Hmmm," she says as she puts the long nail of her middle finger between her teeth and bites down a few times. "A lot," she repeats. "That's interesting. Very, very interesting."

I know where this is headed. I know where this is going. She's backed me into a Psych 101 corner, and she's not going to let me out until I give her, the tape recorder, and the video camera exactly what they all want. I swallow hard, anticipating how I'm going to go about this. I swallow hard, but the lump in my throat is not going down. I reach for the lemonade and take another swig, but it doesn't seem to alleviate the dryness in my mouth. I underestimated O'Hare. She has her own way of going about things, and I wasn't prepared for her style of questioning.

I shook her up some with my audacity, and now, she's back in full force, full swing. Her hateful, hurtful eyes are glaring at me hard. I wiggle in my seat because each second that crawls by, each second that drags on, I know what's going to come.

She re-crosses her legs again. She's wearing nylon stockings, but they're a nude color. Her calf muscles are toned. I see the muscle jut out from the side as she com-fortably rests her leg over her knee.

And then she says it.

It echoes in the room and in my head, deafening me, pushing my back up against the proverbial wall, and I suddenly realize that I never had the upper hand in this session. Her lip pouts out one last time and she asks, "And how does that make you feel?"

Final score: *O'Hare – 4, Griffin – 3.*

SOME TIME AGO, HOLSTON TOLD ME I WOULD have to retrain myself, more importantly—retrain my senses to not be so sensitive. I sincerely have to try because my session with O'Hare yesterday has left me rattled and almost feeling defeated. Her attitude toward me, her glances, her fake sympathy, her subtle underlying fear manifesting itself into sarcasm and hatred, is pretty much how the entire world sees me right now. As I think about O'Hare, I'm having trouble discerning between her brand of contempt for me with that of Graves's. I don't know which is worse—the subtle or the overt. I'll probably never see Dr. Warren Graves, in the flesh, ever again.

But I will.

I'll see him every day in the faces of the humans around me. The world has changed in so many ways. Not because of the infection and the millions it left zombified and/or dead, but it changed those who survived. Reverted them. Brought them back to a dark place of fear and hatred. Just when the world was starting to see the light and accept people and tolerate differences, it gets bitten back into a time of prejudice and fear. This time with a new race of people to hate. *The Altered*. And Graves and O'Hare are the poster children for that contempt.

The more I stay in this room, my dorm, the more I feel its cage walls closing in on me. The pictures with the shiny happy people smiling at me make me feel dizzy. I know the world looks nothing like that anymore. I know the world has barely a smile for each day that passes as families try to rebuild what they once had, as people try to salvage through the corpses left littering the streets searching for some semblance of their former lives. The world was consumed, humanity consumed, and it's time to rebuild life into some form of normalcy. If that's even possible anymore. What do I know? Maybe I'm still a naïve 17-year-old.

One thing I know for sure is that I can't stay here forever. Even with the possibility of the Center's shutdown looming over my head, the time is coming for me to leave. I feel it. I feel that I've outstayed my welcome. The people in the pictures don't appear to be welcoming me anymore; I think they're waving goodbye. *Goodbye.* "Goodbye" insinuates that there's a "Hello" on the opposite side of the fence. Like, one door closes, another one opens. Only *when* I say goodbye, I'm unsure about what type of greeting awaits me out there.

My door clicks open. It's Dr. Eisenberg holding a small paper Dixie cup in his hand.

"Good morning," he says in a quasi-cheery way.

"Morning," I reply unenthusiastically.

"This is for you," he continues as he walks over to my bed and hands me the cup.

I examine the contents. There are pills in it. Pills that they've never given me before. "What is it?" I ask suspiciously. I don't trust anyone here and know that there's an ulterior motive behind everyone's actions. Even Holston's.

"Blue is the vitamin. Red is the antibiotic. Green is the sedative," he answers in his official doctor voice.

No. I don't like this at all. This doesn't add up. Antibiotic? Sedative? I hold the cup in my hand and look back and forth from it to him. He stares at me, his eyes urging me to ingest the concoction, but I don't. I hesitate. I shake my head back and forth. "Dr. Holston's never given me..." I start to say, but he quickly interjects.

"The vitamin is a supplement. Your body is ready for it now. It's one of those chewy kid vitamins to start with and won't upset your stomach so much." He takes out a thermometer from his white lab coat pocket. "Open your mouth," he orders, and I oblige him. "The antibiotic is a precaution," he continues. "Your white blood cell count was on the high side from your last analysis, so if there's any type of infection, we want to head it off at the pass so to speak." He stops and the thermometer beeps. He takes it out of my mouth and reads aloud, "97.6. That seems to be a norm for you. Dr. Holston would like it a little higher, but it's not dipping or spiking like it had been, so I guess we should take what we can get."

He's given me a nice and neat explanation of two of the three. I can handle that. But... "Why a sedative?" I snap at him.

His lips twist at the corner of his mouth, and he wrestles with whether or not he's going to tell me. "Just take it," he says as he waves his hands in my direction. "I'm bringing you to the day room, and everyone will be there. You were supposed to be split into two groups, but the storm isn't going to let up, and Dr. Holston wants all of you to get your rec time."

It's raining? I hadn't even noticed. I guess I was too wrapped up in my own internal dialog that I didn't realize there was rain pounding against the building. But, once he says it, I hear it. The wind howls against the window pane. Sounds pretty bad out there. I'm really surprised that it didn't dawn on me.

"So, why a sedative?" I ask him again, not fully understanding.

"Precaution," he repeats. "More for the others than for you, actually, but Dr. Holston would rather be safe than sorry. It won't knock you out. It's more of a relaxer than anything."

"Like a Valium?"

"Yes," he says nodding his head.

Whatever. I'm over it. I'll play nice. I'll play test subject. I raise the cup to my lips and cock my head back, swallowing all three pills at once. No water. I crush up the cup and hand it back to him. "I'm ready," I say with a big cheesy grin as I hop down from my bed.

He wasn't kidding when he said all of us would be in the day room. The Altered. I scan the room, searching for a familiar face. There's a man sitting in a wheelchair, and it looks as if there's not much there to him. There's a nurse beside him holding up a cup to his lips. Water spills everywhere as he attempts to drink, and I think this must be 1 or 3 or 4, one of the first patients to get the original U Virus vaccine Holston told me about. I count off the others. 23 plus me adds up to my number: 24. I particularly take note that both 16 and 7 are not here. There are three others I recognize from that disastrous group session: 10, the middle-aged man, is at a table playing chess with a middle-aged woman I've never seen before. 20, the young Hispanic guy sits on a couch, reading a magazine. 15, the timid teenage girl is on another couch directly across from 20. Her knees are curled up to her chest and she's wrapping the ends of her long hair around her fingers. She looks up at me, and I give a slight wave, but she quickly looks back down, ignoring my gesture. She must be 15 years old, and I laugh to myself that her name and age are the same. But she ignored me, and when that hard fact actually registers in my brain, I stop my inside giggles. She ignored me. She ignored me. We're supposedly one in the same, and still, she ignored me.

I don't like rec time. I want to go back to my dorm.

I sit down next to 20, and I can feel 15's eyes are popping up every once in a while to watch me.

20 puts his magazine down and looks at me as well "How's it going?" he says quietly.

"Okay," I reply nonchalantly.

"Not gonna cause trouble today, are you?" he asks with real concern in his voice.

"Nah, nah," I say waving my hand back and forth, "I took those pills like a good boy!" and I smile at him.

20 smiles wide. A knowing smile. He took them too, and to be honest, I'm starting to feel the effects of them. I'm starting to feel my muscles collapsing into a bowl of jelly, and the smile on my face is not going away. I consciously struggle to force the edges of my mouth into the downright position, but I can't. It's one of those uncontrollable drug smiles. So is 20's. So, we look at each other, two dopey smiles plastered on our faces, and we start to laugh out loud. 15 stops playing with her hair and looks

up at us. She starts to laugh too. Three dopey smiles and three dopes laughing.

"It's the drugs, man, the drugs!" 20 bursts into an uncontrollable fit, and 15 and I follow suit.

One of the nurses in the room looks sharply in our direction but doesn't move from her post. She's keeping an eye on us. That makes us roar even more.

"You're a funny guy!" I belt out, sending 15 into a wave of witch-like cackles. 20's mouth opens wide, and he laughs so hard there isn't even sound coming out. I'm trying to catch my breath, but it's so hard to. I can't remember the last time I laughed so hard that my sides hurt, 'cause my sides actually hurt right now.

The nurse across the room yells, "Settle down over there!" to us. The three of us instantly stop laughing, and we look at each other with guilty eyes. 15's mouth falls into an "O" shape. "Uh-oh," she whispers, "we're in truuuubbbbllllee," and her childlike song further tailspins our snicker-fest.

"Oh man! Oh man! Stop! Stop! You're killing me! You're killing me!" 20 snorts between laughs, gasping for breath. But it's no use. What he says is cause for more howls and cackles.

I'm cackling now. 15 is snorting. 20's breaths are silent and staggered. Among us, we three have probably killed hundreds of people, now we're killing each other with silliness. We're not eating people; we're tickling funny bones. The irony in what 20 said is moronic. Three cold-blooded killers killing each other with stupidity. Drug-induced stupidity. Drug-induced irony. I don't know what I'm thinking because I feel hazy. And I'm laughing so hard my thoughts are jumbled.

I'm not sure how long it lasts, but it seems like it takes a while for us to settle down.

"You from around here?" 20 asks me when the din of silliness finally dissipates.

I nod my head.

"You?" he asks in 15's direction and she nods her head too.

"You really kill your wife?" I brazenly ask him, but that's the drugs talking. I wouldn't normally blurt that out to someone.

He nods this time, and 15 repositions her legs to her chest like she had them before. Must be her defensive stance.

"I probably wouldn't have if I knew I was gonna change. Maybe we could have been together, ya know? Maybe she could have survived like me and been Altered here with me."

"I hear ya, man," I reply as 15 lets out a nervous squeal.

I remember 15 said she was cutting school and was at the mall when she was attacked. She's cute. Dark hair and light blues eyes. The me of *The Before* probably would have tried to get her phone number if I saw her at the mall with her friends. I could see it now: Josh would go up to her friends and do his usual "wink and point" routine. Her friends would giggle and flirt back like all girls do. I would glance at her, and we would both roll our eyes as if to say we understood each other, we both have crazy friends, and we know what it's like. That would be our connection, my gateway to swoop in and get her number, ask her out. She would hesitate at first, but I would say something witty, and she would give in to my silly charms. I would take her to the movies. Or maybe to get lattes 'cause that's kinda what trendy teenage girls like to do, and let me tell ya, two cups of latte at one of these trendy coffee houses is nearly equivalent to the cost of two movie tickets! We'd chat online and text and see each other exclusively for about a month or two until I got bored, and Lana Anderson managed to weasel herself into my conscious mind. Yeah, that's how it would have gone down 'cause that was my MO. That was the pretty much the story of all of my relationships during *The Before*.

I try to think about how the me of *The Now* would handle this situation. She's cute enough to want to date, but I don't see how that would work. Would we exchange stories about how many people we killed versus how many people we infected? Would we share the tales of our first kill?

"I killed some random mall worker!"

"I ate the first girl I ever had sex with!"

Would we discuss the difference in taste between chunky finger flesh and bony finger flesh (because, trust me, there is a distinct difference)? *Nope. Not gonna work. Not gonna happen.* And that's even assuming she remembers what happened when we were infected because judging from our group session with Graves, she has no recollection. But I find that hard to believe because I remember just fine, and there was something in the way when the others caved in to Graves that makes me believe they remember as much as I do. All of them. I want to ask 15 and 20 what their deal is, but I let it go. Maybe one day when we're in therapy at an "AA" meeting (Altered Anonymous, of course) the truth will come out, but really? What difference would knowing that make any way?

"I have to get out of here," 15 says under her breath so quietly I almost want to ask "What?" but don't. I heard her. 20 heard her. Others around us heard her too because some heads of some other Altereds swing around in our direction.

"Soon," 20 comforts, "soon. It's gotta be soon. They can't keep us here forever."

I keep my mouth shut about a possible Center shut down. I don't know how much they know, and I don't want to cause a panic. Or trouble. "All good things must come to an end at some point," I interject, and she looks up at me with her crystal blue eyes and smiles although I can't tell if it's a real smile or a drugged out one.

"I'm excited," 20 says as he shifts in his seat and my eyebrows rise in confusion. "I'm excited to get back into the swing of things, ya know? Start over. Fresh start. New world." He grins. A real grin. Not a drugged-out one. He means it. His eyes light up with the prospect of starting over. Reset.

"Why?" I ask, and there's a hint of disgust in my voice.

"Second chance," he answers promptly as if he's thought this through many times. "I get to be someone new. I get to start over. There are many new opportunities waiting out there for me. I get to build my life from the bottom up, my way."

I guess he didn't watch the news program I watched. I guess he doesn't know the world outside these hospital walls is not ready to accept us with opened arms. He rubs his hands together in anticipation, and for the first time, I notice there's a gang symbol tattooed on the skin of his hand between his thumb and his forefinger. I want to tell him he's part of a new gang now, and people in the world are now only going to see the tattoo on his face under his right eye, the one that he won't be able to cover up and hide.

In a way, though, he's kinda right. Staying here, while a tempting thought, is not the answer, and regardless of the social perception of me, I too need to start my life over. I'm reconciling *The Before* with *The After* and *The Now* with *The What's-to-Come*. I anticipate my second chance. I welcome it. The longer I stay here, the more I am lulled into a false sense of security because there's so much more outside these walls. Even though the world has changed, I know in my heart I need to be a part of it.

After a little while, Mazzy comes to take me back to my dorm. She's the most genuine person I've met here, and I can only hope there are more people like her on the outside. There's a food tray waiting for me on my desk, and I don't have to open it up to know it's some sort of pasta and meat dish.

"Beef stroganoff?" I ask as I glance at the tray.

She smiles.

I stick out my tongue in disapproval. I never liked beef stroganoff.

She gives a breathy chuckle. Next to the tray is a large envelope, the yellowish-orange kind they use in offices that can hold many documents. She picks it up and holds it out toward me. "Listen," she begins, "the Center is getting shut down."

"Wow, that was fast!" I say in amazement, because really, I thought it would have taken much longer for Graves's petition to go through.

"Yeah," she replies as she lowers her head. "All the Centers are being closed. A team of doctors and head CDC guys are evaluating the status of all the patients.

They reviewed your file in detail, and well, they determined that you were a candidate."

My heart races, and my face flushes with that all-telling pink color of emotion. "A candidate?" I exclaim. "A candidate for what?"

"To leave," she answers softly, a sound in such stark contrast to my previous outburst, and hands me the thick envelope.

Leave? Did she say I was going to leave? I think. *Am I still high and flying from that sedative Eisenberg gave me?*

My fingers accept the envelope and for a moment, Mazzy's finger brushes along the outside of my hand. Her caress sends a surge throughout my body, and I do everything I consciously can from having a full-blown body quiver.

"Dr. Holston is so dedicated to this project and to his research," she says. "He truly put his heart and soul into this. In that packet you'll find all kinds of things. He's arranged temporary housing for you and lined up a few job interviews. He set up a bank account, and I believe he's going to give you an allowance for six months. He's done this all with his own money. This is all from him. I'm sure you'll find other things you'll need in there, too."

My head swims. I'm still not able to fully process what's happening.

"You're scheduled to be released tomorrow. There are instructions on where you need to go and how you will be able to get there."

Released? Like an animal being set free into the wild?

"Will I at least get to see Holston? To thank him?" I ask, cause I don't know what else to say and it kinda seems like the appropriate human response for the situation.

"No," she replies, "he left this morning to go to the other Centers and do final evals on the patients."

What about the others? The other patients? Are they leaving too? What will happen to them?" I ask rapid fire, still trying to digest everything.

Mazzy shrugs her shoulders and makes a slight humming noise in her throat, one that if it had actual words would have been "I don't know."

"Will I see you again?" My voice sounds small and immature, and to be honest, stupid! I have no idea why I ask that question and want to palm my forehead!

Mazzy looks up at me. "Probably not," she answers. "I'm going to California to stay with my aunt. She's the only family I have left." She puts her hand on my shoulder and stares deeply into my eyes. I see my reflection in the black ink dot of her enlarged pupils as the amber and gold shades dance around the darkness in a thin line. "I wish you all the best in the world. I will think about you often. Don't ever give up hope," and she leans in and kisses me on the cheek. On my scar. "*I* forgive you," she whispers into my ear then turns around and walks out of the room.

I ATE THE BEEF STROGANOFF, SHOWERED, slept, and walked around in a daze after I woke up. A note in the envelope said I would be leaving this morning. I would be picked up and escorted out of the facility. Another nurse brought me a new set of clothes last night: new boxer shorts, jeans, a navy-blue t-shirt, socks, and a pair of no-frills sneakers. I'm wearing that outfit now, and I hope that there are some summer-type clothes waiting for me at my new destination. I mean, it is kinda warm in Florida this time of year!

From the time Mazzy left me yesterday afternoon up until right now, I've been processing and digesting, but the weight of this new information, the sheer heaviness of it, still strangles me. After Mazzy had left, I sat back on the bed and held the envelope in my hands for a real long time. I dared not open it because there were too many mixed emotions brewing inside me. I was afraid that the anger and excitement that was seeping out as sweat on my palms might ruin some important document or something. To be honest, I was afraid to look. Afraid to see my instructions. Afraid to take the next step. I knew I had to, but animals can get quite comfortable in their cages, too. The prospect of being out there, being on my own, is something I've both longed for and dreaded at the same time.

After what seemed like hours, I opened the envelope; slowly and carefully as to not damage any of the contents within. Holston was thorough, and I had to admire his sense of dedication. It was all mapped out, every last detail. Upon being discharged from the Center, I would get on the HARTline Bus, pay the fare (like a normal person would), and be dropped off at my designated apartment complex up in town. My instructions say to speak to Annie, the head director of the complex, and she would set me up in my new digs. Apparently, it's already furnished. Holston even left a copy of the floor plan—one bedroom, kitchen, one bathroom, living room, breakfast nook (which is a euphemism for tiny ass dining room).

This bothers me. I've never lived on my own. Probably wasn't going to have to live on my own for a very long time. Probably was going to end up at Hillsborough Community College for two years until I figured out what I was going to do with my life, and even after that, I probably would have stayed at my parents' house and commuted to the university of my choice. According to my calculations, I had about another good four years or so left with my mom and dad. Now, I'm being thrust into an apartment on my own? I can barely boil water! I guess the one good thing about me is I can easily adapt. I don't like change much, but I guess I proved to myself that when the going gets tough... I mean, hell, I wandered the streets as a zombie for three months of my life and survived, I guess living alone in my own apartment is a major step up from that.

Holston also set up a bank account for me with Wells Fargo. Not sure if that's supposed to mean anything, but that's what the papers say. My apartment is paid in full, so I won't have to worry about rent or utilities bills for about a year, give or take, and he's set up an allowance system that will keep me on my feet until I get a job. He's giving me $500 a week until I can find a job. I have a checkbook and everything! I'm a little nervous 'cause I've never written a check before. Once I find a job, the allowance will steadily decrease each month until I'm self-sufficient.

Speaking of finding a job, there's a schedule of job interviews he's set up for me. Says he used his clout as my doctor as a solid reference at all these places. There's an interview scheduled every day for a month! And it's at all types of places: the mall, grocery store, janitor at a school (oh, so I guess some schools are up and running), menial stuff like that. He says I need to start at the bottom and work my way up. Whatever. I get it. There's a stack of applications I need to fill out before each interview. Some of the information is already filled in for me, so I don't think the process will be all that grueling. I've never had a real job. Just a paper route that lasted all of five seconds, and I once worked at a bakery for a day. I couldn't figure out how to operate the espresso machine, so I walked out. My parents never stressed the importance of having a job as a teenager. They always said school should come first, and all that jazz, so if I actually land one of these positions, it'll be my first.

An Altered's gotta start somewhere!

One thing's for sure: it seems like Holston is trying to help me out as much as he possibly can. It seems like he's trying to make this process, this transition, this re-assimilation as easy as possible for me.

The one thing I do notice right away is the lack of a car. Holston has laid out maps and bus routes to help me navigate the city, and I suppose that's pretty much all I can ask for at this point. I mean, hell, he's doing all this for me out of the kindness of his own heart, out of the kindness of his own wallet, for me to ask for a car is unreasonable and downright selfish. Besides, I haven't driven a car since before the outbreak, and don't know if I would still know how. Or if I really even want to. Cars and me don't have such a good track record.

There's a wallet in the envelope. In it is some cash (I'm guessing for the bus), a credit card (probably with a minimal limit) and an ID card with all my pertinent information. The picture on it is a still shot from one of my video sessions with Graves. I was actually smiling. I wonder what I could have possibly been talking or thinking about at that particular moment. I find it curious on the section of the card that says "Name," I'm listed as "Griffin King 024." As a matter of fact, as I thumb through the papers and applications and other materials, that's how my name appears. Griffin King 024. Griffin King 024. Griffin King 024. Is this my new name, now? Is that how they're going to also identify us? The Altered. Name and number. Is that how I have to sign legal documents and other papers? Griffin King 024.

Even my name... altered.

The door to my room opens, and I quickly hop down from the bed. I stuff the wallet into the back pocket of my jeans and gather the last of the loose papers beside me and neatly place them back into the envelope. It's the nurse who brought the clothes to me last night.

"Are you ready?" she asks with no real emotion in her voice. Like, this is a job for her.

"Yeah," I answer, "is Mazzy at the nurse's station? I'd like to say goodbye to her before I leave."

She wrinkles her fat nose, and it looks like a ball in the center of her face. "Mazzy?" she spits out like the word is pure poison.

"Nurse Madeline," I correct myself.

"Oh, no. She's gone," she huffs.

"Oh," I mumble pitifully. I really wanted that to be an inside thought.

"You're all set with where you need to go, right?" she barks at me.

I nod my head and walk to the door.

She guides me down the hallway, and as I walk by each room and nurse's desk, everyone's eyes are glued on me. It's quiet. Not the usual hallway hospital quiet; I mean, it's *dead* silent. And they're all watching me. The other nurses, the doctors. They're all watching me walk, watching me saunter, watching me slip out the doors of this controlled environment and back into the big bad world. Like releasing an animal back into the wild. I smell all of their smells. My heightened senses are still intact because I know that scent. The scent of anxiety and fear is like roasted chicken on an open grill. It fills my nostrils and makes my stomach muscles tighten a bit. Not a full-blown hunger growl, but a little rumble letting me know that, yeah, I could go for a snack right now.

I remember this one time I had to do this project for biology class. Some extra credit assignment thing. I read all these articles and watched videos about animals in captivity and how some programs were successful, and others were complete failures. This one lady had saved a Bengal Tiger cub that had lost its mother and siblings to poachers. The lady raised the cub, loved it, cared for it, the whole nine. Well, the day came when the lady felt the tiger had grown up enough and was ready to be reintroduced into the wild. There was a whole crew there to document the animal's return into its natural habitat; it was like a big party. The lady was so proud. She was crying and sad and happy at the same time. Well, she's got that big tiger on a leash. She's petting it. Whispering into its ear. Crying. Standing at the edge of some national park in India, ready to unleash him and set him free. She pets him one last time, unhooks the leash, and sends him on his way. The big cat saunters down like ten feet or something, pauses, turns around and charges at the lady, knocking her down, mauling her to death.

The nurse and I go down the elevator in silence and step into the main lobby. There are two guards stationed at the main entrance armed with semi-automatic weapons. Just in case. Just in case I get ten feet out the door, have a tiger freak out and decide to eat the nurse, I suppose.

The main entrance doors were once made of glass but are now reinforced with steel. The nurse points at them, and something jumps inside my stomach and up to my throat. I gulp it down. Acid and bile sting the roof of my mouth. My grip tightens on the thick envelope in my hands. My lifeline.

"Out the doors, through the front parking lot to the main road. You'll see the sign for the bus stop. Bus'll be coming in about ten minutes or so," she instructs.

I don't say anything else to her. I nod my head again and walk. I pass the guards with their guns and feel their eyes boring holes in my body. They smell like burnt pork roast. That must be hatred. I don't look back at either them or the nurse, but I hear the ding of the elevator and assume she's gone back upstairs to her post.

I open the doors and step into the brightness of the morning. My eyes squint from natural light glaring off the blacktop of the parking lot, and I remember the first line from one of my favorite books, *The Outsiders*. I feel like Ponyboy stepping out of the darkness of the movie theatre, the place where he escaped into his daydreams and fantasies, and into the brightness of the real world where he was forced to face reality and the oppression of his rival gang. Now, that would be nice if it were like that.

The world outside the hospital is quiet. Hushed. Desolate. My senses can pick up sounds and smells, but only faintly. Traffic is barely existent. It's like the population was cut in half and has left a feeling of a gaping void in the morning air. No, this scene isn't like the romantic vision of S.E. Hinton's coming-of-age novel. This is more reminiscent of one of those movie scenes where the bad guy is released from prison and there's no one waiting at the gates to pick him up. There's no one here to pick me up. To greet me. No beautiful girlfriend who's waited years for me, leaning her slender body against a nice-looking sports car, her brown curls blowing in the morning breeze, a smile plastered on her hooker red lips when she sees me pass through the prison gates to freedom.

Either the nurse was wrong, or I've dallied in the parking lot in a daze because the bus pulls up to the slot almost immediately. I pick up the pace and do an awkward jog as the doors open with their breathy hiss.

"I always wanted to do that," Josh's voice echoes in my memory, and I close my eyes as the painful thought of my best friend stabs me like a knife in my brain.

The driver glares at me. "One seventy-five," he grunts.

I'm taken off guard for a second but realize that's how much I have to pay to ride. I fumble for the wallet in my back pocket, take out two dollars, and hand it to him.

"I don't give change," he says in disgust as he barely takes the money into the tips of his thumb and forefinger.

"That's okay," I reply. 'Cause really, I couldn't care less about a quarter.

He closes the doors behind me. The hissing sound creeps into the back of my brain like another painful stab. I survey the bus. There are people on it. Scattered. And as I look for an empty seat, I realize they're all staring at me. Their eyes say to me: Don't sit next to me! Don't even think about sitting across from me! Don't sit behind or in front of me! My free hand instinctively rises to my face. I touch the welt of the scar raised under my right eye and realize their staring eyes are all fixated on that. My mark. My visual. That which screams to the world I am a killer, a mutilator, a demon, a zombie, a sinner, an infidel, a monster, a barbarian, an animal. *An Altered.* My face flushes with heat, and my stomach does one of those low rumbles. For a split second, I want so very badly to hiss and growl at them, to gnash my teeth in their direction, maybe even do the high-pitched screech, maybe even rip their fearful and hateful eyeballs out of their sockets with my own teeth. I want so very badly to give them something to be truly afraid of. Fear me, human! I probably ate your dog and your husband, and if you don't watch your step, I may very well eat you too!

But I hold myself back. I suppress the instinct inside of me. I realize as the days have passed, it's gotten easier to calm those feelings and to control those urges. I find a seat in the back of the bus away from everyone else and lean my head against the glass window as the driver pulls away. This is my reboot. Restart. Life Part 2.

"Let's start at the beginning," I remember Graves saying to me a million years ago. Well, the beginning is now. A new beginning. I place Holston's envelope in my lap and put both hands over it, protecting it. Protecting the start of my new Life. *The What's-to-Come.* I know I'm in for a lot of looks and stares and glares, and quite possibly retaliation. But I'm ready. I have to be. I have to know what this near desolate world has in store for me. I think I'm ready for the journey. For *The What's-to-Come.*

The rumbling of the engine rattles my head gently back and forth on the glass, and it gives the empty world vrooming outside a fuzzy look to it. A jagged look. Like it's still shaking violently.

1. Discuss Griffin's journey of self-discovery throughout the story. How does his understanding of himself change as he comes to grips with what happened?

2. What is the relationship between Griffin and Graves? Griffin and Holston? Compare and contrast how each doctor plays a role in who Griffin is becoming now that he's Altered.

3. Discuss the setting. How does the environment play a pivotal role in in the contribution to the mood and atmosphere?

4. Explore the moral dilemma faced by Griffin. Are there any instances where his actions blur the lines between right and wrong?

5. Why do you think it takes Griffin so long to have the full realization that his family is gone?

6. Griffin's ordeal is certainly a traumatic one, but often-times he reflects on what he went through with a very flippant attitude. Why do you think he acts this way?

7. Why do you think Graves has a hard time believing that Griffin (and quite possibly, the other Altereds) was sentient when he was infected? Do you think the others had the same thoughts and feelings as Griffin?

8. Consider the novel's ending and its implications for the characters and the world they are now trying to rebuild. What lingering questions do you still have? Do you think Griffin will be able to have a normal life again? Why or why not?

9. Food tends to be a common theme throughout the novel. Griffin often struggles with bouts of hunger and the feeling of not being hungry. What is the significance of food? What does food now represent for Griffin?

10. Consider the portrayal of friendship and loyalty in the novel. How do the characters navigate trust and betrayal in their relationships with one another?

MARIA DEVIVO WRITES HORROR AND DARK fantasy for both a YA and an adult audience. Each of her series has been Amazon best-sellers and has won multiple awards since 2012. A lover of all things dark and demented, the worlds she creates are fantastical and immersive. Get swept away in the lands of elves, zombies, angels, demons, and witches (but not all in the same place). Maria takes great pleasure in warping the comfort factor in her readers' minds—just when you think you've reached a safe space in her stories, she snaps you back into her twisted reality.

Discover more at
4HorsemenPublications.com

10% off using HORSEMEN10